© All Rights Reserved

Khara Campbell

Edition License Notes

This Book is licensed for your personal enjoyment only and may not be reproduced or re-sold for monetary gain. If you would like to share this book with another person, please purchase an additional copy for each recipient. If you're reading this book and did not purchase it or it was not purchased for your enjoyment only, then please return to your favorite retailer and purchase your own copy. Thank you for respecting the hard work of this author.

The church is your typical cathedral style from the outside. Gabriel's parents insisted it be built this way years ago because they love the architecture. On the inside, it is modernly decorated with purple and gold as the overall color scheme for the carpets, drapes, and seats. One may feel like they've stepped into a luxury hotel when entering Everlasting Love Ministry.

Ms. Urma, one of the ushers at the door, greets me with a fake smile. For whatever reason, the woman doesn't like me.

"Good morning, Ms. Urma."

I watch her eyes scan my 5'5 body from head to toe. My natural hair is in its signature bob cut that falls right above my shoulders. I have on a pair of red framed glasses today. They match my ruby red shoes, which gives a pop of color to my black and white skater dress that stops right above my knees. Ms. Urma makes a clucking sound like she's chastising me.

I do get a genuine smile from Lilly, the other greeter, who also gives me a hug. I'm not much of a hugger but I don't mind hugs from her. My coffee hasn't kicked in enough nor do I have the energy to pretend to give a genuine hug to Ms. Urma.

"Sabrina, I've been meaning to tell you, the weight you've put on looks great on you," Lilly whispers in my ear. She's a 40-year-old white woman.

All of this attention that I have been receiving from my weight gain makes me wonder what people thought of me when I was a size two about a year ago. I try not to let it get to me and cause my self-esteem to take a nosedive by pushing the negative thoughts away. At 34, I just gradually gained my womanly curves over a year ago and apparently, everyone is taking notice to my size 6 almost size 8 frame. It's like my metabolism went to sleep. It doesn't help that I love to eat. I know that I've added on a few pounds over the holidays. I've been working out to keep my body toned.

Knowing that the girls are settled in children's church, I walk through one of the side doors to the sanctuary and head for my seat in the front row. I hate sitting up front. My husband is already at the podium when I take my seat. His eyes find mine and I can see that he's upset with my lateness, but he doesn't have to deal with two preteens in the mornings. He's up and gone every Sunday by 6 a.m., and doesn't return home until maybe 4 p.m.

I sit through the service doing my duty of nodding, clapping and occasionally throwing in an "amen" when necessary. Not that the service or his teaching is bad, he's an amazing preacher, but God forbid I don't look like I'm playing my part as "First Lady".

I didn't want to be a pastor's wife. I know I married a PK, but I didn't sign up for this. Maybe I'm abnormal. Many women tell me I should be blessed to be married to a pastor, but many of them don't know the pressures this role carries.

"Make sure your house is in order!" Gabriel preaches and I fight my eye roll. He continues to quote 2 Kings 20:1.

He needs to make sure his house is in order.

"You were late, again," my husband whispers to me at the end of service. We were walking towards the lobby to greet the congregation.

"I like that tie on you." I say ignoring his comment. I try not to be late and I'm tired of explaining the reason every Sunday when I am.

He smiles reaching for my hand and I almost flinch away from his touch, but I catch myself and allow my hand to slip into his. His touch feels like a stranger's. It's sad what years of being unappreciated can do. I used to be the one reaching for his hand when he didn't want to be bothered. Now, he's become a familiar stranger to me. The intimacy in our marriage is long gone— at least on my end. Ironically, Gabriel now has the desire to touch me all the time. *Was I too skinny for him to love up on me before?* I shake my head. *Get away from me negativity.*

TWO - SABRINA

It's close to five in the evening when Gabriel returns home from church. After the third service, which ends at 1 p.m., he usually stays longer to talk in-depth to any church member that wants further clarification on his preaching, or if there's some sort of church activity that needs his attention. As the pastor of a 2500 member church, he stays busy.

Since he took over the position of the lead pastor from his dad two years ago, he's been trying to get me to be more involved in church ministries. I do head the women's ministry but more so as an advisor. Minister Tabitha spearheads most of it, but I have my input and attend all the ministry events. It's too exhausting for me to grit and grin like my life is in a good place. Being the First Lady of Everlasting Love Ministry is too much and because of it, my heart isn't into being fake and phony while involved in church ministry.

"Hey daddy!" the girls exclaim when Gabriel enters the house. They are in one of their rare moments of getting along as sisters while playing video games in the family room. Especially since I gave them only an hour to enjoy it.

I watch as he hugs then kisses them both on the forehead before coming over to me for a kiss. I indulge him in a quick peck because it feels weird kissing my husband. In the past, almost 11 years, the only time I've ever found his tongue deep down my throat was during sex. Now, he wants to tongue kiss me all the time but mentally I can't do it. This touchy-feely husband of mine is new to me.

He runs his hand up my now thick thighs. "You look good enough to eat. Sitting here reading on your kindle, wearing your glasses."

His breath tickles my ear. His words and actions do nothing but make me want to push him away, but I refrain myself.

"You want me to fix your plate?" I move to stand.

"Yes, thanks. I'll go change first."

He playfully smacks me on my butt when I turn for the kitchen. I internally shake my head thinking how oblivious he is to how I feel.

"Ms. Urma said you didn't speak to her this morning." Gabriel has a displeased look on this face.

Ms. Urma is 67 years old and I'm convinced she wants my husband. The way she runs and tells him everything she doesn't like about me proves it.

"You can't go around being rude to the congregation. You're the first lady, you help set the tone of the church and you're representing me." He looks at my hibiscus tattoo that's on the inside of my forearm. "Maybe you should cover that with makeup when you're not wearing long sleeves. I don't know why you got that tattoo anyway."

"Ms. Urma is a rude old woman that needs to mind her business. I did greet her this morning. She was the one that said nothing back. First Lady or not I don't have to deal with rude people if I choose not to. If you or *Ms. Urma* don't like my tattoo, look elsewhere when it's on display."

Gabriel regards me and sits across from me at the granite kitchen island. We live modestly good, our home and simple elegant décor reflects it. "You're right, I'm sorry. She is rude when she wants to be."

I lift my brow.

He chuckles. "Okay, she's rude most of the time and you know I like your tattoo. It's cute."

Interesting.

When I came home with it on my 30th birthday you would've thought I told him I cheated on him by the way he carried on.

Maybe I should've divorced him then.

"What time will you get to Miah's soccer game tomorrow?" I ask.

He picks up a forkful of salad and places it into his mouth.

"I won't. I have a hospital visit at the same time of Miah's game. Bria just put it on my calendar."

Of course he won't be there, but I dutifully ask anyway. He will have to tell Nehemiah that he won't be in attendance himself. I'm over making excuses for his absence.

"Let her know I can't make it."

I shake my head. "Nope. You tell her."

His absence doesn't bother me anymore. At least not for my sake--for my daughters, yes. They should have their father active in their lives. I couldn't care less anymore whether he was home or not. I prefer when he isn't.

I can breathe.

I can be Sabrina.

No masks are present.

I feel that all these years of God not answering my prayers, regarding my husband, means that my marriage is my "thorn in the flesh" that I have to endure--at least until Genesis and Nehemiah are older and I could leave.

Then sometimes I feel I should just be grateful that Gabriel doesn't physically and verbally abuse me. He takes care of things financially, he isn't cheating on me, and comes home every night. Yet, those things are to be expected and there's a lot more to a relationship than that. Love, affection, attention, and appreciation is what I lack. That's what I needed from him. Now, I don't want it from him anymore.

"The girls are asleep." Gabriel drapes his arm around me, pulling me towards him. I can feel his erection.

I internally groan. Why couldn't I be on my period? I envision the play by play of our lovemaking, if it can even be called that, praying for God to help me get my mind right.

I give in because it would be best for me to just get it over with verses be nagged for the rest of the night. I never understood how a person could have emotionless sex until the last few years of my marriage.

The next day I can't remember whether I had an orgasm or not.

THREE - SABRINA

After ensuring the girls made it safely on the school bus, I enter the kitchen to tidy up before I grab my things to head into the office. I own a small design firm in Delray Beach, Florida called DesignHer. I'm the head graphic designer with a small staff of five: three men and two females. We do both commercial and end-user businesses. Our work ranges from book covers and author materials to large commercial ads. I partnered up with a company that takes care of our printing needs. I need to stop by the printer to review prints before heading into the office.

"Good morning, did you make breakfast?" Gabriel asks as he comes strolling into the kitchen in a t-shirt and boxers. The clock on the stove read 8:50 a.m.

"Microwave." I reply letting him know where to find his food.

"Thanks! Can you start the coffee machine?"

This dude just got up after I had to wake two children up for school, listen to them complain about getting up early, and then fuss over their lunch and snack choices. I folded a load of clothes, that I forgot were in the dryer, made breakfast and waited fifteen minutes for the school bus, now he wants me to start his coffee?

"Sure, anything else?" I ask. I was already near the machine, so it wouldn't take much effort.

Oblivious to my passive-aggressive response, he says, "No, thanks."

He sits to eat his scrambled eggs, bacon and blueberry muffin. I leave the kitchen to gather my purse and laptop bag to leave.

"Can I get a kiss?" He asks after I tell him bye on my way to the front door.

I guess as a dutiful wife I should. Funny how when I wanted this in the past, it went ignored.

I walk back to him and quickly press my lips against his. He tries to make the kiss deeper, but I pull away quickly feigning that I'm running late.

***

I listen to Tasha Cobbs for a while on my drive to the printer before switching it to Chris Brown. If I was driving with Gabriel, I would keep it on gospel because it was best to not hear him complain about my music choices. I hate having to get a lecture from him about the things I do that he doesn't agree with.

I'm not a perfect Christian but being the First Lady makes me feel like I need to pretend to be. Sometimes, Gabriel comes across judgmental with some of his Christian viewpoints. Being his wife, I can attest to the fact that he isn't perfect either.

"Good morning, Sabrina." Kian greets me when I step into the print shop he owns.

It's a small print shop with top of the line printing machines. He can print just about anything, which is why our business deal works— that and he's an honest hardworking business owner, and he's black-owned, if I can keep it real. I like supporting my own.

Kian is in his early 40's with a sprinkle of gray in his hair. He's clean-shaven, 3 inches taller than Gabriel, standing at 6'3, and has a muscular build. I also notice that he is not wearing a wedding ring like I'm clearly sporting.

Recently, I've found myself acutely aware of men more than I've been before. I know it's because I'm not in a good place in my marriage and it pisses me off. Gabriel used to be the center of my attention since we got together in college…not anymore.

Butterflies go wild in my belly when my eyes lift to meet Kian's. I ignore the effect he has on me and greet him with a pleasant smile, while keeping it strictly professional.

"Good morning, Kian."

He smiles back and says, "I hope you didn't stop for coffee, I knew you were coming in and I stopped by Wawa and got you a cup."

My face breaks into a wide grin. "That was nice of you. Thanks!"

"No problem. I love their coffee too. Come to the back to review your prints and I'll get the coffee from the kitchen." He leads me to the back room.

"These came out great." I tell him as I look over the large print ads for billboards that will be advertising a stage play.

"I thought so, too. With your design firm and my print shop we make a great team."

He's standing too close to me at the table. We aren't touching, but he is close enough for me to enjoy the enticing scent of his cologne.

"Hmm, we do make a good team." I step back from the table and take a sip of coffee. "I believe the customer will be pleased. Can you get it ready so I can take it with me?"

"Yeah, sure." He begins preparing the items. I watch him get the prints ready to go. "How was church yesterday?"

"Good. My husband taught on keeping your house in order which can take on several different meanings. Two of which are, our house as in our body being the temple of the Lord or our house as in our home life being in order. Those things must properly be in order so we can successfully fulfill the will of God."

"Interesting. I've been looking for a church home, I may come visit. What's the name of your church again?"

"Everlasting Love Ministry, it's not far from here in Boca Raton."

"Cool. That's not far from my home either. Maybe I'll come on Sunday."

"That would be nice."

What the heck?! Would it be nice?

"Okay, prints are ready to go. I'll bring them out to your car." He says, pulling me away from my own thoughts.

I turn to leave feeling his eyes on me. He follows me outside. I disengage the locks to my SUV. I quickly open the trunk and push the button to lay the back seats down to fit the prints inside.

"All set. I guess I'll see you on Sunday or if I'm lucky, sometime sooner...for prints." Kian closes the trunk.

I need to leave. Now. I can't tell if he's flirting or playing around. Either way, I need to go. Our friendship and work relationship have always been cool, but this feels...

"Thanks, Kian." I hop in my car and leave.

FOUR - SABRINA

"Do you think ripped jeans are appropriate for a church meeting?" Ms. Urma asks with her top lip curled up taking in my attire of light washed ripped jeans and a plain white t-shirt under my black blazer. "It's not acceptable attire for a first lady."

Jesus, help me to respect my elders.

"And what exactly do you deem appropriate?" I decide to indulge her for a moment.

The Women's ministry brunch is set to begin in twenty minutes. I was here last night helping Tabitha and a few of the ladies on the ministry set up the church hall. There are enough round tables to seat about 300 women which is the average size that attends the monthly brunch. Each table is decorated with a small vase of fresh tropical flowers. The place settings have unique inspiring quotes for the attendees. I noticed some of the women were reading there's already.

"Not those raggedy jeans showing flesh on your thighs and knees. You young women in the church ought to be ashamed of the way you carry yourselves.

Tight clothes, stiletto heels, tattoos. Trying to have a *hot girl summer* in the house of the Lord..."

I bite my lip to avoid laughing at her quoting Megan Thee Stallion.

"...what I'm wearing is what's appropriate attire. It's holy."

I take in Ms. Urma's attire. She has on a hideous green floral muumuu dress that falls right above her ankles and she's wearing white sandals that look like they came out the year she was born. Her outfit isn't my taste but I'm not going to chastise her for it. She's a sturdy woman with fully gray, almost white, relaxed hair that lays limp on her shoulders. She's about 5'5 and wears about a size 10, judging by that muumuu dress. She is a nice-looking woman in the face, her attitude takes away most of her beauty though.

"With all due respect, Ms. Urma, you wear what you feel comfortable wearing and I wear what I feel comfortable wearing. I'm not dressed provocatively. Not only do I respect myself, I respect Jesus and the church. Just because you don't like my outfit doesn't make it wrong. Maybe you should read Acts ten verse fifteen."

"Hmph! Pastor Dean will hear about this." I hear her say as I walk away.

"I'm sure he will."

Tabitha loops her arm in mine. "Ms. Urma is trying to be the lady of the church. You better watch your man."

She can have him, I want to say but keep it to myself.

"She needs to find a better hobby than harassing me."

Tabitha is the only true friend I have at church. She's a year older than me at 35. Her outgoing personality drew me in and the fact that she's an extrovert who forced her way into my life. She's a beautiful chocolate woman with a boho-chic style that I admire.

"So, first lady Sabrina," Bria says. She's the church secretary, like Ms. Urma, the woman has a vendetta against me and for the life of me, I don't know why. "What's it like being a pastor's wife?"

We are at the questions and answers portion of the brunch. The part I don't like because personal questions are often thrown my way.

"It's great," My fake genuine smile displays on my face. "I have my *personal* bible rolodex right at home." I say referring to Gabriel.

"I know it must be perfect being married to a man of God. A man that truly loves the Lord, church, and his family. To be equally yoked to a person must be great." A lady in the back says.

I nod. I don't doubt my husband's love for me and our family. He's just taken me for granted for many years and slowly pushed me away. His love for the church is more of a priority. My husband is having an affair with the church and I can no longer compete with her. I no longer care about the matter or about our marriage. I've divorced myself years ago. I'm just bidding my time. Saving face—at least until the girls are older. Doing anything about it now will bring a scandal to the church that I'm not ready to deal with.

I definitely won't tell these women that. For one, they don't need to be in my business; two, it's not just my business to tell, though it seems Gabriel has buried his head in the sand regarding issues in our marriage; three, there's an image of perfection I can't ruin, it's been drilled enough in my head by my husband and in-laws.

"I know if I was pastor's wife..." Bria starts. See this is the nonsense I have to deal with. "I would be a dutiful stay at home mom to our children and be actively involved in the church."

Bria and I are the same age, 34. She's a beautiful black woman. She's been divorced for six years and is a single parent to her eight-year-old son.

"Or you can find your own husband to be a housewife for. Pastor Dean is spoken for." I flash her my diamond rings. I may not be in a good place in my marriage, but I won't be disrespected by Bria taking shots. He's still my husband, regardless.

She laughs trying to play it off. "Who said anything about Pastor Dean? I meant being married to a pastor, period."

Tabitha gives me a knowing look.

"Bria does have a point about a pastor's wife being active in the church. Sure would be nice if you attend all church events. Poor Pastor Dean dealing with all the responsibilities without his better-half." of course Ms. Urma has something to say on the matter.

"Being the pastor of this church is my husband's job. His attending functions and events is part of that. My job as a graphic artist and business owner has responsibilities I must carry out. It won't be fair for me to expect my husband to do all those things with me. Same as it's unfair to expect me to attend and be a part of all church business. It's an unrealistic expectation, especially for a congregation with twenty-five hundred members. We also have two children with activities outside of the church."

"The lady of the church should have more of a pivotal role. Senior First Lady Evelyn Dean sure did." Ms. Urma mentions my mother in law.

"I sure miss her since they retired." Bria says.

After turning the church over to Gabriel, my in-laws moved to Barbados. They visited the country many years ago and fell in love with the island.

"Okay, let's move the questions on." Tabitha steers the group in another direction for which I am thankful.

FIVE - SABRINA

Today is a stress-free day getting the girls up, ready and in the car for church.

"Mom, can we stop at Five Below after church? I need to get some supplies for my project. Daddy is going to help me with my project for art class." Genesis says sitting next to me in the passenger seat.

"Really? When is the project due?"

"Tomorrow."

"Why are you just doing it the day before?" I ask.

"I was waiting on daddy to get everything, but I figure we can do it when he gets home from church."

"Okay. We can stop. Next time, try not to wait until the day before a project is due to do it."

We make it to church ten minutes before the second service starts. The girls hurry in. I'm so grateful for their love of Jesus and church.

"You must be new here. I haven't seen you before. I'm Ms. Urma and this Miss Lilly. We're the greeters here at the north side doors. At the south side doors is Mrs. Kala and Mr. Kenny."

I watch the exchange in front of me.

"It's nice to meet you both. Yes, I'm new here. I was invited by Sabrina Dean." Kian says.

Ms. Urma's eyes widen in surprise. "Oh really? And how do you know the First Lady?"

Lilly sees me approaching. "Here comes Sabrina now."

Kian turns towards me causing me to almost stumble in my steps. He's breathtaking in a suit. I internally check myself and continue towards them. I don't miss the way Kian's eyes approvingly sweep over me. I peep Ms. Urma doesn't miss it either.

He catches me completely off guard embracing me in a hug and darn if it isn't a hug I don't hate. I pull away quickly. It was an innocent embrace but I'm emotionally too vulnerable to analyze my reaction to him further.

"It's nice that you decided to visit today." I tell him. Ms. Urma is burning a hole in the side of my face with her eyes. She's so busy staring at us she doesn't greet the couple that just entered.

"I told you I would." He blesses me with a smile.

"Come, let me help you find a seat." After saying a quick hello to Lilly and Ms. Urma, Kian follows me.

"Can't I sit with you?"

Again, he almost causes me to misstep. He's walking beside me now. I wave at a few members as we walk towards the sanctuary doors.

"As the pastor's wife, I have a designated seat up front."

I see him looking at me from the corner of my eye. "I've known you for years, you don't seem like the first-row type, pastor's wife or not."

I shrug my shoulder. "I'm not, but it comes with the territory."

He says, "Play hooky this one Sunday and sit with me."

I smile. "I can't, but I will help you find a good seat in the back."

"Since I'm your guest, can I at least sit behind you?" He flashes me his smile again.

"Sure. Let's enter this way." I make a beeline for the side entrance into the sanctuary.

Throughout the service, I can feel Kian's eyes on me and it's making me nervous. I don't know what to make about him being here today.

After service, I obligatorily meet Gabriel near the pulpit, and we make our way to the lobby.

"I enjoyed the service." Kian shakes Gabriel's hand. "I was invited by your lovely wife and I'm happy I accepted her invite." Kian's eyes move to me.

"Is that so?" Gabriel asks shifting his eyes on me too.

What the heck?

"Kian's the owner of the print shop I partnered with three years ago."

Gabriel nods, but I know he doesn't remember that fact. I'd given up talking to him about the ins and outs of my business because he seemed uninterested and doesn't ask. "I think I recall her telling me about her partnership with a printer. Nice to meet you."

"She and her staff are a talented bunch, it was a no brainer working with her."

"Yeah. She was always into that drawing stuff."

That drawing stuff? Really, Gabriel?

"It's more than just drawing, it's art. She brings people's vision to life."

Gabriel quirks a brow at how passionately Kian speaks of me and my team's work. I inwardly blush.

"Yeah, she's great at what she does." Gabriel flatly replies. I can tell he's getting irritated by Kian.

Kian must have picked up on it too. "It was nice meeting you. I will be visiting again."

Kian surprises the heck out of me again with another hug. "See you soon," he says near my ear before releasing me and walking away.

The anger radiating off Gabriel is enough to start a fire. "What was that about?" he asks through gritted teeth.

"What?" I ask because I don't know myself.

Gabriel looks at me, studying my face. "Do I need to be concerned about him?"

I've never seen Gabriel jealous over me and although my heart is dead to him, I'm surprisingly turned on. It's been forever since I've felt this way and it shocks and confuses me because I'm not sure who my arousal is really for. Him or Kian.

I shake my head. "No."

"Keep it that way."

We greet a few more people before the girls make their way to us.

He hugs and kisses the girls.

Genesis asks, "Daddy, are you still going to help me with my project today?"

"When is it due again?"

"Tomorrow."

Shaking his head, "Oh baby, I won't be able to help. I'm sure mommy can help you with it."

The sadness in my daughter's eyes breaks my heart. "But you promised, and I've been waiting for you to help for a week and you didn't get the supplies like you said."

Gabriel hugs her to his side. "Daddy's sorry baby. I will make it up to you. Remember that video game you asked for? I will tell mommy to get it for you."

Genesis sadness seems to quickly evaporate. "Really? Thank you, daddy!" She hugs him tight.

"Mommy, can we get two hours of playtime today after you get the game?" Nehemiah asks sharing in her sister's excitement.

I'm fuming mad. Not only has Gabriel broken his promise to Genesis, but he's also pushing his responsibilities on me. Because I'm always here. I'm always picking up his slack.

I silently count to ten to stop myself from going off on him in front of our daughters and churchgoers that are still mingling around in the lobby.

Usually, I stand by his side for a few minutes greeting guests then getting the girls and leaving. However, today I follow him to his office.

"Why can't you help Genesis with her project?" I slam the office door shut no longer able to control my anger.

"What is your problem? Why are you slamming the door?" He asks.

"Because I'm pissed the hell off!"

"We got word earlier this morning that Erica Smith's sister died last night and I have to go and show my support to her and her family."

"Why can't one of the other pastors do it?"

"Because I'm a senior pastor and it's my obligation. I've only been in this position for two years and I still have a lot to prove. Following in my father's footsteps isn't easy."

"And losing your family is?" I fold my arms across my chest.

"What's that supposed to mean?"

I stare at him while shaking my head. For a man so knowledgeable about the word of God he can be dense sometimes about applying the bible to his own life. I'm so tired of having this conversation with him.

"Give my condolences to Erica and her family." I turn and leave not having the energy to deal with him further.

Gabriel doesn't get home until close to seven in the evening. He finds me and the girls curled up on the couch watching a Disney movie. He places a kiss on the top of all our heads before heading to our bedroom to shower and change.

Minutes later, I hear him in the kitchen warming up his dinner. I don't move from my spot. After he eats, he comes into the family room and sits on the couch with us watching the movie.

Later that night, when he initiates sex, I give in without a fight. I'm sexually frustrated. Still angry from church, and the arousal I felt earlier for either him or Kian, still lingers. I have a toe-curling climax that has me hollering in pleasure. I'm so loud Gabriel has to cover my mouth and whisper in my ear that I might wake up the girls. It's been so long since I've reached this height of pleasure, I want to savor every second of it until I blissfully fall asleep.

SIX - GABRIEL

I'm sitting in my office at the church thinking about sex with my wife last night. It was the best we've had in… a very long time. I shake my head at the realization of it. She was so passionate and didn't put up a fight when I initiated it. I'm almost ashamed to admit I haven't felt that from her in years.

In the past year or so, she's developed womanly curves that I can't get enough of. I've always thought Sabrina was beautiful. When we met in college, and just over a year ago, she was a size two. Which I had no problem with, but now she's just – wow!

I wasn't in love with Sabrina when we got married. I cared about her a lot, but love wasn't there yet. Our relationship took off so fast. And when she got pregnant, I knew I had to take care of my responsibility, but it was my parents that convinced me that the best thing to do was to marry her. I'd only known Sabrina for six months when she got pregnant and two months later, we were husband and wife. That was a lot to deal with at twenty-four.

Now, here we are. I'd grown to love my wife over the years. I'm completely in love with her. She's my helpmate. I wouldn't have the successes I have without her. Not only is she beautiful, but she's also smart, talented, and has a great sense of humor. She's an awesome mother to Genesis and Nehemiah. She's truly my blessing from God.

Sitting here thinking things over, I'm aware that things aren't great in my marriage. I've felt her pulling away for a long time, but I'm clueless on what to do, which is why I've inadvertently put church business ahead of my issues at home. I've been doing a terrible job of showing Sabrina how much I love and appreciate her.

One may think that my being raised by parents, who've been married for almost forty years, I would have a clue on how to have a happy marriage – but I don't. Or at least I haven't tried hard enough to figure it out. My parents were always in the church. My mom never worked outside of home and church. She raised me and my sisters and took on almost every ministry in the church supporting my dad.

My dad preached the gospel and financially took care of the home. I didn't see them as husband and wife, they were always Pastor and First Lady. No romantic dates. No surprise gifts. No open display of affection. Though now that they've retired, I'm just now really seeing them interacting as a couple.

I don't know anything about planning romantic dates. Sabrina always did that stuff. I always brushed her off or had other obligations. I wanted her more involved in the church like my mom was. However, she has her own business. *When was the last time that I asked her how her business was doing?*

Sabrina always wanted to go on family vacations and romantic getaways for us to stay connected, but I'm not into traveling. She and girls went on the last few trips without me. I even refused to go on romantic getaways for our anniversaries. The last time she'd asked was five years ago, and she hasn't bothered me about vacations since. Or date nights.

"I don't want years down the line for us to become strangers to each other..."

I recall the words she spoke years ago. I groan internally. *You've been messing up big time, Gabriel.*

Jesus, help me!

I call for Bria to come into my office.

"You called?" she takes a seat in one of the visitor chairs in front of my desk.

"If a guy was taking you on a date, where would you like to go?"

Her eyes grow wide with my question. I need help. I need to do something nice for my wife.

"Well," her voice now takes on a girly tone. "If a man was taking me out on a date. It would have to be romantic and fun, but it doesn't need to be fancy. Maybe lunch or dinner near the beach. Or drive down to Miami for a show. Go to the aquarium…"

I think Sabrina would like to go to the aquarium. "I need a day on my calendar to take Sabrina on a date."

She stops talking leaving her mouth open. "Oh… ah. Sure, I will check your calendar to see if you have any availability. But I doubt it."

"Well, make it fit. I want to do something special for Sabrina."

She stands to leave. "Of course. But like I said, you're a busy man and your calendar is pretty much filled up. However, I will *try* to pencil her in."

I need to win my wife back.

SEVEN - SABRINA

I wake up feeling guilty as sin. Sex with my husband was absolutely amazing last night but it was filled with fantasies of a faceless man. A man pleasing me and loving me the way my husband hasn't for years.

My therapist would probably tell me I shouldn't feel guilty, but I do. I'm married! I shouldn't be fantasizing about anyone but my husband during sex. Now I'm angry because I shouldn't be at this place in my life. In my marriage. But here I am. And I question myself daily as to why. Why haven't I left Gabriel already? Why do I put up with him disregarding me and the kids?

There have been many reasons over the years why I've stayed; we were newlyweds figuring out life, marriage, and a baby; then baby number two came; financial struggles; his meddling parents; his full-time associate pastor position in the church; my starting my business; the kids are too young and I don't want to disrupt their lives; praying and believing God for things to get better; his new senior pastor position…

I don't know how much more of this I can take. I no longer like this version of myself being married to him. I find myself angry and irritable often. Switching between multiple masks hiding what I'm emotionally dealing with. Suppressing my desires to keep the peace. Biting my tongue and always having to be *understanding* of his absence because of his position in the church. I'm exhausted!

I just left a client's office with a new project, but before heading into the office, I make a stop at the printer. I need to talk to Kian about yesterday. Yesterday was weird.

"Hey Stacey, is Kian in this morning?" I ask the front clerk.

"Yeah. He's in the office. Just knock first." She returns her attention to the computer.

I knock on Kian's office door.

"Come in."

I find him doing work on his computer. His eyes smile when he sees me.

His office is masculine to the core. Blacks and grays, no sight of a pop of color in the décor. The view through the small window, behind his desk, of a Yellow Elder tree, adds some life to the space.

"Good morning," I greet him leaving the door open.

He stands. "Good morning. To what do I owe this pleasure? I wasn't aware you have an order to pick up."

"No orders. I came to talk to you about church yesterday."

He gestures for me to take a seat before he returns to his.

"What about church?"

I decided to bite the bullet. "I've known you for years, and yesterday your interaction with me was *different*. The hugging and asking to sit with me and then the exchange with my husband. I was getting a weird vibe."

"I'm attracted to you, Sabrina. I have been since I met you. I know you're married, and I have no desire to overstep bounds. I just got a little carried away yesterday, but it won't happen again."

Okay. So there's *that*.

I decide not to acknowledge his attraction because there's no need for opening those can of worms. "I would appreciate it if things remain professional between us. We have a great business relationship I want to keep."

"I agree. Things will remain professional... I do have one question though."

"What's that?"

"Are you happy?"

My eyes blink rapidly, caught off guard by his question. That's one of the first questions my therapist asked me when I started seeing her a few months ago. The honest answer is "no". But I'm not telling him that.

"Yes, I'm happy. The weather is good, I had my cup of coffee and I have a new project I'm eager to start on." I'm a master of deflecting.

Kian places his forearms on the desk leaning forward. "Sabrina, are *you* happy?"

My heart is speeding like a freight train. He's trying to puncture the wall around my emotions. I stand. "I should go. See ya." I hightail out of his office and to my car.

My cellphone rings when I turn onto the highway. I click a button on the dashboard for Gabriel's call to come through the Bluetooth.

"Good morning," I reply with my eyes on the road.

"Good morning Sabrina. I was able to schedule for us to go on a date on Thursday…"

I almost skid off the road.

"…We can spend most of the day together." He sounds so excited.

"I can't on Thursday."

"Why? I had to move things around just to fit that in."

"Why? Because I have a business to run. My staff and I are attending a workshop in Miami that day."

"Come on Sabrina, you can't get out of it? It's not often I have free time like this."

"Oh, so I must bend over backward and do flips because you were able to pencil me into your *precious* schedule? The same schedule you told me last week you couldn't rearrange when I told you about my workshop and that the girls have a half-day and I can't pick them up. But I was able to get Frankie, their old daycare teacher to pick them up and have them stay at her daycare until the evening. Is it that same Thursday, Gabriel?"

He blows a breath. "Okay, I get it. I'm sorry."

I'm so freaking tired of his sorry's!

"Why don't you use that time to do something special with the girls, I'm sure they'll love that. Don't tell them just pick them up from school, it would be a nice surprise."

I can hear the smile in his voice. "That's a great idea! And I want to cook dinner tonight…"

I almost skid off the road, again. Who is this man?

"Oooookay. I was going to cook salmon, but I'm good with whatever you decide."

"I'll surprise you."

"Mmm, kay."

"I love you, hope you have a great day."

"Okay, you too. Bye."

EIGHT - SABRINA

Once upon a time, I loved date nights. I used to be so excited to spend quality time with my man. I would find the perfect thing for us to do. I would make sure the babysitter was booked. Pick out my outfit. Then be giddy the entire day until it was time to leave.

Gabriel killed that desire in me a long time ago. One way or another my planned dates left me in disappointment. Either he forgot, canceled or didn't like what I had planned and complained making the time less fun. He was tired. We arrive late because he had *things* to take care of first. Etc. Etc.

It's been a month since he called me that day about clearing his schedule for a Thursday date. Since then I've been dragging my feet in agreeing to go out with him. I finally relented a couple of days ago and tonight's the night.

Ugh!

I don't feel like pretending to be lovey-dovey with him. It's funny too because I'd prayed for years for Gabriel to give me undivided attention and treat me like a lady. Quality time is my love language after all. I wanted him to surprise me with dates and small gestures that show me he cares. Now he's doing it and I couldn't care less.

He's a day late and a dollar short and I can't wait for this night to be over.

I dress simply in a cute yellow maxi dress with wedged sandals, large gold hoop earrings and, bangles on my wrist. I bypass putting on makeup other than shaping and shading my brows and applying clear lip-gloss. After spritzing myself with perfume I put on my favorite neutral pair of glasses then head out the bedroom door.

"Wow, you look nice," Gabriel compliments me when I walk into the family room.

"Thank you!" I appreciate it but other than that his words do nothing for me.

After walking the girls to the neighbor to babysit, he took his things and got dressed in the guest bedroom. I'm pleasantly surprised to see him dressed down in dark slacks, a designer button-down shirt untucked with loafers. I'm used to him in a suit.

"You look nice, too."

He smiles big reminding me of how handsome he is. "Thank you." He pulls his cellphone from his pocket. "I want to take a picture of you in that dress."

I go to the door. "Okay. Take it outside by the bougainvillea plant."

I pose for a couple of pictures for him. His attention is making me leery. I'm not used to this. After he assures me he got the perfect shot I walk towards the garage. My cellphone chimes in my purse. Taking it out I see a notification from Facebook that I was tagged in a photo from Gabriel. I don't bother looking at the post.

"Do you have gas in your car? I'm low and I don't want us to miss the beginning of the show by stopping for gas."

"Yeah, I filled up earlier today." I hand him my car keys.

After unlocking the doors, he walks to the passenger side opening my door for me. I can't help the shocked look on my face. I tell him thanks while slipping into the seat. It feels weird. We haven't driven in the car together in a while. Our lives are so separate.

After starting the car, Buju Banton's voice flows through the speakers. I was listening to his old school songs on my way home.

"Can I change this?" Gabriel asks immediately reaching for the radio dial.

"Sure."

He changes it to a Christian music station. I love Christian music, but wouldn't now be a good time to listen to Jazz, RnB, love songs? But whatever!

"How is your business going."

"Good."

"Are you working on any interesting projects?"

"Yes."

"You still have three people on staff?"

"Five now." I gaze out the window watching the palm trees go by.

"Why are you being so short with me?"

"Am I? I'm just answering your questions."

"But I'm trying to have a conversation with my wife and you're making it hard."

I internally roll my eyes. "I'm sorry Gabriel but I'm not in the talking mood."

"You're not in the mood for a lot of things lately."

"Can we not do this now?" Even though I didn't want to be on this date I'm on it now and the last thing I want is an argument.

We're quiet for the final five minutes it takes us to arrive at the event center. After shutting off the car Gabriel looks over at me. "Sabrina, I get it. I have not been the best husband. But I've made a vow to do better. Can't you see I'm trying?"

I've heard those lines too many times before. But hey, why don't I give him the benefit of the doubt again? Too bad I have nothing left in me to try.

"Okay," I reply because I just want this night over with. I could be home happy reading a novel.

I go to open my door, but he prompts me to stop. His chivalry is nice.

Gabriel got us tickets for a clean comedy and improv show. The line-up looks great with B and C list celebrities and some local artists. Unfortunately, the seats aren't reserved and so far with us being 15 minutes early, there's a good size turnout already.

"Go in line for snacks and I will find us good seats," Gabriel tells me. I nod and watch him walk away into the room for the show.

After ordering a cheese and fruit plate and a glass of wine for me and water for Gabriel I stand to the side to wait for it to be ready.

"Dang, baby, you are killing it in that dress." A man with a thick Caribbean accent says from behind me. I look over my shoulder finding him shamelessly checking me out.

"Thanks, my husband thinks so too."

He moves to stand in front of me. We're eye level with me wearing four-inch heels, which means he's 5' 10" tall.

"Nice glasses," he compliments me again.

"I like your frames too." His rectangular shaped frames compliment his facial features. It gives him a bad-boy sophisticated look.

"Thank you. I found this online store that has nice frames and lens prices real cheap."

"Well you have to give up the details," I take my phone out of my purse and type the info he gives me.

His voice trails off and I feel a possessive arm snake around my waist. Knowing it's Gabriel doesn't stop my urge to flinch. But I do my best not to. His hand presses against my midsection.

"You good?" He asks leaning near my ear while looking over my shoulder at my phone in my hand that now has a dark screen.

The Caribbean Guy steps back out of my personal space. "It's all good bruh, she told me she's married, and I respect that."

Gabriel gives a head nod and the guy walks away. My order is called and Gabriel gets the tray and escorts me to our seats near the front.

I'm barely seated when he asks, "What was that all about? You're getting guys numbers now?"

"Please don't insult my integrity, Gabriel." I take my glass of wine from the tray and take a much-needed sip.

The show host is on stage getting the night started with jokes.

"I don't want to but with your cold shoulder lately, that dude hugging on you at church a few weeks ago, and the way he was looking at you according to Ms. Urma..."

Of course, nosey Urma. I sip my wine.

"...then that guy all up in your face just now, I have to wonder."

"This is our first date in forever outside of church, can we *please* discuss this later and enjoy the show?"

He sighs. "You're right. Let's enjoy the show."

***

I walk into our bedroom after kissing the girls good night. The sitter has the code to enter our house and she brought the girls back over before their bedtime, putting them to sleep and waiting for our return. It is so convenient having our 16-year-old neighbor babysit though I don't use her often because I almost always have the girls with me.

I find Gabriel sitting on the edge of our bed still fully dressed.

The master bedroom is one of my favorite spots in our Spanish style one level, four-bedroom home. I wanted a romantic tropical oasis in here. I think I achieved it with a four-poster bed with white sheer material draping the corners. Mint green walls with tropical artwork adorning it. White tile floors with a large multicolored rug under and surrounding the bed. Potted palm trees are by the windows facing the expansive, beautifully decorated, back lawn.

"Can we talk now?"

I go into our walk-in closet to take my heels off. "Sure."

"Why are you so short with me? Tonight was supposed to be special. I planned for us to have fun together and you've been acting like you didn't want to go."

I calmly reply. "Gabriel, this was the *first* date you've planned in our almost ten years of marriage but unfortunately it doesn't matter to me anymore. So yes, I didn't feel like going which was why I blew off your first attempts in taking me out on a date. But regardless, I enjoyed the show." I turn and start slipping off my dress.

"Are you cheating on me?"

"No Gabriel, I'm your loyal and faithful wife. But is that why you planned a date? Because you feel threatened?" I turn to face him.

"No, tonight was about me wanting to reconnect with my wife."

"How sweet."

"Why are you acting like this?"

"Because this is what you made me!" I snap. "I'm sorry tonight wasn't the perfect date night you've envisioned but trust me I have years of experience of knowing how you feel."

"Is this payback?"

I laugh but it's void of humor. "No this isn't payback. This is the result of you not giving a fuck about me for too long."

He blanches, either shocked by words, tone or use of profanity. But it's the perfect way to convey what I feel. What I've been feeling.

He stands and takes one step towards me. I shake my head "no".

"Baby I'm sorry. Please forgive me, Sabrina. I never meant to hurt you or make you feel like I don't care. I love you..."

I can't even muster any sentimental emotions at his words. If I recall, he said something similar a few years ago. Though this time it does feel different.

"...Do you love me?"

"Yeah, I love you." I hang my dress on a hanger.

"Are you *in* love with me?"

My hand stills and I close my eyes with my back to him.

"Look at me Sabrina, *please*." I turn to face him. The sadness in his eyes chips at a brick around my heart. "Are you still in love with me?"

"No."

His eyes close and I can see him fighting back tears. He opens them and looks me in the eyes. "I don't want to lose you. I love you and I will fight for you. You're going to fall in love with me again." He closes the distance between us gently pulling me into his strong chest, enveloping me.

And it's a hug I don't hate.

NINE - SABRINA

Sitting on my bed, I close the book to my daily devotions then look at the clock on the nightstand. I still have thirty minutes before I need to get the girls up for church. Gabriel left two hours ago to be on time for the 8 a.m. service.

I close my eyes and pray. "Jesus, thank you, God, for blessing me and my family with a brand-new day. Thank you for your grace and mercy that's new every day. Thank you for perfect health and strength...Heal my heart towards my husband Lord...and You." My heart is so heavy. "Jesus, you know I have given up on my marriage a long time ago.

I've prayed for years for Gabriel to love and appreciate me the way I need to be loved. For him to be present in both my and the girl's lives. For him not to push most of the parenting responsibilities on my shoulder and taking care of the home. I don't care anymore. I just want to be happy...and I feel I can only truly get it by no longer being his wife. But Jesus I place my desires...my hurt and pain in your hands. Heal me, Lord. I'm tired of being angry and frustrated and walking on a tight rope that can lead to depression.

I've also come to realize my heart has become a little bitter towards You because I felt You have failed me with not answering my prayers. Forgive me. I'm sorry. I believe with my whole heart that You want the best for me. Things may not be how I want them but I trust You have a master plan and it will all work out."

I switch to praying in my heavenly language. I need the Holy Spirit to intervene on my behalf. I think about the scripture Romans 8:26, *"And the Holy Spirit helps us in our weakness. For example, we don't know what God wants us to pray for. But the Holy Spirit prays for us with groanings that cannot be expressed in words."*

I successfully make it pass Ms. Urma without drama. I only enter through that door because it's nearer to my reserved parking. I guess my midi style wrap dress meets her approval and with the long sleeves, my tattoo isn't on display. I get the girls checked in for children's church though it's not necessary that I sign them in or out. It's one of the perks of being Lady of the church.

I love our praise and worship team. They can sing!!! And do an amazing job getting the congregation on their feet in the mood for worship. I'm especially feeling the choir this morning because I'm convinced God is speaking to me through every song they sing.

My arms are lifted in praise and remorse. "I give myself away..." I sing off-key with tears in my eyes. Even when I felt bitterness towards God, He forgives me and loves me. "Thank you, Jesus!"

I feel Gabriel's eyes on me from where he sits on the stage near the pulpit with the other pastors and church leaders. It's been a while since I've gotten this emotional.

Moments later Gabriel is standing at the pulpit delivering his message.

He reads Revelations 3:2, the New Life Version. "Wake up! Make stronger what you have before it dies. I have not found your work complete in God's sight."

He looks right at me. My heart is knocking rapidly against my rib cage. Usually, I would be upset about Gabriel speaking to me through his sermons, but I feel it's God, not my husband, that truly needs me to hear this word.

He repeats, "Wake up! Make stronger what you have before it dies. I have not found your work complete in God's sight."

I'm not the only one the scripture resonates with. There are some claps and Hmm, hmms throughout the congregation.

Your marriage is on life support, but it's not dead yet. There's still time for it to come back to life. The voice of God booms in my ear. I know I prayed this morning. But I shake my head at the words because it's not what I want to hear. I no longer trust Gabriel with my heart. He's broken it too many times. I'm tired. Tired of fighting. Tired of standing by a man I no longer love because he's pushed me away. I have no more fight left in me.

"Some of you may be weary. You've given up hope. You're just sitting and waiting to die. But don't you know you're exactly where the enemy wants you. Like a predator after its prey, the perfect time to attack is when they're weak. Their guard is down. Their hope is gone. But I'm here to prompt you to WAKE UP!

Your prayers and your efforts have not gone unnoticed by God…"

I fight back the tears stinging my eyes. *Jesusssssss!*

"…Your savior has not forgotten you! Your work for Him is not complete. God wants you to wake up and renew your strength. To not let die what you've worked so hard for. What you prayed for. Life can be hard, man…" Some in the congregation laugh. Gabriel chuckles too. "I don't recall anyone telling me life will be easy. We all face challenges. It's unavoidable. But dealing with challenges with Jesus makes things a whole lot better. Surrender your will to Him. Trust Him. Don't let the enemy conquer you. Stand your guard against visible and invisible attacks because your heavenly Father wants you to win. He has not brought you this far to fail you…"

After service, I make my way to Gabriel. "I enjoyed your sermon today."

He smiles causing my heart to skip a beat. I press my palm against my chest. He notices and asks, "Are you okay?"

"Yes. I think I have heartburn or something," I look away from him with the lie.

"What did you eat for breakfast?"

"Cereal."

"Okay, take some tums if you keep feeling anything..." He shakes his head with a smile on his face. "Remember when you were pregnant with Nehemiah? You had heartburn most of your pregnancy."

I smile at the memory. "Yeah, she had me popping tums nonstop for six months and she came out with a head full of hair."

We laugh at the memory and it's surprisingly refreshing to have this moment with him.

After greeting people in the lobby, I leave Gabriel and head towards children's church to get the girls. Bria is walking in my direction. I see the slight frown on her face when she notices me but then she plasters on a fake smile.

"How was your date last night?" She stops in front of me.

My brow arches at her question. "It was great. But how do you know about it?"

"I do handle Pastor's calendar, I'm his *secretary*. I know everything he has going on. Besides, I'm the one he asked to purchase the tickets." Bria smirks.

Too bad what she's trying to do doesn't work. Sometimes I wish Gabriel was cheating on me to give me a clean break.

"You did good! We had a great time laughing and enjoying each other's company. Later that night I showed him just how appreciative I was. All thanks to you. Keep up the good work, *secretary*." The deep frown on her face has me doing cartwheels on the inside. I walk around her to retrieve the girls from the children's church.

TEN – GABRIEL

"You sure brought a word today Pastor Gabriel…" Ms. Urma says standing at my side.

My eyes are locked on Sabrina and the girls walking towards her SUV. I have a full view of them through the large cathedral windows in the church foyer. Genesis is animatedly talking, then Sabrina and Nehemiah are laughing at what she said. I smile at my family, then I have a feeling like I'm missing out.

"…That scripture was perfect too…" Ms. Urma continues.

"Thank you, Ms. Urma. I know if no one else enjoys my sermon, you certainly will." I thank the older woman kindly. She's faithfully been attending Everlasting Love Ministry for eight years.

"You're doing a great job as the pastor of the church." She places her hand on my arm, rubbing up and down. If she was any other woman I would step out of her reach, but she means no harm. "I knew you would do a great job after your father retired. How are they in Barbados?"

"They're doing well. They attend a smaller church on the island. And they have a nice house near the beach with amazing views. It's going to be a while before they come back to Florida for a visit."

She smiles. "I don't blame them."

My stomach growls embarrassingly loud. I skipped on breakfast this morning now I'm paying for it.

"Oh, you poor man. Didn't Sabrina cook you a hot breakfast this morning?"

"I didn't get a chance to eat this morning. But –"

"Your young wife needs to learn how to take care of a strong man like you. Why don't you come over to my house for lunch? I have ribs that will fall off the bones cooking in the crockpot. I made the potato salad yesterday and the mac and cheese are prepped so I only have to pop it in the oven."

That sounds really good.

I shake my head, "Thank you for the invite but I'll be eating at home…"

"Excuse me Ms. Urma. Gabriel, I need to talk to you before I leave," Pastor Jason interrupts us.

"Ms. Urma, you enjoy the rest of your Sunday," I tell her before quickly walking away with Jason.

He chuckles when we're out of earshot heading towards my office. "I thought you needed some rescuing."

"Thanks, man."

"You know that old woman wants to jump your bones, right?"

I almost vomit in my mouth. "Bruh, please don't put that image in my head." Not only is Jason an associate pastor at the church he's also my best friend since elementary school. We go way back. Some people say he resembles actor Omari Hardwick.

He laughs at my expense. "Just saying. I know you're a one-woman man."

"Absolutely!" We reach my office and step in. "I'm glad you interrupted though. Is it possible for you to visit Brother Cedric Miller at his home for a sick visit today at three?"

I sit behind my desk and he sits in one of the visitor's seats. "Yeah, I should be able to. I will have to check with Tabitha first to make sure she's good with the kids for a couple of hours."

"Thanks, man I would appreciate it. I want to go straight home today and spend QT with my family."

"Bout time you took time to chill. You've been running like a machine since you took the senior pastor position. On top of preaching at three services on Sunday to twenty-five hundred people. I bet Sabrina would be happy."

I must have a telling look on my face.

"What's wrong? Is there trouble in paradise?"

Jason has been my friend for a long time, and we've experienced a lot together. But what man wants to admit to another that your wife is no longer in love with you? Hearing my wife admit that was a sobering experience.

"I just need to properly balance my personal and professional life. You're right, I've been so busy building my career as a pastor that I've been neglectful to my wife and kids. But it's nothing that can't be easily fixed."

"Our family is our first ministry, so take care of home. And get the rest of the pastors on staff to pitch in more with church responsibilities."

"I plan on doing that."

He stands to leave. "I better go if I'm to make it to Brother Cedric's house by three. I'll check in with you later."

"Ok, later."

***

I walk into the house a little after 2 p.m. and I can hear Sabrina and the girls in the kitchen. After talking with Jason at church, I grabbed my things and took the back exit to my car to avoid bumping into anyone to delay my departure.

"It smells good in here," I say catching them off guard. I'm surprised they didn't hear the door chime announcing my entrance into the house.

The girls exclaim at my presence.

"Daddy!" I can't tell you just how great their excitement for me makes me feel. I remember when their mother used to at least smile when I came home.

Now, she wears a blank expression on her beautiful face.

"Are those for mommy, daddy?" Miah asks about the flowers in my hand.

"They are. And I got some for you and Genesis too." I walk further into the kitchen and give my daughters each their own small vase of sunflowers. "Go put those in your rooms."

"Thank you, daddy!" I give them a one-arm hug before they skip off to their rooms.

"Come back so we can finish the cookies," Sabrina calls after them.

"These are for you," I hand her the large vase of assortorted hibiscus flowers. Her favorite.

"They're beautiful, thank you."

She blesses me with a smile showcasing the indent in her right cheek that I find adorable. I step closer to her, leaning in and kissing her lips. She doesn't pull away, for which I'm thankful. I take that small feat further by deepening the kiss. Her mouth opens for me and I dive in. She moans. *Music to my ears.* I'm about to lose my senses and slide the bowl of cookie dough and ingredients off the kitchen island and devour her.

I hear the girls running back towards the kitchen and I reluctantly pull away. I watch Sabrina as she opens her eyes, blinking away desire I haven't seen in her eyes for me in forever.

"Let's finish making the cookies. Daddy do you want to help?" Nehemiah asks.

"Yes. Let me change and wash up first."

I return to the kitchen to bake cookies with my family. Then we give the girls the okay to play video games while we cook.

I'm not the best cook but I'm not terrible either. I'm good at following a recipe or being directed. Sabrina tasks me with making coleslaw while she fries the red snappers.

"Sabrina, I want things to get better in our marriage."

"Does that mean going to counseling?"

"No. I don't think we need to. I just need to work on balancing home and church."

She looks at me over her shoulder. "And wouldn't seeing a therapist help? I need you to *hear* me, it hasn't worked over the years so having a third party may be beneficial." She huffs a breath. "I don't even know why I'm even –"

I stop her train of thought. "Babe…" She looks at me like a deer in headlights. Yeah, we don't even have pet names for each other and maybe *babe* isn't it for her. "Sabrina. What I'm saying is, as a senior pastor I counsel people, it would be weird for me to sit with a therapist about my marriage. Our problems can be fixed by us both opening our hearts to move forward for better. I need you to forgive me for letting you down all these years and see that I'm going to do everything I can to do things differently and better."

She studies my face for a while before shrugging her shoulders and saying, "Fine."

"I've also been thinking, with our eleventh anniversary in three months, what do you think about us going on a cruise to the Bahamas?" I look at her at the stove while I ask the question.

She places the hot fish she pulled out of the grease onto a dish covered with a paper towel. She turns to face me. I can tell she's trying to find the right words to reply. "*You*...want to go on vacation, for our anniversary?" I nod my head. She busies herself tending to the fish. I wait because I know she needs time to process what I'm asking. As an introvert, she needs a moment to gather her words. "Are you sure you're going to follow through if I agree?"

"Yes. I *want* to do this for us." I know she's skeptical. I've flat out turned her down before about taking trips for our anniversary.

"When?"

"We can leave the day before our anniversary for a five-day cruise from Fort Lauderdale or Miami."

"Okay…do you want me to book the trip?" I can tell she's a bit hesitant but I'm happy she easily agreed.

"No, I'll take care of it."

"Or you'll get Bria to do it for you," she mumbles under her breath, but I let it slide without a response. We're in a good vibe right now that I don't want it to be ruined.

"I will also arrange for someone to take care of the girls while we're gone."

Her eyes enlarge in size. It's almost comical. But sad that me doing this is such a surprise for her. I want me doing things like this to become normal.

ELEVEN – SABRINA

"Hey," Sunni pops her head into my office. She's a 39-year-old white woman that still looks like she's in her 20s. She's the only nonblack employee. And she's a beast with graphics. Her animated ads are a hit and a huge boost to business. "Your hubby's here."

"Send him in. Thanks."

Gabriel came home early yesterday, brought flowers, baked cookies with us then cooked dinner with me, suggested and is planning our anniversary trip, now this. I'm pleasantly surprised. He hasn't been to my office since I opened almost five years ago.

"Good afternoon." Kian walks into my office carrying a huge bag of takeout. I'm partially disappointed that it's not Gabriel. I forgot my staff jokingly refer to Kian as my work-husband. Only Josh and Zaiden, my first two employees, have met Gabriel. "I brought lunch for everyone."

I smile big because I'm starving. I've been holed up in my office working since nine this morning.

I giddily clap my hands. "Please tell me you have a brisket sub in that bag."

"You have to meet me in your breakroom to find out," Kian teases.

I'm out my seat and hot on his trail. Josh, Zaiden, Sunni, Aubree, and Tyreke are also following behind the food.

"Can you visit your wife often and bring us food?" Tyreke tells Kian after taking another bite of his sub. Tyreke is the youngest on staff at 26 years old.

We're all sitting at the large breakroom table eating subs and French fries.

I'm in food paradise with this brisket sub with southwest chipotle sauce.

"My wife?" Kian asks lifting his brow. He's sitting next to me to my left.

"Yeah, Sabrina's your work wife," Aubree tells him. She's 30 and the life of the party here. I just love her spunky personality. "You two act like it at least. You bring her coffee or food. You talk about watching the same show on TV and you both love everything graphics and print related. And weren't you two discussing a book you two read a few months ago?"

Things have gone back to normal between Kian and I since he admitted his attraction to me and he's agreed to keep things professional.

"Work-wife, huh?" Kian smirks at me.

"Yeah. But she is married, to a pastor. So everything stays PG." Zaiden acts as my unofficial big brother. He's 36 and has a heart of gold.

"Don't they at least kiss in PG movies?" Josh teases. He's also 36 and the jokester around here, but he means no harm.

I almost choke on the bottled water I'm drinking. Kian smirks at me again, saying, "I do like PG movies."

"Nah, homie. No PG either," Zaiden tells him. Not only has Zaiden met Gabriel he's a member of the church.

Kian lets him know, "Don't worry. Mrs. Sabrina has already told me where she stands."

"Exactly. Our business relationship and friendship are cool but I am a real-life married woman…" I start.

But Zaiden finishes. "That loves her husband."

As a married man himself, Zaiden doesn't mess around with infidelity or anything close to it. He's admitted to me once that growing up watching his mother cry over, and constantly take back her cheating husband showed him the value of respecting his woman, marriage, and family enough to not bring anything in it that can tear it down.

I admire him so much for that.

"Y'all know we're only playing about the work-wife, work-husband thing," Sunni says. "Plus, there's nothing wrong with a man and woman being friends."

"Not when there's mutual attraction though. I don't care what no one says. I don't want my fiancée being friends with a dude that wants her." Tyreke shakes his head adamantly. "Nope, not going for it, period."

"Same here for my wife," Zaiden says.

Josh speaks up. "A person's going to do what they want to regardless of restrictions. I'm not saying my girl can have a sleepover at her friend who may be a dude's house. But I'm not going to tell her to stop being friends with a dude either unless there's some disrespect. If not, we cool. If she loves me, I trust her to respect me and stay loyal as I will be for her."

"I agree with Josh," Aubree tells us. "I can barely control what my two-year-old does, so I'm for sure not going to be monitoring my man and his friends."

"I don't have a woman right now, but if I did, I'm not sure I will be comfortable with her being friends with someone I know wants her." I turn to look at

Kian. He continues, "But like you said Josh, as long as she loves and respects me, I would trust her loyalty."

"Hmmm," is my only contribution to the conversation before sipping on my water.

"Sabrina, what are your plans for your five years in business anniversary?" Sunni asks moments later.

"I want to have a party."

TWELVE – SABRINA

I have a dedicated *work from home Friday's* for my business. We all do a conference call at 9:30 in the morning to keep everyone abreast of the status of projects and discuss any necessary issues, after that we finish our projects at home. I like to use Friday's to do my bookkeeping. I have an accountant that takes care of the business taxes at the end of the year, but I handle all the weekly and monthly transactions.

Each employee is responsible for invoicing their jobs and ensuring payment at completion and inputting info into the billing software. On Fridays, I transfer the info to QuickBooks ensuring everything is in order. I do payroll biweekly and bank reconciliation at the beginning of the month.

I'm done with my business tasks by noon and start doing work around the house. I add a load of laundry for the girls in the washer before I play *The Miseducation of Lauryn Hill* album on the Bluetooth speakers.

I'm dancing to the song "Doo Wop (That Thing)" blasting loudly as I mop the kitchen floor. I hold the mop like a microphone as I sing and dance, enjoying my one-woman concert.

Strong arms encircle my waist causing me to scream. The enticing scent of Gabriel's cologne and his kiss on my cheek calm my nerves.

"Sorry I scared you, *babe*." He begins to move to the beat of the music. When it comes to the hook of the song he sings off-key making me giggle like a schoolgirl. "Guys you know you'd better watch out…"

He spins me around, the mop drops from my hands and we start to dance. *Oh my gosh, we've never danced before*. Not even on our wedding day because it was a shotgun wedding at the courthouse.

We dance the entire song. I've never had this much fun with my husband outside of the kids.

I turn down the speaker. "I didn't know you knew Lauryn Hill," I say picking up the mop and placing it to the side. I'll finish the floor later.

"Who doesn't know Lauryn Hill? That album came out when we were what, thirteen? Everybody was jamming to that. Even me as a Preacher's kid."

"I didn't mean that, I just meant I'm surprised. You even know some of the lyrics…We've never danced before."

He moves closer to me, caging me in against the granite kitchen counter. "Which means we need to do it more. I meant what I told you Sabrina, I'm going to make you fall in love with me all over again." Butterflies go wild in my belly. He kisses me on the tip of my nose. "I came home to eat lunch with you before my meeting with the church board at three. Want me to make you a sandwich?" He steps away to the fridge.

"Yes, thanks." I go to the sink to wash my hands, then sit at the kitchen island watching him.

"I booked our trip." He spreads mayo on a slice of bread.

I perk up. I know he said he would, but I wasn't expecting him to follow through with it. With his track record, it's hard for me not to doubt his word. But I'm lowkey excited to go on a romantic vacation.

"Yeah? What are the destinations?" I take a pickle from the jar and take a bite.

"Key West, Freeport, Nassau, and Great Stirrup Cay. We leave and return from Miami."

"Sounds good."

"Make sure you buy a yellow bikini when you go shopping for the trip. That color looks great on you." He adds meat to the sandwiches.

I blush.

"Yeah. Maybe I should get you a matching speedo."

He playfully throws a piece of lunch meat at me I move to the side and it falls to the tiled floor.

I laugh.

"I will not be caught dead wearing those things. We, manly men, wear swim trunks." He puffs out his chest doing the superman pose with his fists to his hips.

I laugh louder.

He watches me with a smile. "I love when you laugh." He leans over the kitchen island and kisses me briefly.

"I do too," I say against his lips.

THIRTEEN – GABRIEL

"I know you love Sabrina but why do you have a miniature version of her on your desk?" Jason asks after walking into my office seeing me play with the bobblehead of Sabrina.

"It was just delivered. I got it as a gift for her business anniversary party."

"A bobblehead?" He raises his eyebrow.

"What? It's a creative gift for a creative. I think she'll like it. I also got her this," I open my desk drawer and pull out the jewelry box. I open it to reveal a white gold chain with a diamond-encrusted pendant of the year she opened her business.

"Now that, she's going to love." He sits.

There's a knock on my open office door, "Hey pastor Jason," Bria walks in while Jason says his hello. "Pastor Gabriel here's a draft of the newsletter for your review." She places the document on my desk.

She notices the necklace. "That's beautiful. Who's it for?"

"Sabrina," I tell her closing the jewelry box.

"I guess she'll like it. Is there a special occasion?" She flicks the bobblehead with her finger making it shake.

"My wife will be celebrating five years in business in a couple weeks. I got her the bobblehead too as a gift."

"Nice." She steps back from the desk. "I'm going to be running out for lunch. Do you need anything before I leave?"

"No, thanks. I'll review these while you're gone." I lift the document.

She nods then turns and leaves.

Jason gets up and closes my office door. "I still don't understand why you have her working for you." He returns to his seat.

"She's a great secretary and she needed a job."

"But y'all have history. You were going to marry her, remember?"

I wave him off. "She's harmless."

Jason shakes his head. "I'm just saying. Couldn't be me. Tabitha would hang me by my nuts."

I chuckle.

There's a knock on the door.

"Come in," I call out before the door is pushed open.

"Good afternoon, pastor Gabriel," Ms. Urma steps in carrying a plate covered in foil. She notices Jason. "Oh, and hi there pastor Jason. Aren't I lucky to be in the presence of you two fine godly men."

The bright yellow sleeveless muumuu dress she's wearing is like a beacon.

"Hi Ms. Urma," Jason and I say in unison.

"I brought you some home cooked lunch." She places the plate on my desk. "And there's enough for you too, pastor Jason."

"Thank you, Ms. Urma. I am hungry. I will bum some of Gabriel's food for sure. It smells real good."

She blushes and for a moment it makes her look a bit younger than her 67 years. "Well, I'll leave you two to finish your meeting and eat. I just wanted to drop that by before I start my errands."

"Thank you, Ms. Urma, I appreciate it." I stand as she leaves.

"I know you probably don't get a homecooked meal often with Sabrina working and all, it's the least I can do." She leaves.

And Jason is now having a fit laughing.

I sit back down. "What are you laughing at?"

"Dude, I think that is the first time I've seen Ms. Urma in anything sleeveless. And if I'm not mistaken, her dress was not sweeping the floor, it was right below her knees."

"You checking out Ms. Urma now?" I tease.

"With that dress on it's hard for anyone not to notice. And I do believe she wore it just for you." He barks a laugh.

I pick up a pen and fling it at him, hitting him on the chest. "Shut up! She's just being motherly."

"Yeah, I bet she wants to call you *daddy*." This joker continues to laugh at my expense.

"Here, why don't you enjoy lunch, on me." I shove the plate on my desk towards him.

He shakes his head. "I was just being polite to her. All twenty-five hundred members of this church knows Ms. Urma can't cook."

I shake my head and chuckle. "And no matter how many times Minister Betty tells her not to volunteer to cook at functions she always does. And now I don't know how to tell her not to bring me food."

"Just be honest. Say, Ms. Urma, if I had a dog, even he wouldn't want to eat your food, so please stop bringing me some."

"You want that woman to cuss me out? Saved or not she will call me everything but a child of God."

"You know I'm just playing. I don't know, just keep accepting her food. She seems to enjoy doing something for you."

"Yeah but I don't eat it. Next time I'll just tell her thanks, but please don't bring me food anymore."

He stands. "Okay. But speaking of food, let's go grab something edible to eat."

FOURTEEN – SABRINA

At first, I didn't want to do anything big for my 5th business anniversary, but this is a huge milestone that ought to be celebrated. Sunni and Aubree were both completely on board with the idea and helped me with the planning. DesignHer design studio was my dream child since high school. A few times I doubted it would become reality. I was blessed with a gig right out of college designing book covers for an indie publisher, I earned enough over the years for me to save enough money to finally rent my own space, purchase computers, software, and to hire my initial staff of three.

"You're happy this morning, excited about your party tonight?" Gabriel asks stepping behind me and kissing me on my exposed shoulder. I was at the kitchen counter singing along to "Lovely Day" by Kirk Franklin.

"Mommy's been singing all morning," Nehemiah tells him. She and Genesis are helping me cut fruit for the homemade yogurt we made for breakfast. It's Friday and they're out of school for teachers in service.

Gabriel spins me around causing me to squeal and start dancing to the song. He's not a dancer – neither am I. But we have fun making up moves. The girls join us while singing along to the song.

"That was fun," Genesis admits when the song ends. Our 11-year-old is at the stage where she still likes doing some things with her parents but sometimes she doesn't and thinks we're weird.

We all sit and eat breakfast together. Then the girls leave to grudgingly do their chores. Gabriel and I remain at the kitchen table.

"Everything is set for the party tonight. About sixty people RSVP'd. The caterer that Aubree found is amazing so I know the food will be great. And the DJ knows to play clean music." I smile. "I'm so excited. Five years of business, this is so amazing."

"I'm proud of you, babe." I'm starting to get used to him calling me that.

"Thank you! I'll be at the hall early, so you'll have to meet me there."

"Ok, no problem. I'm leaving church at four." He stands to leave.

I do something I haven't willingly done in ages, I get up from the table and go to give him a kiss bye. "See you later."

He smiles against my lips. "Later."

***

"Hey, boss lady." Josh walks up beside me. I'm standing talking to one of my former clients, Ashley. A couple years ago I designed t-shirts for her bachelorette party. We've kept in touch since. "Come dance with me." He starts tugging on my arm. "I see you over here swaying to the beat." The DJ was playing a 90s track by Missy Elliott.

I shake my head. "Nope! I only dance in the privacy of my home. I have no desire to make a fool of myself."

"It's your party which means you must dance." He takes my hand and tugs me forward.

Ashley laughs at the horror on my face. "He's right. It is your party and you can dance badly if you want to."

"No one better record this," I say before giving in.

It is my party and I should have fun.

"I solemnly promise you will not go viral on social media and no awful memes will be made from it." Josh laughs pulling me to the dance floor.

I swat at his arm. "I'm serious, Josh. If I see any phones out pointing at us I'm leaving you here."

He starts dancing encouraging me to do so as well. With the music and the energy of the party, I start to loosen up and – dance badly. One song turns to three. Soon my entire staff are all on the dance floor dancing with me.

"Everyone has gotten a chance to dance with the lady of the hour, I think it's my turn now." A deep voice says over my shoulder.

I turn and come face to face with Kian.

Kirk Franklin's song, "Stomp" starts to play. I start moving to the beat and Kian follows suit. I'm impressed by his moves – clapping and stomping to the beat. Everyone starts dancing like the people in the music video.

I start to rap Salt's part of the song. Aubree and Sunni join in with me.

I'm having so much fun.

I've mentally been in a bad place for too long, it's great to have a reprieve.

After the song ends, I make my way off the dance floor. I need some water.

"You're a good dancer," Kian says following behind me.

I laugh. "Yeah right. But I've been having too much fun to think too much about it."

"My motto is as long as you don't trip over your own feet, you can dance."

"I guess I can sign-up for America's Got Talent, then?"

"On second thought…"

I playfully swat him on the arm. "Ha! I knew it." I hand him a bottled water from the drinks table then take one for myself.

He takes a sip while looking around the room. "Where's your husband?"

A great question. The party started two hours ago and Gabriel isn't here yet. He texted me earlier and said he would be a little late. I'm giving him the benefit of a doubt. I know he's busy being the pastor of a steadily growing church, but tonight is a special and monumental night for me. I want to celebrate along with my husband. And I haven't wanted to do that in a while.

"He'll be here soon." I sip my water.

"Well, I want one more dance until then." Kian pitches his empty bottle in the trash can then beckons for me to follow him back on the dance floor.

This used to be my jam. Beenie Man's, "Girls Dem Sugar," thumps through the speakers. My hips move involuntarily, and I get lost in the beat. Kian is a good hype man, making me feel like I'm Ciara on the dancefloor. We're dancing together at a respectable distance.

"Okay, I see you, first lady," Tabitha says dancing beside me.

I throw my arms around her. "Hey, thanks for coming."

"Of course. Congratulations on five years in business!" She hugs me back. "Sorry, I'm late. I was waiting on Jason, but he called and said they had a last-minute meeting at church."

"It's okay." I excuse myself from Kian and Tabitha and I walk off the dance floor.

"I got you a gift." She holds up the gift bag.

"You didn't have to get me anything."

"Jason and I wanted to though." She hands it to me.

"Thank you." I open it to find a mug that reads, *Happy 5 Years* and it's filled with several gift cards I can use for my business. "Aww thank you, guys!"

"You're welcome." She looks around. "This is a nice party." She turns back to me. "And it's great seeing you *happy* and carefree. It's been a minute since I've seen you like this."

It's been hard wearing a smile on my face when my personal life is falling apart. But maybe things are looking up.

Gabriel still hasn't arrived...

"Yeah, it feels good to be Sabrina."

"Excuse me, Sabrina," Aubree walks up to us. "It's time for your celebratory speech."

I take the microphone from the Deejay. "Thank you all for coming out tonight to celebrate my five years in business." Everyone applauds and I can't help but kick myself for letting my guard down and expecting Gabriel to be here to celebrate with me. "I thank God for His blessings and favor for DesignHer. I'm thankful to all our clients new and old. Thanks for trusting us with your vision. We appreciate your business. I wouldn't be standing here a success today without the help from my staff. Josh, Tyreke, Zaiden,

Sunni and Aubree, my success is yours too!" There's applause. "Please if you all can join me here." I wait for them all to stand with me near the deejay. I hand each of them an envelope with a check for $1500. "You all are extraordinarily talented, and I'm blessed to have you as part of my team. I love you guys!"

"We love you too!" They tell me.

"Here's to many more successful years in business." I raise a fake glass. Everyone cheers.

I sneak away a short time later to get some fresh air out on the back patio of the venue. The lush gardens are welcoming but the humid night here in Boca Raton, Florida, isn't.

I silently pray in my heavenly language because I don't want my overthinking negative thoughts to consume me.

Why can't he put me first for once?

"I thought I saw you sneak out here."

I open my eyes at the sound of Kian's voice.

"Mind if I join you."

Yes!

But I shake my head "no".

He silently stands next to me. Moments pass before he asks, "Are you happy?"

Damn my tears.

Damn you, Gabriel.

"No," I whisper wiping tears from my eyes.

"You are too beautiful. Too talented. Too admirable to be unhappy. He doesn't deserve you if he doesn't appreciate *all* of you."

The heat of him nearing me sends my heart racing.

"Look at me, Sabrina." I lift my eyes to meet his. "You deserve better." He leans into me leaving only a hairsbreadth space between our lips.

"Watch and pray so that you will not be tempted. Man's spirit is willing, but the body does not have the power to do it." Matthew 26:41 pops into my head.

I close my eyes and step back. The temptation is overwhelmingly strong. And although Gabriel has broken my heart yet *again*, I'm still his wife.

"I can't do this. I'm married and the First Lady of a church. And a mother of two daughters. And above all that I'm a child of God. I'm not going to commit adultery because I'm heartbroken. No matter how tempting you are."

I step back even further.

"I respect that. Yet another thing to admire about you." He nods his head. "You're right and I'm glad you stopped what was going to happen. Please forgive me." He sounds genuinely sincere.

"I forgive you."

"Don't let his absence ruin your celebration. You deserve this night. Come back and finish enjoying the rest of the party."

The party ends in thirty minutes, I might as well enjoy it till the end.

We walk back into the party and I immediately lock eyes with Gabriel. He frowns when he notices Kian by my side.

FIFTEEN – GABRIEL

"You're in a good mood," Bria says when I walk into the office. She's sitting behind her desk in the reception area.

"I am. I'm excited about Sabrina's business anniversary party tonight."

"Oh, her thing is tonight?"

"Yes. And I'll be leaving here at four today."

"Hmmm," she picks up some papers off her desk. "Here's the list of the recent high school students with 2.0 to 2.5 GPA's for the scholarship fund. The board agreed to five thousand dollars each. There are thirty-seven students signed up for university, community college or trade school."

I take the document from her. "Thank you." Since I came on board as a senior pastor I thought it was important for the church to offer scholarships to those students that didn't get the perfect grades in school and have a hard time getting scholarships because of it.

I head into my office to finish working on my sermon for Sunday. There are a few notes I want to add before I handle church business. As soon as I sit in the leather seat my desk phone rings.

I see that it's Bria calling from the front desk. "Yes."

"James from maintenance is here to see you."

"Okay, send him in."

"Good morning James."

He takes a seat. "Good morning Pastor Gabriel. I've checked out the AC unit in the Sanctuary building and it's not cooling properly. Especially with this Florida heat, it's working hard to cool down if it's not repaired soon it will go out completely. I'm going to need to order parts to repair it before church on Sunday. What I need can be delivered tomorrow morning if I can order them before noon."

He slides a piece of paper on my desk and I pick it up. "Okay. Use your card and I'll let Kimberly in accounting know to lift your daily limit for the charge." The parts he needs will cost close to $2,000. Everyone on staff that has a church issued card for expenses have a daily transaction limit of $500.

He stands. "Okay. I'll wait for her to call to give me the okay. Everything is already saved in my cart."

"Great, thank you, James. I appreciate you and the maintenance staff."

"You're welcome."

Not even an hour later I hear a ruckus outside my office door before it's abruptly pushed open.

"You can't just barge in here and –"

"And what?" the disgruntled woman cuts Bria off. "I've called five times this morning and your irritating voice keeps telling me I have to fill out some form to get help from my church! I've been paying tithes here for years. I shouldn't have to fill out no form to wait…"

I step from around my desk. "Miss, I understand you're upset but please have some respect and take a seat and talk to me about what the problem is."

The woman who appears to be in her mid-forties turns her angry gaze from Bria and I watch them soften a bit when she looks at me. "Okay." She sits in one of the visitor's seat. Bria is shooting daggers at the woman.

"Bria, I'll handle this from here, thank you." She nods then turns and walks away.

"Please tell me your name?"

"I'm Cassie."

I extend my hand to her for a handshake, which she accepts. "Hi Cassie, I'm pastor Gabriel."

"Hi."

I go back and sit behind my desk. "So tell me how I can help you, Cassie." The woman is a disheveled mess. Her eyes are bloodshot and with the tank top she's wearing I can see her exposed arm with track marks on them.

Cassie starts rocking slightly while scratching her dirty fingernails against her arm. "I need help. That's what I was trying to tell *that* woman out there. I ahh…I need money for food and a place to stay."

"Okay, I can help you with that. We sponsor a woman's shelter not far from here which provides three hot meals a day."

She shakes her head. "No… no I just need the money so I can find my own place. I don't like being around a bunch of people."

"How much money do you need?"

She perks up. "Hmmm, I mean I don't need that much. Maybe like ten thousand dollars. You know, to rent me a place and ah…buy a bed and stuff…oh and food. So can I get that in cash?"

"Ma'am we're not able to give that kind of money out in cash and though I'm the senior pastor, a decision like that will have to go through the board. But like I told you, there's a woman's shelter that we sponsor where you can stay and eat hot meals. I can also have someone on staff assist you with finding a job to help you get on your feet."

"Okay…okay. What about one thousand? I need to pay Ricky back…I mean, I mean, I know it's risky giving out ten thousand so I'll settle for one."

"Tell you what. You go and sign up to the shelter today and once the director Missy calls me to let me know you're settled and have been there for a couple days, we'll write you a check for $300 to help you buy clothes, shoes and any toiletries you may need." The women's shelter that the church sponsors is great with not only providing a clean and safe place for women and children, but hot meals are provided three times a day and there's medical staff on the team to help women with drug addiction, and counselors for mental support. I know Cassie doesn't want money for food and shelter, but I have to be diplomatic in my approach to her.

"This is some BS! I've been paying tithes in this church for years and y'all can't give me nothing back?" She stands completely irate.

"Cassie I'm trying to help you but your disrespect won't be tolerated. If you truly want a safe clean place to stay and food, staying at the woman's shelter would be beneficial and in doing so the church can formulate a plan to assist you further."

"I've told you I don't like being around a bunch of people. So just give me the money. Please."

"Do you want the money for food and shelter, or to pay for drugs?"

"How dare you? Now I have to be a druggie because I need money?" She can't help scratching the tracks on her arms. I really want her to go to the shelter so Missy and her team can help her. Cassie fruitlessly tries to smooth down her wrinkle tank top and pants trying to appear presentable. "I'm not on drugs. I'm just hard on luck."

"If you don't want to go to the shelter we won't be able to help you."

"Okay, okay, how about fifty dollars? *Please*. I just need fifty dollars and you won't be bothered with me again."

I shake my head.

"Okay fine! I'll go to the shelter. But you have to give me fifty dollars for it."

"Deal." I stand. "Follow me out front and we'll get you over to the shelter."

I have Bria call ahead to the shelter to let Missy know that Cassie is coming and that I suspect she is on drugs. I have Christian counseling certification, but Missy is much more experienced in situations like this and I hope Cassie takes the help offered. She will get $50 cash after she sat and talked with Missy.

Back at my desk, I follow up on calls I received for speaking engagements. Lunch comes and go and I'm just now reviewing the scholarship list Bria had given me this morning and signing the checks. Mine is one of two signatures needed. Kimberly, the church's controller, signed her signature already.

The time on the bottom right of my computer says is 3:30. *Maybe I can cut out of here now.* I finish up my email response to a man that didn't like that I quoted a scripture from the New Living translation instead of the King James version.

My desk phone rings, it's Bria calling. "Hey."

"Hey, Mr. and Mrs. Cox are here for their 3:30 appointment."

"What appointment? I have that time blocked on my calendar."

"Oh, I must have forgotten to tell you. They're here now and are eager to meet with you."

I sigh deeply. Maybe this won't take long. "What is the appointment for?"

"They have emotional and religious conflicts they want to discuss with you and get your guidance."

"Okay. Send them in."

I close out of my email and stand to greet the couple at the door.

"Pastor Gabriel, my wife thinks it's a sin for me to want to have sex every day, twice a day."

"And my husband thinks it's ungodly for women to wear weave and too much makeup."

Oh boy, this is going to be long.

Almost three hours go by without me realizing it. But the couple is now gone with another appointment set for a month from today.

Sabrina's party starts in thirty minutes. I know she's probably busy getting things ready, I pick up my cellphone to send her a quick text.

6:33 PM Gabriel: Babe, I will be a little late. See you soon.

I go to put my phone down when I see the three dots dance...

6:33 PM Babe: Okay ☐

I reach for the handle on my desk drawer to get Sabrina's gifts when there's a knock on my office door followed by Jason barging in.

"Bro, KJAC 95.5 FM Radio is here! How did you get a meeting set up with the producers?"

I look at him like he's crazy. "What?"

"Bria called and told me we have a meeting with the radio show producers about potentially having a daily segment where you and I drop words of wisdom during the weekday 6-9 p.m. segment."

I had pitched the idea to the radio station months ago with a tape of Jason and I having a 15-minute discussion about relevant topics from a biblical perspective, but I hadn't heard anything back. This opportunity will be great for us and the church.

Bria walks into the office. "I guess Jason told you already. The Producers are waiting in the meeting room."

The question is why she hadn't told me about this sooner. But this is great news.

"Thanks Bria!" I stand excitedly. "Do you have water and snacks available in the meeting room?"

"Yup, everything is set. I have a feeling this is going to be a long but interesting meeting." She steps out of the office ahead of us.

"We will be able to reach so many more people with the Word. This is dope," Jason says heading out the door. I can't agree with him more.

***

The producers loved our idea and have agreed for us to start just doing our segment once a week on a Monday to start and if it garners enough interest, they will increase days of segment. The good thing is Jason and I can pre-record our 15-minute discussion and not have to be live in the studio. We will have our test run in two weeks.

It's 9:15 p.m. by the time I'm walking to my car. Sabrina's party ends at ten because the hall has to be cleaned and set up again for a brunch event tomorrow. I won't have time to go home and change and the venue is about twenty minutes away. I'm sorry I pretty much missed her party, but the meeting with the radio producers was huge.

Minutes after entering the hall I lock eyes with Sabrina. God, she's gorgeous! *Thank you.* My focus shifts to the figure at her side and I frown. I don't like this clown, especially being near my wife. And where are they coming from and what were they doing?

I purposely walk towards them, stopping in front of Sabrina, embracing her in my arms then I devour her lips. I have something to prove to her...and *him.* She's reluctant at first but soon willingly opens to me and that's all the encouragement I need. She moans in my mouth and I enjoy the satisfaction of it and the defeated look on this loser's face when I peek an eye open. *She's mine!*

"AhhhHmmm," someone clears their throat. "Things will get X-rated if y'all don't stop." I recognize Jason's voice. He and I arrived at the same time.

I give Sabrina one last kiss before releasing her now swollen lips. She bashfully buries her face in my chest. It's fair to say we both got lost in the moment.

"I think he got the message," Jason leans in and tells me. I can hear the smile in his voice.

I look to where Kian was standing moments ago and he's not there. *Good.*

The DJ announces the last song. "Won't He Do It" by Koryn Hawthorne begins to play and it's quite fitting.

"Dance with me?" I ask Sabrina. She nods, takes my hand and leads me to the dance floor.

SIXTEEN – SABRINA

I'm still a little salty over Gabriel practically missing my party. But my guilt, his explanation and cute gifts he gave me, softened me up a bit.

I lift my hand to touch the gorgeous necklace around my neck.

We danced to the last song last night then we said goodbye to my guests and he helped load my SUV with my gifts. When we got home, though I was upset with him, I pounced on him the second we walked into our bedroom. I needed to be reminded that he's my husband in every way and to rid any lingering desire for Kian.

God, this cycle I'm in is frustrating. And now I'm sitting here drinking my coffee on the deck, angry at Gabriel all over again. I wouldn't be in this confusing state if he had just loved, appreciated and gave me the affection I needed. I'm his wife! Now I'm no longer in love with him. I can no longer be vulnerable with him. I no longer trust him with my heart. And now I'm guilty of almost kissing another man.

"It's a beautiful day, isn't it?" I almost jump out of my skin at the sound of Gabriel's voice behind me. I was so lost in thought.

"Hmmm," is my reply. I sip my coffee.

He takes a seat next to me on the patio chair holding his cup of coffee. We silently sip our hot beverage and enjoy the cool early morning air.

"Is something going on with you and Kian?"

I knew the question was coming but I'm still not prepared.

"No. We're only friends and business partners of sorts." Kian and I don't share finances we just have a deal where we exclusively benefit from each other's business. I do my printing needs with him and he sends graphic design business my way. It's a win-win and we review our contract every year.

"Do you want him to be more than a friend?"

Do I?

I shake my head. "No."

"He wants you..."

I know.

And this isn't helping my guilt and maybe I should tell Gabriel what almost happened last night, but not now.

"...Where were you two coming from when I got there?" Gabriel tugs on his full beard which lets me know he's trying to stay calm.

My heartbeat speeds up. Maybe I should tell him. Maybe it's the out I need.

"I went outside to get a breather and he came to get me to go back to the party."

I feel Gabriel shift next to me and I feel him looking at my profile but I refuse to look at him.

"I love you, Sabrina. I don't want to lose you. And if something is going on between you two I want to know so –"

I shift in the chair to face him. "There's nothing between us but friendship and business."

He visibly relaxes.

And there I go again trying to protect his heart when mine is all the way screwed up.

***

Gabriel preached a good message about faith today. His scripture was Mark 11:22-24. "Then Jesus said to the disciples, "Have faith in God. I tell you the truth, you can say to this mountain, 'May you be lifted up and thrown into the sea,' and it will happen. But you must really believe it will happen and have no doubt in your heart. I tell you, you can pray for anything, and if you believe that you've received it, it will be yours."

Not going to lie, my faith has been wavering. Especially when my most important relationship after God has me unhappy. Sitting in service today I've realized my thoughts and prayers are contradicting. I feel Gabriel is trying but God I just can't relinquish my heart to him anymore. I can't. I'm terrified. He's broken my heart too many times to count. Marriage is bullshit! Ugh. It shouldn't hurt this badly.

One of my favorite scriptures pops into my head, 2 Timothy 1:7. *"For God did not give us a spirit of fear. He gave us a spirit of power and of love and of a good mind."*

A bubbly couple comes over to greet us. "Good afternoon Pastor Gabriel and First Lady." The Woman says. Gabriel and I say our hellos. "That was a powerful message today, the scripture really spoke to me."

"Me too," her husband says. I tune them out afterward, smiling and nodding when necessary.

They're holding hands and the look in their eyes when they look at each other makes me swoon. How cute. And how sad I've never really had that. Almost eleven years. It seems like a life sentence rather than happily ever after. But that's my problem and I pray they never experience even an ounce of what I feel in my marriage.

He's trying, my conscience tells me. My therapist has said the same thing. But, whatever.

After my obligation, I walk towards children's church to get the girls. I see Bria in a room picking up a small box. She looks up, our eyes connect, then she quickly looks away as if she doesn't notice me. Whatever. I'm not in the mood for fake pleasantries. I'm about to turn the corner to walk past the door when she steps out and bumps into my shoulder, hard.

"Oh, I'm sorry, I didn't see you there." Her voice is dripping with malice.

Jesussssss

"Bitc –" I bite down on my tongue until it hurts.

I am a child of God. I will not stoop to her level. I will not Jackie Chan her in the throat. I will not backslide and cuss her out in the house of the Lord. Jesus you are my strength and help.

"I heard you had your lil' business anniversary party on Friday. Too bad pastor and I were working late that night and he made it there too late."

I will not punch her in her mouth. Thank you, Jesus, for your grace and mercy which is new every day. Every second.

"What is it that you want, Bria?" My voice is calm.

She looks over my shoulder then hisses in my ear. "He was mine first! I should be First Lady. He was going to marry me." She slaps her free hand against her chest. "But you being a THOT got pregnant and ruined everything."

Okay, I was *not* expecting that. Now I want to knock her out for whole other reasons.

"And here it is almost eleven years later and he still hasn't chosen you."

"Or has he." She leans closer. "Church is his second home and I'm *always* here with him."

Her words sucker punch the hell out of me. And my insecurities run wild.

She steps around me and walks away. I don't know what to think. I'm so numb to Gabriel that him having an affair doesn't anger me. It's the principle of him stepping outside our marriage and keeping his situation-ship with her when we met in college from me. And he hired her as his secretary. *Are they sleeping together?* If I had known this a few years ago I would be livid. Now I just don't know.

SEVENTEEN – GABRIEL

I feel Sabrina pulling away from me again, not that I made any leeway since I told her I'm going to make things right between us. She was, however, open to us working things out. I felt it. She wasn't so standoffish. She smiled. But since I practically missed her party over a week ago, she's been a little more distant. Which makes me wonder if there's something really going on with her and Kian. Did I already lose her...to him?

The thought causes a physical ache in my chest. I love my wife. I was a fool to have neglected her for so long. I realize my mistake and I'm correcting them. I don't want my family broken apart.

I slam my car door shut and make my way to the entrance of the building. "Welcome to Best Prints," a redhead behind the counter pleasantly greets me.

I smile at her. "Good morning. I'm here to see Kian, is he available?"

"Yup, he's in the back in his office. What's your name, I can let him know you're here." Her blue eyes rake over my face and she smiles flirtatiously. I guess she has a thing for black men with beards.

"Can you just point me in the direction of his office?"

"Sure. It's the last door on the right." She points down a corridor.

"Thank you."

I reach Kian's office door and knock. He asks who is it but I just turn the knob and push the door open. He'll see who I am.

"Pastor Gabriel." The shocked look on his face is evidence he wasn't expecting to see me. "To what do I owe this meeting?"

I recall the prayer I prayed earlier to keep my cool. I shut the door then sit before answering him where he sits behind his desk. "My wife."

"What about Sabrina?"

I don't even like her name on his lips, but I push the thought aside and remain my cool. "Are you sleeping with my wife?"

He's taken aback at my directness. My suit and tie and cool as a cucumber demeanor must be part of it. Add the fact that I'm a pastor. But I'm not here to play about my wife.

"No! I'm not sleeping with *your* wife." He leans against his high back desk chair. I'm itching for him to leap out of it so I can justifiably knock the smug look off his face.

"But you want to. I get it. She's gorgeous. But she's my wife. Which makes her off limits."

"It's good to know you finally realize she is *your* wife."

What's that supposed to mean? Has she been talking to him about me?

"Don't worry. She hasn't told me about how unhappy she is in her marriage. But it's evident. Like you said, she's gorgeous and she should always have a beautiful smile on her face. But her smile has been dimmed for a long time. Her business is going well. Your children seem to be doing well from the way she brags about them. Which leaves *you*. A woman that doesn't talk about her man… makes one wonder if said man is worth talking about."

His words sting and ring true. Have I been that clueless about how sad Sabrina's been in our marriage?

"Regardless of what you think is going on in my marriage she's still my wife and you will stay away from her. Keep things strictly professional. The moment I feel you are compromising that I will have her look into finding another printer. Don't let my position as pastor fool you, Peter was a disciple and he drew his sword – I come from his side of God's family. Don't mess with my wife."

He sits up straighter moving closer to his desk. "I promise you nothing is going on between me and Sabrina. We have a good working relationship. You won't have any problems from me."

I feel I can believe him. But he's still a man that's attracted to my wife and he works with her often. The last thing I need to be doing is dictating to her who she can and cannot work with. Especially if there's no concrete reason to justify it. My being uncomfortable about it is valid but it also speaks of my shortcomings and current insecurities about the state of my marriage. For now, I have to trust her words and his, that there's nothing inappropriate going on.

I rise to my feet. "Keep things that way and we won't have a problem." I open the door. "Have a blessed day." It was best to leave with those words rather than the profanity floating around in my head.

***

I make it to the church office to find the reception area empty. Bria isn't at her desk. She's probably chatting with Kimberly in accounting. Those two and their church gossip. I shake my head. I walk past her desk, down the corridor passing a few more closed doors before reaching my office. I take my suit jacket off and hang it on the coat rack before taking a seat behind my desk.

First things first, I need to tackle my emails. I have over a hundred unread emails. I could task Bria with filtering through them, but I prefer to do it myself. It keeps me connected to our church members. I never want my position as pastor to get too big to where I'm not able to fully connect and be accessible to the body of Christ.

"Good morning Gabriel," I lift my head from my computer to find Bria standing in the open doorway. She looks...*different*. "I didn't realize you were in the office yet." She remains standing there moving her feet slightly to the left, slightly to the right.

I lift my brow. "I got in fifteen minutes ago." I turn my attention back to the email I was responding to.

I hear her walk further into my office. "I was in Kimberly's office. She wanted the number for the woman that did my hair."

My eyes remain focused on the computer. "Hmmm. Okay."

I hear her huff a breath. "So ah, what do you think?"

"Think about what?"

"My hair. It's different, right?"

Yeah, different. Familiar. And better suited for my wife. She has her hair cut in a bob style similar to Sabrina's. Though Sabrina's hair is in its kinky straight state – thick and full and I love running my fingers through it. Bria has her hair bone straight.

I look up briefly then back at the email. "Yeah, it's nice."

"Thank you. I thought I should try something new. So far I've gotten lots of compliments.

"Okay," I respond while typing.

"What are you doing that's got your full attention?" From the corner of my eye, I see her take a seat.

"I'm working Bria. Is there something you needed other than showing me your new hair cut?"

I see my curtness bothers her by the slight frown on her face. I'm trying to work I don't have time for whatever this is she's doing. And I'm still processing my drop-in at Kian's business.

"What's bothering you?"

You sitting here interrupting me.

"Is there anything church related that I need to know, if not I want to get back to reading and answering emails."

"You know as a pastor you have people coming to you with their problems all the time, but who do you have to talk to? Vent with? I can help. You can tell me if Sabrina isn't being a *good* wife."

My head snaps in her direction. "Bria, you are the church secretary. That's your job. Me venting to you or talking to you about whatever problems you *think* I may have is not part of your job description."

Jason is probably right, I shouldn't have her working for me.

She frowns again. Maybe this time she gets up and leaves.

"I'm just trying to help. You seem tense today. I know if you were my husband I wouldn't let you leave the house tense. You'll always leave relaxed with a huge smile on your face."

I turn from the computer and rest my forearms on the desk. "That was inappropriate. Not only am I your pastor I'm a married man which you're very much aware of. If this happens again I will have a third party intervene. But hopefully, it won't come to that, right?"

She visibly swallows. There's no way I can read Kian the riot act and let Bria's behavior slide.

"I'm supposed to be your wife!" She softly replies.

I shake my head and sigh deeply. I feel a headache coming on. "Why do you think that?"

"We were destined to get married. Our parents had it all arranged. Then you went to college and got Sabrina pregnant and ruined our chance."

"There hasn't and never will be a *you* and *me*, Bria. Just because our parents had some fantasy that their children would get married doesn't mean I wanted the same thing."

"I did and I still do. I know in my heart God wants you to be my husband."

How? Maybe she needs to see a therapist for her delusion.

"I'm already married. I love my wife. Why would God give you someone else's husband? Maybe you should find another position –"

"No. No. I get it. You're married and I respect that. I do. I just wanted you to know how I feel. I have always been professional and it will stay that way. You don't have to replace me." She stands. "Please keep this between us. I promise this is the last I will speak of this." She moves closer to the door.

"All right. I want to finish up some more emails before my noon appointment." I pray this doesn't come back to bite me.

She nods before leaving my office. I mentally sigh. More and more I'm looking forward to mine and Sabrina's anniversary trip.

***

I pull into my garage right at 4:26 p.m. I've been doing better at getting home earlier, it's not always easy. Before I wouldn't get home until close to 8 p.m. during the week and a bit later on Wednesdays for bible study and Thursdays for men's ministry meetings. And evenings are more accommodating for Christian counseling sessions with members who can't take off from work during the day. It's Tuesday, a day I usually schedule a few Christian counseling sessions, but I had Bria reschedule them so I can get home and give Sabrina a break and cook dinner.

I take the few grocery bags from the trunk then make my way into the kitchen from the garage. Usually, the girls hear the door chime and run out to greet me or call out "daddy". I'm met with neither. I place the bags on the kitchen counter and head towards the family room.

Empty.

I know they're home because Sabrina's SUV is in the garage.

I find them in Nehemiah's room playing with their American Dolls. Genesis, Nehemiah, and Sabrina each have a doll in their hands pretending to talk for them.

Once they notice me standing in the doorway, three pairs of evil eyes turn in my direction. I almost shrink back.

I lift my arms playfully in surrender. "Is this a no boys allowed zone?"

"Yes! Because you missed our awards ceremony." Miah pouts.

What? No! "I thought that was tomorrow. It's on my calendar for tomorrow." *How did I mix the days up?* When Sabrina told me about it, I put in on my calendar right away so I nor Bria would schedule anything in its place. I walk into the girlie décor bedroom. I cop a squat between my baby girls placing my arms around them. "Daddy's really sorry. I really wanted to be there. I was going to show up with flowers too. I guess I will have to bring them home tomorrow."

"It's okay, daddy. If you're really, really sorry we forgive you," Genesis says. They each hug me and I place kisses on their foreheads.

Looking across at Sabrina I have a feeling I won't be forgiven so easily. She stands up from the carpet. "I'm going to get some work finished before I start dinner. Miah and Gen you can finish playing with your dad."

"Actually, I'm cooking dinner tonight."

Sabrina cut her eyes at me. "Fine. Gives me more time to work." She spins on her heels and leaves.

I'm officially in the doghouse, again.

It's not until 8:30 p.m. when Sabrina and I have a chance to talk alone. The girls are sound asleep.

I volunteered to get the girls in bed giving Sabrina the opportunity to shower and get ready for bed early. I walk into our bedroom to find her on the bed dressed in a silk pajama dress with her hair tied up in a scarf. She's sitting against the headboard with her reading tablet and a glass of wine. She pushes her glasses further up the bridge of her nose before taking a sip of the red liquid.

"I really did think the awards ceremony was tomorrow."

"Of course you did." She swipes her finger across the tablet screen. She has yet to look up at me.

"Babe, I know you're pissed at me, but please look at me when I'm talking to you." She lifts her head. "I'm sorry I missed the ceremony because I wanted to be there for our daughters. I really did."

"Fine, Gabriel." She picks her tablet up.

"Don't shut me out, Sabrina. Nothing will get resolved if you shut me out. And you're doing it in your passive aggressive way."

"Because I don't believe you. I don't believe you "accidentally" mixed the days up." She uses air quotes. "You didn't come because church business... or someone else was more important."

Someone else?

"I'm telling you the truth. Don't hold my shortcomings from the past against me. I'm trying."

"Your past was a few weeks ago so forgive me for being skeptical." She throws her hands up.

I tug at my beard in frustration.

I sit next to her on the bed. "I'm telling you the truth. I wanted to be there."

"I guess going to Best Prints was more important."

Is that why she's really upset? "Your *friend* called and told on me?" I bite out.

"No. Zaiden saw you as you were leaving."

"I don't like Kian. I went to him man to man to make him understand you're my wife and he's not to overstep his boundaries. And I'm not apologizing for it either."

Her eyes darken a bit behind her frames. Though she's pissed she's turned on by my aggressiveness about the matter. But she tries to cover it by saying, "I told you there is nothing for you to worry about with me and Kian."

"I know." I stand with her following my every move. "I'm going to get in the shower." I unbutton my shirt purposely making a show of it. She's giving me attention and I'm not gonna let it go to waste. She still watches me but tries to pretend not to by lifting her tablet, faking that she's reading. I pull my shirt off then go and put it in the dry clean basket in the walk-in closet. I walk back out in the nude. I see her watching me over the rim of her stylish black frames. "Care to join me?" I'm standing in the doorway of the bathroom.

Sabrina bites down on her bottom lip. She sees how serious I am about my request. We haven't had sex in over a week since before her party, which is not from my lack of trying. I *need* her. She needs me too.

"I can probably shower again." She rises from the bed.

I smirk turning my back walking away to get the shower ready.

EIGHTEEN – SABRINA

Gabriel loads the dishwasher from breakfast, and I put the items away from making the girls sandwiches for lunch. Once that's done, I close the fridge after pouring myself a glass of orange juice, then take a sip.

"Mommy, why are you walking so funny?" Nehemiah blurts out. She and Genesis are sitting at the kitchen island putting their snacks in their lunch boxes.

I almost choke on the juice going down my throat.

Gabriel chuckles from behind me at the sink. "Mommy fell on something hard last night, but she'll be fine."

I choke a laugh at his comment. I had a moment of weakness last night and willingly gave in to Gabriel... okay, though I was upset with him since last week, he's wearing me down and I'm starting to get some of the old sparks again. It's disconcerting. I'm afraid of him hurting me and this time would be far worse. If that happens, I don't know how I will survive it. The Holy Spirit has been whipping my butt telling me to release my heart again, but I have that vessel in a death grip.

But last night was amazing. I smile at the thought.

"Okay girls, time to go for the school bus." Gabriel picks up their packed book bags from the counter. He comes over to me. "Have a great day, babe," I blush at his term of endearment. "Maybe you should soak in the jacuzzi when you come home tonight." He places a kiss behind my ear then usher the girls outside.

Please, please don't break my heart again.

I go back into our bedroom to finish getting dressed for work.

***

"Ugh!" Aubree whines. Her, Sunni and I are in the breakroom eating lunch. "Being single sucks!"

"I thought you had a man. What happened to Jericho?" I bite a piece of my sandwich.

She dramatically groans slamming her cellphone down on the table. "He's the main reason why being single sucks. He's thirty and still playing games. We've been doing this on-again, off-again nonsense for so long I have whiplash. I'm done with him! One chick came to *my* house two days ago telling me to leave her man alone. But that's not the worst part, she looks to be nine months pregnant with his second child, according to her."

I shake my head.

"Damn! Some men ain't sh –" Sunni looks at me and amends her profanity. "Nothing. They ain't nothing."

I appreciate that they try to censor themselves around me though I don't mind them being themselves.

"What did he say?" I ask.

"Believe it or not he told me the truth the first time I asked. Usually, he tries to turn the table on me and try to make me out to be the insecure one, but this time he manned up. Our son is his second child, not the first like I thought. And ole' girl is actually his wife, pregnant with his third child."

My mouth drops open.

"Damn!" Sunni exclaims.

I drop my sandwich and reach over for Aubree's hand on the table giving it a comforting pat. "I'm so sorry. Are you okay?"

She nods. "After I spoke with him I told him to leave and take our son with him to give me a break. I gave myself a couple hours to cry over him then I was done."

I'm curious. "How long were you two together?"

"Five, almost six years. And I had no clue he was married. None." She doesn't look overly affected by it, but I see hurt and sadness in her eyes. "But before finding out about his wife and kids things weren't great with us. I couldn't go more than two months without drama and confusion from him. That explains the times he would go MIA for days and weeks at a time."

"I'm surprised his wife doesn't divorce him. If it was me I wouldn't be knocking on a woman's door telling her to leave my man. She can have him all she wants because I would be out of the picture." Sunni picks up her soda can and takes a sip.

I readily agree. "Me too. There are way too many things to deal with in a relationship to have another person added into the mix."

"Well not only is she not divorcing Jericho, but he keeps blowing up my phone asking for another chance. I can't exactly delete his number because of our son. So now that I've gotten over being in a relationship with his trifling behind, I'm pissed I will be tied to him for another sixteen years."

"That's why I'm not dating. After my breakup three years ago I've been solo. I mean I'm thirty-nine and would love to have a husband and a child, but it's tough out there. Dating isn't like when our parents were doing it. People respected each other more. Guys weren't asking you for nudes and wanting you to have sex with them the moment you meet. At least not as much as things are now."

"You're saying with dating white men you have the same problems I have dating black men?" Aubree asks.

Sunni lifts her dark wavy hair in a ponytail using the hair-tie from her wrist. "I'm not dating now, but I didn't discriminate either. So yes, the white, black, Hispanic, and Asian men I have dated gave me similar issues. But I think part of it too was because I was dating younger men. I think when I'm ready I'll date men my age and older. Maybe they're mature enough now to properly commit."

"Sunni, if you want the husband and child, I think you should get back out there and date. Try changing up places you meet men too. I know at my church we have a singles ministry and they plan fun monthly outings. You should consider it too Aubree when you're ready. If nothing else it would be good social networking with Christian singles."

"You know, I would be interested in that. I've been celibate for three years and in doing so I feel more in touch with myself. More empowered. At my age, it's time for me to try something different. Willingly hopping into bed with men without serious commitment hasn't worked. They never had to earn it. This time around they will have to. I want the next time I have sex for it to be with my husband," Sunni tells us.

"Good for you!" I high-five her.

"Though, when I do find *the one*, we would have to get married quickly. I don't know how long I will be able to hold out being around his goodness. And sidenote, Sabrina, don't think I haven't noticed you walking funny today." She winks at me.

Aubree and I laugh then Sunni joins us.

"I don't know if I can abstain from sex with the man I'm in a relationship with. But I've also never tried. Maybe if I had held out on sex, I may have found out about Jericho being married sooner before I wasted six years of my life with him." Aubree says.

"Honestly, who knows. Sometimes even with our best intentions, we get screwed over. But that's life. Wallowing in the what if's won't change what happened. Just don't let what he did to you close you off from having love and happiness again." *Maybe you should follow your own advice.* I push my conscious thought away. *Her situation is different.*

Sunni looks over at me. "Being married to a pastor you don't have to deal with the nonsense we have to deal with."

"You do realize Gabriel is human, right? I'm not saying he cheats on me or abuses me, but being married period, is hard work." *And you just want to give up.*

Sunni replies, "Yeah but I've never heard of any scandals from him or your church in general. I know just because a person is a pastor or minister in the church doesn't mean they're perfect. But the good ones know scripture and how to apply it to their lives. I've never met your husband, but from the picture I've seen on your church website, you two are couple goals." She helps me with upkeeping the church website and designing the monthly newsletter.

Couple goals, really? I must fake it well.

"Hmmm. Thank you. But never idolize another couple, you never know their real struggle or the fact that they may be faking their way through it." Truer words have never been spoken.

Aubree begins packing up her lunch and trash. "All I know is if I had a good man like Gabriel I wasn't letting him go. Good men, unfortunately, are hard to find. As long as he isn't cheating on me or beating me upside my head, my husband and I will work everything out through thick and thin. If sex is getting boring, then we will figure out how to keep it spicy. If communication is getting worse, we will find a therapist to help us out. If money get funky, we'll come up with a plan to build up our finances. If he starts pulling away, I'll move closer. We'll do mandatory date nights and baecations. And for sure we will put each other first before the kids – that's not saying we neglect our children, but we won't let our children pull us apart."

Sunni cosigns, "Preach, Aubree. Preach! When my future husband says "I do" it's til death. No divorce allowed."

I can't help but think it's easy for them to say those things when they haven't been in my shoes – *for almost eleven years.* Not that they're talking about my marriage – but they could be. Why fight when you're the only one in the ring? Why stay when your needs aren't being met?

Yet you're still there which means you haven't completely given up. And Gabriel is doing better. He's seeking your affection. Your forgiveness. He's making himself more available to you and Genesis and Nehemiah.

I don't need this mental guilt trip.

I Sabrina Cox take you, Gabriel Dean, to be my wedded husband, to have and to hold, from this day forward, for better, for worse, for richer, for poorer, in sickness… My wedding vows pop into my head.

I plaster on a fake smile. "A good and lasting marriage takes work that's for sure." I pick up my trash and stand. "I will let you both know when there's another singles ministry meeting. And I have a women's ministry brunch coming up soon that I will like for you to attend."

"Cool, I'm game." Aubree stands to dump her trash.

Sunni pushes away from the table. "Me too. I want to try dating the Jesus way."

NINETEEN – SABRINA

"I say get a swimsuit for every day of the trip." Tabitha has a blue and orange designed high-waist two-piece swimsuit in her hand. We're digging through the racks of a department store.

"I don't like the high-waist bottoms, they look so odd on me," I tell her. I'm holding a one-piece purple and pink swimsuit.

"They make my belly look like I haven't given birth to two children. The illusion is what I need. It's a winner for me." She adds it to her cart. Living in Southern Florida you can never have too many swimsuits.

I'm shopping for me and Gabriel's upcoming anniversary cruise. I'm now all the way excited about the trip. For so long Gabriel had denied me baecations and to know it's going to happen in a couple weeks has me giddy. He arranged for my parents to come down from Maryland to take care of the girls while we're away. All I have to do is be ready with my passport and luggage packed.

"Okay. And I agree with you. A swimsuit for every day of vacation." I smile adding the one-piece to my cart. I already have a yellow bikini in there too – Gabriel's special request. *I can't wait for him to see me in it.*

"I never got a chance to ask you, who was that fine specimen of a man you were dancing with at your party?"

I give her a mock shocked expression.

She laughs. "I'm very happily married but ya girl is not blind. He is a silver fox."

He is.

"That's Kian. I have a partnership with his printing company." I hold up a two-piece white swimsuit, debating if I should add it to my cart.

"Well, I almost fell out when Gabriel showed up and walked up to y'all like he was about to *lay hands* on Kian." She laughs. I do too at the memory. "He staked his claim when he kissed the soul out of you." She playfully fans herself with her hand. "Whew child."

I laugh. "Nothing is going on between me and Kian other than business." *And it will remain that way.*

"Hmmm, well Gabriel made sure Kian knows to keep it that way. Jason would've done the same if it were me. Sometimes people think because a person is a pastor that they are passive."

"You're so right about that."

"Your party was fun. But I couldn't help but think Ms. Urma would've had a hissy fit. You know she acts like she was born saved and sanctified." Tabitha rolls her eyes while looking at another high-waisted two-piece polka dot swimsuit.

"She would've condemned all of us to hell for dancing. Then she may have started throwing holy oil on us because some of the songs were "secular".

"And don't forget you served wine." Tabitha shakes her head. "That woman is too religious for her own good."

"I wonder if her heart is as connected to Jesus as her false and misguided religious beliefs." I look over Tabitha's shoulder noticing a familiar face in the men's department. "Girl, we talked Ms. Urma up cause she's over there shopping for a man."

Tabitha discreetly looks over her shoulder. Ms. Urma is in one of her signature muumuu dresses because she's against women wearing pants. She's holding up a pack of men's briefs. What male over the age of 10 wears briefs?

Tabitha turns back to face me. "Owwww, you think Ms. Urma got a man?"

My nose scrunches up. "I mean, I guess anything is possible."

Tabitha barks a laugh. "Oh my gosh, you should see your face."

Tabitha's outburst garnered Ms. Urma's attention. Her wrinkled face frowns at us, she's still holding the pack of men's briefs. "So y'all loud and unladylike in public too?" She sasses.

I roll my eyes. *This woman.* "Good afternoon to you too Ms. Urma." My voice is sweet like sugarcane.

She sneers and Tabitha snickers.

"God don't like ugly Ms. Urma, so fix ya face." I hold in my grin when she pats her face while relaxing it from a frown.

Tabitha is dying laughing.

"Umph! You young women need to learn decorum. Up in here carrying on. You're both married to pastors, act like it!" She snaps then turns her back dismissing us.

"Sabrina lets buy our swimsuits and get out of here before I tell this woman off."

I couldn't agree more.

TWENTY – GABRIEL

"Man, I almost thought that was Sabrina sitting at the reception desk." Jason takes a seat next to me in the soundproof music room for us to record our 15-minute discussions about relevant topics from a biblical perspective for our radio segment with KJAC 95.5 FM Radio. We plan on recording four weeks of shows today to get them out of the way. "Why is Bria looking like a knockoff Sabrina?"

I shake my head suppressing a laugh. "Only God knows," I tell him not wanting to talk about it. Since our talk, Bria has kept things professional which I appreciate.

I look over our notes for the recording today. Drake, the church's recording technician, has our mics set up and ready, we were just waiting on Jason to arrive.

"That's weird man. I thought the same thing too," Drake says from his spot in front of the soundboard. "The style doesn't look bad on her though."

"Has the lady of the church seen her yet?" Jason picks up the notes Bria typed up.

"I'm not sure. If she has, she hasn't said anything. And it's a hairstyle, it's not patented. Anyone can wear that style." This conversation is making me a bit uncomfortable especially because of Bria's admission. But I believe everything is under control.

"You're right. But it's still kinda strange though." Jason leans in closer so only I can hear him. "You better watch out for Bria, bro."

"Trust me, she knows I'm a happily married man and not to overstep. I had a conversation with her already."

He looks me in the face, being friends for so long, he reads into more than what I've said. "Word? And she's *still* your secretary?"

"She respects my position as the pastor and a married man and promised to keep things professional. I haven't had an issue since."

He shakes his head. "Gabe, man. I know you don't want any church drama, but I think you should find her another position."

"I will if things change. For now, I trust she's going to respect my position."

"All right. Let's get started on the recording."

We position ourselves in front of the mics. Drake counts us down for when the recording begins.

"Welcome to fifttreen minutes with Senior pastor Gabriel Dean and Associate pastor Jason Forbes of Everlasting Love Ministry in Boca Raton, Florida." Drake plays the radio DJ's announcement which will be played at the beginning of each segment.

"I'm Pastor Gabriel."

"And I'm Pastor Jason."

"Now that you've gotten a little familiar with our voices, let's get into our topic for tonight. Soul-ties. Yes folks, if you have little children now will be a good fifteen minute break for them. We're about to talk about sex. This is a topic that was recently brought up in our men's ministry group. In the bible, soul-ties are mentioned as souls becoming one flesh. You can read Ephesians 5:31.

Some of you may have heard that when you have sex with someone your souls become intertwined. This is true. Now imagine having sex with multiple people and or someone harmful, emotionally or physically, against you or others. When you engage in sex, even casual emotionless sex, you are creating an emotional connection to that person. Your soul becomes attached and may cause a negative magnetic pull to that individual. Have you ever wondered sometimes why you keep attracting the wrong mate? A certain soul-tie could be the cause of it."

Jason joins in. "Yes, and from a male's perspective, having sex with multiple women before marriage may create a problem in your marriage. For instance, if a man has gotten certain needs met from several different women, imagine the burden he places on his spouse to compete with the many different soul-ties he's had. This is *a* reason why God wants us to wait to engage in sex until we're married. It helps eliminate your soul being tied to so many individuals other than your spouse."

I add, "Some people may argue it's better to "test-drive" before marriage. I get it, and I'm a pastor but I wasn't always walking fully in the Word of God and had sex before I was married. However, I've come to realize that God's way is better. Why do you need a test drive before marriage?

If two individuals learn to fulfill each other's needs together, it allows them an unbiased opportunity to meet those needs and desires. No other soul-ties are hindering their experience. And if there is a hinderance – together they should seek the help they need. Believe it or not, sometimes the negative soul-tie could be your spouse. But that's a topic for another day."

"In conclusion. Soul-ties are real. Pray in the name of Jesus for negative soul-ties to be removed because those soul-ties can be the cause of destructive behavior and or difficult relationships in your life. For those that aren't married, practice abstinence. And for those that are married and struggling with the effects of soul-ties from others, seek counseling and prayer."

"That's it for us for now. Join us again next week same time, same place. And you can also join us every Sunday or during one of our weekly services or groups, at Everlasting Love Ministry, seventy-seven James Hastings Ave, Boca Raton, Florida. Check us out on the web – www.everlastingloveministry.nas. I'm Pastor Gabriel."

"And I'm Pastor Jason."

Simultaneously we end with, "Good night!"

"That was a good clean run guys. Want to move on to the next one?" Drake asks.

I nod.

"Yeah, let's keep rolling," Jason tells him.

An hour later we finished up the other three segments for the radio show. Drake will get the recordings ready and sent to KJAC 95.5 FM Radio for review. In a week Jason and I will be heard on the radio.

"I think we did well with the topics." Jason and I head out the door of the music room.

I pat him on the back. "I think so too. The radio show will reach a lot more people than we're able to on Sundays."

"This makes me feel like Steve Harvey, without the studio audience and live cameras, but you know what I mean." He chuckles.

"I know what you mean. And Steve Harvey does have a radio show." We walk down a corridor heading towards the reception area. "Ready for the meeting with the board?"

"Yeah."

Voices can be heard from the reception area as we near the entrance of the church office.

"Oh good, Pastor Gabriel, I was hoping I got a chance to see you," Ms. Urma says upon my appearance. "I always like to take the opportunity to bless the man of God." She thrusts a wrapped package toward me. "I got you a gift."

It isn't my birthday or any other special occasion, however, members of the church occasionally give me gifts as they saw fit. I appreciate it, but it wasn't necessary.

I humbly accept the gift from her hands. "Thank you, Ms. Urma. I do appreciate it."

"You're welcome. Since you didn't want me bringing you meals anymore, I decided to find another way to show my appreciation for the wonderful work you do pastoring the church."

She pulls another wrapped package from her oversized purse. "And I've got a gift for you too Pastor Jason." She gives him the gift. "Your work is appreciated too."

Jason smiles. "Thank you, Ms. Urma." He shakes the package. "It sounds like something good."

"It is." She beams then just so quickly she has a sour expression on her face. "I saw your wives earlier. You know for pastors, you ought to tell your wives to conduct themselves more appropriately in public."

Bria, sitting behind her desk pretending to type a document, perks up at the mention of our wives.

Jason asks. "What do you mean, Ms. Urma?"

"They were in the department store shopping for skimpy swimsuits, laughing and being loud." She shakes her head in disgust. "Such a shame I tell you. Pastor's wives should not conduct themselves in such a way."

I can't wait to see what swimsuits Sabrina bought for our trip. I hope she bought a yellow bikini like I suggested.

Jason defends our wives. "Women shopping and laughing are not inappropriate Ms. Urma. And swimsuits are for swimming and being at the pool or beach. It's not like they will be wearing them in church."

"Hmpf! Well, they're your wives so I expect you to defend them. But I feel women should wear long t-shirts and tights for swimming."

I look at my watch. "We have a board meeting we need to get to, Ms. Urma. Thanks again for the gifts."

"Okay. You're welcome. I'll see you two on Wednesday at bible study." She pats me on the arm, then does the same to Jason. "Such young strong men." She turns and leaves the office with her White Diamonds perfume lingering in the air.

TWENTY-ONE – GABRIEL

Still standing in the reception area, Jason excitedly rips into Ms. Urma's gift. His face drops when he pulls out a pack of white briefs.

I bark a laugh at his expression and the gift. What was Ms. Urma thinking?

Bria stands up and comes over to take a look at what's in Jason's hand, I see she tries to hold it, but the giggles take over.

"Ms. Urma bought me drawers? And not just any drawers but briefs? What man wears briefs?" Jason holds the pack with two fingers like it's infected.

I wipe the tears from my eyes, this is too funny.

Jason frowns facing me. "Oh, you think this is funny. Open up your gift. Let's see what Ms. Urma got you." He drops his pack of briefs back into the torn box.

I open the gift in my hand, cringing as I rip the decorative paper.

"Haaaa Haaaa...!" Jason and Bria laugh as I pull a similar pack of briefs from the wrapping.

"How you like them *briefs*?" Jason pats me on the back laughing. "Well, at least she bought us extra-large." He says for only me to hear.

I don't know if that's a good or bad thing. I don't want Ms. Urma thinking about my junk. Who buys a non-relative underwear?

"Is this considered an inappropriate gift or not?" I ask no one in particular.

"I vote inappropriate. If you want, I can donate them to the men's shelter." Bria holds out her hands to take our gifts which we eagerly give her.

"Thanks, Bria," Jason says walking to the trash can to dump the wrapping.

"Yeah, thanks, Bria. I have to have a talk with Ms. Urma with you Jason and other ministers and pastors present. Between her mouth being a little reckless at times and the inappropriate gifts, I need her to stop."

"Ms. Urma moves to the beat of her own drums. All God's best with *that*." Bria walks back to her desk.

"Bro, we just had a sit down with Ms. Urma eight months ago and nothing's changed. That woman is set in her ways."

I nod at Jason. "Which means it's time for another one."

The main door to the church office opens, Mitch and Renee, two members of the church board, have arrived. I look at my watch. The meeting is in 15 minutes.

***

I'm the Chairman of the board, being that I'm the senior pastor. Jason is vice chairman. Then there are eleven other board members, including my parents that are with us via skype from their residence in Barbados.

Though I'm the "coach" for Everlasting Love Ministry and can make my own rules and vision for the church, I must adhere to the guidelines of the board. They make sure nothing I do is illegal, unethical, imprudent, or unbiblical. And they can vote to remove me from my position as they see fit.

That is why for the past two years of my senior position appointment I've been doing everything I can to improve the church and bring in members.

"I must say the church is steadily growing under your leadership, Pastor Gabriel," Renee, a mid-fifty-year-old woman, addresses me. "I know I noticed an influx of attendance these past few months. She's reviewing the quarterly "status of the church" report that I had Bria type up.

"According to this report, looks like church membership has increased by twenty-three percent. Everlasting Love Ministries now has about three thousand members." My father proudly boasts from his living room with views of the ocean in the background. My mother is sitting at his side. Bria emailed my parents a copy of the report prior to the meeting. My dad looks like me just older and grayer. My mom dyes her graying hair black which makes her look more youthful than her 66 years of age. She's a gorgeous petite woman and next to my father she seems even smaller.

"Yes, this is marvelous news." My mother claps. "Now if you can just get Sabrina to become more active, she too can help build church membership. Members need to see the First Lady more regularly."

Here we go. Not a meeting goes by without my mother putting in her two cents about my wife and her *nonactive* role.

"Sabrina doesn't have a big physical presence in the church but she does her part. She takes care of all the print media, graphics and manages the website. She also works with Tabitha on the women's ministry –"

My mother interrupts me, "And shouldn't the first lady be head of the women's ministry?"

"Says who?" I challenge. "There's no law that the first lady of the church has to run the women's ministry."

"Be that as it may, *I* believe, and I'm sure many others do too, that the first lady should be head of the women's ministry and actively involved in many other areas. I did as first lady and Sabrina can too."

"Tabitha enjoys being head of the women's ministry and she gets input and assistance from Sabrina," Jason says by my side at the large conference room table.

My mother purses her lips.

Renee speaks up. "I do agree with senior first lady Evelyn," she says referring to my mother. "First lady Sabrina should have more of an active position in the church. It will be good for the congregation to see. It lets them know your family is intact."

My brow raises at her insinuation.

"It's a sense of security. Members want to see the senior pastor and first lady together, *regularly*. It will further boost a strong front," Mitch contributes to the conversation. He's a 45-year-old white man.

"She does show up late quite often," Katherine a 38-year-old Caribbean-American says with a thick Haitian accent.

Does she watch the doors and time Sabrina's arrival to church?

"Gabriel, have a conversation with your wife and get her to understand her *role*." My father looks at me pointedly. His tone rubs me the wrong way. He is my father, but I am the senior pastor of this church.

"My *wife* does what she can. Not only is she raising our daughters she runs her own business. She shouldn't be forced to commit herself to multiple ministries on top of her busy schedule."

"She can work for the church full-time and get a salary. Any good First Lady would commit fully to the church," My mother jabs.

I bite my tongue to stop myself from saying anything disrespectful. I detest them ganging up on Sabrina. But maybe they have a point. The Lady of the church should be more active and accessible.

I have been wanting Sabrina to be more involved. I will bring it up during our trip in two weeks.

"With all due respect, how is Sabrina potentially taking over the women's ministry fair to Tabitha? And I agree with pastor Gabriel, that position isn't and doesn't have to be a requirement for the First Lady. Ministries should be led by those called to it and are passionate and or talented to do so. Sabrina does an amazing job with print media and the website. A website that has garnered many visits since she revamped it."

Renee nods approvingly at Jason's words. I notice a few other nonverbal members agree too.

My mother speaks up. "First Lady can share lead of women's ministry and Tabitha won't be affected…"

Jason shakes his head at me as if saying "I tried."

"…And as the first lady please tell her to cover her tattoo it's –"

"Mother, stop! That's enough of you ganging up on my wife. It's uncalled for at this meeting or any other time. And if you have a problem with her tattoo take it up with Jesus. As I recall He has our names engraved in the palm of His hands. Is a tattoo unfitting for our Lord and Savior too?" I'm sure my statement is highly debatable, but she needs to quit it.

My mother clams her mouth shut. My father gives me a disapproving look, but he needs to direct that at his wife. I love my parents, but they can be overbearing at times.

"I understand you all are the board of the church but as a senior pastor, I won't tolerate any disrespect towards me or my wife and children. I'm sure you expect that same level of respect in turn. Unless myself or my family have done anything illegal, unethical, imprudent, or unbiblical, please refrain from bringing them up here. My wife and I will decide if she would like to take on any additional roles at the church. It's not up to you to decide," I defiantly tell them.

"Oh, but we do get to decide. Your wife is an extension of you and should fulfill her role wholeheartedly." My father states authoritatively.

Exodus 20:12 pops into my head, *"Honor your father and mother, that you may have a long, good life in the land the Lord your God will give you."* They are making this extremely difficult right now.

I grit my teeth.

Mitch clears his throat. "He's right Pastor Gabriel, we do."

This is nonsense!

"Are you going to vote to remove me from my position?"

Most of the members quickly voice there "no" to my question. My parents stare on the screen. We can see them from the flatscreen television mounted on the conference room wall.

"Son, you know that's not what we want." My mother's sweet response flows through the speakers.

"Then don't try to dictate what my wife should or shouldn't be doing. Like I said, she and I will discuss which, if any, other positions she wants to take on." I let out an aspirated breath. "Now let's finish up the other items on the agenda."

TWENTY-TWO – SABRINA

Gabriel steps into our bedroom and I place my tablet down on my lap to acknowledge him. It's almost 9 p.m. I was expecting him home sooner, at least before the girl's bedtime. He's been doing well getting home at a decent hour especially on nights there isn't bible study or men's meeting.

I'm not going to fuss though because he's been making an honest effort which is all I wanted and it's not necessary to be dogmatic.

"How was your day?"

He blows a breath while loosening his tie. "It would be better if my wife got more involved in the church." He walks into the walk-in closet.

I sit up straighter in bed. "What?"

He returns to the doorframe of the closet, less a dress shirt, and tie. "I have a lot of pressure as senior pastor and not having your full support at church is adding to it. Can't you split your time between DesignHer and Everlasting Love Ministry? Or just sell the business and come on fulltime at the church?"

I cross my arm across my chest. "So, I should just throw away my dream, passion and hard work to make your position as senior pastor less difficult?"

"It would help. You can still do what you enjoy doing by continuing with the print media and managing the website." He says all this with a straight face.

And this is the foolishness I've had to deal with for years. He can be so selfish at times. This is a big fat exhibit K.

"I see your parents got into your head today. And I want no parts of it!"

"This has nothing to do with my parents. It's what I've felt for a long time now. You know how much I've been asking you to be more active around the church. There's no reason for you not to."

I shake my head. "I love the Lord. I pray. I tithe. I worship. And I'm involved in a couple of ministries in the church. But what I'm not going to do is feel forced to do more than I'm willing and able. I have a life outside of Everlasting Love Ministries. I run a business. I take care of our household and I'm a mother to two girls with busy schedules of their own. On top of that, I'm not going to squash my dreams and aspirations for you to get brownie points with your parents and the church board. What about what I want, Gabriel." I suppress the tears. I hate *having* to defend my dreams to my husband.

God knows I didn't want to be a pastor's wife. But it's Gabriel's dream and I would never stand in the way of him fulfilling it. Yet he's disregarding mine.

"My mother..." Now here he goes with this nonsense. "...Was able to raise me and my sister and help at the church."

"Because that's what your mother *wanted* to do Gabriel! She wanted to be a stay at home wife and fulltime first lady. I'm not your mother!" My fists slap against the bed as I speak.

He watches me for a moment not saying anything, which agitates me more. "I told myself I wasn't going to talk to you about this until our trip. Let's shelf this for now." He walks back into the closet.

I raise my voice after him. "Nothing will change my decision now or then, Gabriel. I'm not doing more at church than I already am. I'm not giving up my business. I'm not going to switch to part-time hours there and do part-time hours at the church office. Tell your parents and the board that's what it is and to stay out of my business."

He walks back into view shirtless with his suit pants hanging low on his hips. The desirable sight doesn't distract me from my stance on the matter at hand.

"Why won't you do this for me, Sabrina?"

"Why would you ask me to give up my business and goals? Because in everything I've said it seems you're not getting that point to sink in. I support you, Gabriel! Everything I do in this household and taking care of Genesis and Nehemiah is in support of you. I'm at your side every Sunday to greet the congregation after service. And I really don't like being around a bunch of people seeing as I'm an introvert. I make sure you have breakfast and a hot meal for dinner. I sometimes even pack your lunch."

"I make sure your suits are dry-cleaned. I give you words of affirmation and feedback on your sermons. I'm the wife that sacrifices time with her husband so he can be available to the congregation. I'm not giving up my goals. Period." Because I've already given up too much of myself in this marriage. I lift the blanket that covers my legs and get out of bed.

"You're right. You do support me, and I appreciate it, Sabrina. I do. I'll drop it, okay."

Grrrrrr, this man!

I go to walk past him to head for the bedroom door. "I'm going to make some tea." *Because you are about to give me a headache.*

He stops me by gently tugging me into his arms, hugging me. My arms are limp at my side. Moments like these pushes all the crap I've dealt with in my marriage, crashing to the forefront of my mind. I've forgiven Gabriel for every time he's emotionally hurt me, but I can't forget the pain.

My heart doesn't trust him anymore. The past almost three months since he's been making an effort to *hear* my needs and meet them, I've been feeling a bit of a spark. That familiar yearning I had for him when we first met. His attitude tonight makes me question why I would even entertain my feelings being rekindled for him.

Does he want Sabrina his wife or Sabrina his mother?

"I'm sorry." Here he goes again with this damn sorry!

I don't want Gabriel to be perfect. I'm not perfect. I know I grate on his nerves sometimes. I know apologies are part of relationships because we make mistakes. However, having to accept *sorry* constantly over the same things is draining. I want a husband that loves me. That supports me. That stands up for me. That gives me quality time and acts of service, which are my two main love languages. I want my feelings and desires considered. I want to be valued. I want to be desired. I want to be appreciated. I want to be respected. I want to be cherished. I want to be understood. I want to be an equal partner.

TWENTY-THREE – SABRINA

The next day, I'm dealing with a dull headache and not much sleep. The way Gabriel came at me last night when he got home still bothers me. It took everything in me not to kick him while he slept next to me last night. He must have been tired because he slept past his alarm and I didn't bother to wake him up until I was leaving the house after getting the girls on the school bus. I didn't want to deal with him this morning. I hope whatever reason he needed to get up early wasn't important because he will definitely be late.

I make a stop at Wawa for coffee before heading into the office. I hope the caffeine and pain meds kick in so I can have a productive day.

"Good morning, boss lady, thanks!" Tyreke greets me after I walk into our quaint and artsy decorated office. It is full of vibrant colors. You can't walk in here without smiling. And this place makes my heart smile. Tyreke takes one of the trays of coffee from my hand. I bought coffee for everyone.

"You're welcome. Take those to Zaiden and Josh." Sunni and Aubree's cubicles are closer to my office.

"Got it." He continues walking towards the left and I head towards the right. The office set up wasn't intentionally done where the men are on one side and the women on the other. When I hired everyone, they chose their cubicles and well, this is the result. But it kinda works for the best. Because it gives us ladies the freedom to have our girl chats without bothering the guys.

"Yesssssss!" Sunni praises when I stick my arm with a cup of coffee in front of her computer screen. She takes it from my hand. "Thank you! We are out of coffee pods in the breakroom."

"You're welcome. A package should be here today with the reorder of coffee pods."

"I smell and heard someone say coffee." Aubree's head pops out from the other side of Sunni's cubicle. She pushes her chair back further at the sight of the coffee tray in my hand. "You are awesome! Not only do you pay us well, but you also bring coffee." I hand her a cup.

She and Sunni both stand I assume to go to the breakroom for cream and sugar.

"It's my pleasure. You guys rock! Meet me in my office after you fix your coffees. I want to discuss the booklet layout for Broward County's Annual Debutante ball."

I get to my office, throwing the cup tray away in the trash near my desk. I store my purse and messenger bag away and boot up my computer. "Hey Zaiden, get the guys and meet me in my office, thanks." I hang up the phone then log into my computer.

Aubree makes it in my office first, followed by Sunni, then Zaiden, Josh and Tyreke. Everyone decides to stand around my desk despite the two guest chairs and small couch in my office.

"Okay, we got the job to design, layout and print the Annual Debutante ball booklet. There are sixty-four debutantes and numerous sponsors that have to be added. I want your input on how to make it the best booklet they've had in forty-two years. And to have them hire us again next year."

"Did they provide copies of booklets from previous years?" Josh asks before taking a sip of coffee.

"I have one from last year." I reach for my messenger bag to pull it out. "And they're going to give me copies of the two previous years."

Josh takes the booklet from my hand. "Ugh. No wonder they want a new designer."

The booklet is your typical 8 ½ x 11. But the cover has no creativity, just simple boxes, lines, and blah colors. It doesn't scream "pick me up and read."

Sunni looks the booklet over after Josh passed it to her. "I think all sixty-four debutantes should be on the cover in a creative collage. Their faces should be front and center before you even open the booklet."

I nod. "I like that."

Tyreke asks, "Do they have a theme or color preference?"

I shake my head. "Nope. They've given us free rein."

Aubree salivates at that. She loves it when customers give complete creative freedom. I do too. But I also enjoy the challenge of meeting their tight criteria. "My type of customer," she confirms.

Tyreke scratches his chin. "This may take a lot, but maybe you should do a short questionnaire for the girls to fill out and use their answers to design their individual pages. Favorite color, career goals, favorite thing, that type of stuff."

Zaiden pats Tyreke on the back. "Dang bro, that's a really good idea."

Tyreke playfully shrugs his handoff. "Don't try to play me like I don't create dopeness."

I smile. "I'm going with that idea Tyreke. It's perfect. And I like the idea of doing a collage cover with all the debutantes' faces. Thank you all for helping."

Josh replies, "Not a problem. We all need our creative juice stirred once and a while." They all file out of my office and I get to work on the preliminary design layout. All the files I need are on a zip drive the Debutante committee gave me.

"Knock, knock." I lift my head at the sound of Kian's voice. "Whatever you're working on has your full attention. I've been standing here for five minutes."

I shake my head and move my eyes to look at the time at the bottom of my computer screen. It's past lunch.

My stomach growls loudly causing Kian to laugh. He steps further into my office. "Sorry, I don't have lunch with me today."

I wave him off. "It's fine. I'll grab a snack from the breakroom. What's up?"

"Nothing really. I dropped off some print samples for Aubree, I saw your door opened and wanted to say hi."

He sits in one of the chairs in front of my desk.

"To say hi and shoot the breeze I see," I smirk watching him cross his outstretched legs at the ankles.

He chuckles. "It's what we do."

I scan his face, noticing the scruff on his face. "I see you have a lot more salt than pepper going on now."

Kian rubs his jaw. "Yeah. And I haven't shaved because Cici likes it."

"I bet she does," I tease.

He recently got back together with his ex-fiancée from five years ago. Not going to lie, I was slightly jealous. Although I wouldn't indulge in his attraction to me, I liked it. Especially when I was lacking it from Gabriel for too long.

"How is it being an instant daddy?"

A bright smile appears on his face. "Good actually. You know I was a bit skeptical at first. I'm forty-two with no children. And to get back with my ex who has a *three-year-old* was a lot to consider. I feel more comfortable around older children. But Sophia has me wrapped around her chubby little finger."

"That's great Kian. You make a great bonus dad."

"Thanks. I'm surprised at how quickly Sophia warmed up to me. Cici and I remained cordial over the years and on occasions, I would see her and Sophia out and about, but I thought it would take months before Sophia would *like* me being around often."

"Kids are perceptive. They can tell if a person has a good heart or not."

"Yeah, I guess you're right. How are things with you?"

I look away from him, focusing my attention on my computer screen. "I'm good. I'm looking forward to the Bahamas cruise Gabriel and I are going on to celebrate our eleventh anniversary."

"Eleven years. Wow. That's a milestone. You both will enjoy yourselves. If you think Florida beaches are nice, you're going to be even more impressed with the Bahamas beaches. And you have to swim with the pigs."

I turn back to face him. "Swimming pigs?"

"Yes! Add it to your to-do list."

I'm feeling even more excited now, especially after last night's blow up. "That sounds like fun.

"Yeah, it's a fun experience." He stands. "Well, I need to get back to the shop. Chat with you later." He heads for the open door.

"Okay. And thanks for the swimming pigs' suggestion."

"You're welcome," he calls over his shoulder leaving my office.

I pull up a search bar on my computer and type in: swimming pigs in the Bahamas.

TWENTY-FOUR – SABRINA

"You are alpha and omega, we worship you our Lord, you are worthy to be praised, we give you all the glory..." Tears are racing down my face with my arms lifted in praise. This song, *Alpha and Omega* by Israel and New Breed always put me in praise mode. I see Sunni and Aubree standing to the left of me at the table are affected by the song too. Their arms are raised in worship. I'm so happy they came out for the Women's Ministry brunch today.

When I assisted Tabitha with the planning for this month's brunch, I insisted that the songstress for today sing this song. We need to be reminded of the awesome and powerful God we serve. Despite our frustrations, despite our fears, despite our disappointments, Jehovah is God almighty. And He will make everything all right. Daily I have to surrender my will to Jesus. Daily I have to cast my concerns regarding my marriage to over to the Lord. *It is well!*

I go to the podium greeted with a round of applause. "Thank you, ladies, for showing up today. Man, you all are gorgeous!" I truly mean that. They respond with "thank you", "you too!" I struggle sometimes with whether their response to me is genuine or not. But this isn't about me, it's about me serving God. "Today's motto is, *It is well!* Minister Tabitha, you did an amazing job teaching on this topic from second Kings, four, verses eight through thirty-seven." (2 Kings 4:8-37). Everyone gives a round of applause. I look to where Tabitha is sitting at the table directly in front of me and give her a proud smile.

"A Shunammite woman was blessed at an old age with her first child, a son. When he grew a little older he became ill one day and died with his head on his mother's lap. Just imagine the pain and agony this woman felt. Not only did her child die, but he was her *only*. I'm with Minister Tabitha, I would have lost it, y'all. I would have been screaming and crying. But this woman picked her son up and laid him in bed. Then she went to find the man of God, Elisha, who prophesied that she would conceive her son. Her husband was looking at her sideways like are you crazy, our son is dead and you're leaving? But mama had things to do. She told her husband, "it shall be well." Listen to me, this woman was either crazy or she had serious faith." The ladies murmur in agreement, nodding and clapping.

"She meets up with the servant of Elisha at the gate, he asks her how she was doing, how her husband was doing and how her son is doing. She answered him, "it is well." I look around acting confused. "This woman's only child just died and she's telling the servant, it is well. It is well? How?

Then she finally speaks to the man of God, Elisha telling him what happened. Elisha returns to her house and through prayer and complete utter faith, the Shunammite woman's son regained life. What in your life is dead but needs your complete utter faith in Jesus to be brought back to life?" Tears are prickling my eyes. *Jesusssssss strengthen my faith. Bless my husband, bless my children, bless our family, bless my marriage. Heal my marriage. Bring it back to life!*

"Be like the Shunammite woman. Despite the obvious in her life, despite the death of her son, despite her family looking at her crazy, she had faith that it is well!"

The songstress begins to sing the song, "It is Well" the version by Kristene DiMarco & Bethel Music.

We're now eating, and this food is delicious. My cousin Dawn did an amazing job catering the brunch spread. I'm shamelessly in the buffet line again to get a second helping.

"You know they have makeup that covers scribbling on your body." I don't have to turn to know who it is. Her intense White Diamonds perfume announced her presence already. I'm wearing a sleeveless pale pink sheath dress. This means my flower tattoo on the inside of my forearm is on display.

I take a deep breath then turn to face Ms. Urma. She must sew these muumuu dresses herself because I didn't realize so many existed. Today she has on a decent looking one. It's pink with a hibiscus flower pattern at the bottom.

"Good morning, Ms. Urma, did you enjoy minister Tabitha's message this morning?" Ignoring her remark may help her lose interest and she can leave me along sooner.

"It was okay. She kept mistakenly switching between Elisha and Elijah. Did she not read the scripture before she taught from it?" She shakes her head. "And the bible doesn't say the woman was old it said her husband was old and couldn't give her a son."

I fight my eyeroll. I can't believe she's nitpicking over trivial things. Speaking to a group of people isn't easy and Tabitha did a fantastic job. And there are about three hundred women in attendance this morning.

I turn to move up in the line after saying, "Did you at least get the message about faith?"

"Hmmm," is her only reply.

Thankfully she leaves me alone. I fill my plate up with the spinach and mushroom omelet, ham, fried apples, and blueberry French toast.

"Whoever catered put their foot in this spread," I overhear Ms. Urma saying. "So good."

I turn to her. "My cousin Dawn is the caterer. I can give you her card if you want."

Her face falls into a scowl. "No, that won't be necessary. I know someone *better*." She walks off the line with a plate full of food.

Walking away from the buffet line I cross paths with Bria, she acts like she doesn't see me, I do the same to her. I've had enough negativity with Ms. Urma. I internally laugh at Bria trying to copy my style with her bob style hairdo. It's hilarious every time I see her since she did it.

I return to my table where Sunni and Tabitha are chatting while eating.

"The blueberry French toast is amazing!" Sunni praises. "You think your cousin will share the recipe with me?"

I shake my head. "Nope! I've tried getting it from her myself but she's not giving it up. As you confirmed it's a hit and makes her lots of money catering."

"She must be filthy rich then." Tabitha forks a mouthful of blueberry French toast in her mouth.

Aubree returns to the table. "I know everyone in the church doesn't have an intimate relationship with Jesus, but there is an old woman over there in her umbrella dress that keeps giving me the stink eye. I have been celibate for a few weeks now, and she just doesn't know me knocking her dentures out will be orgasmic. I will enjoy every second of it." She says it with a straight face causing us to double over in laughter.

"That's Ms. Urma. Just try to ignore her. Cause no matter how many times people correct her she finds a way to flip it back at you," I let her know.

"Well, she about to buck with the worse one. My mama taught me to respect my elders but she also taught me not to let anyone disrespect me either. And Ms. Urma on my hit list if she don't check herself. She too old to be rude."

Tabitha shakes her head. "We are in the house of the Lord, but I sure want a front row seat if something goes down. Ms. Urma is not going to stop until someone properly puts her in her place."

Sunni asks, "Wait, are you all talking about the woman wearing a pink dress with the hibiscus flower pattern at the bottom?"

"Yeah, that's her," Aubree confirms.

Sunni shakes her head. "When I walked in she greeted me at the door then had the nerve to ask me to remove my nose piercing." Sunni has a small diamond stud earring in her nose, she doesn't wear the piercing often. I think it's cute. "I thought she was joking for a second but the scowl on her face told me otherwise."

I pick up my glass of juice. "I'm going to talk to Gabriel about doing something to stop her. What she does can be a huge deterrent to guests. People shouldn't be judged and ridiculed stepping into the house of the Lord."

TWENTY-FIVE – GABRIEL

"They love it!" Jason's fist pumps the air.

Bria squeals.

I just hung up a call from the radio station producers. Me and Jason's 15-minute segment aired last night receiving rave reviews. The producers said they had 7 negative calls out of the 106 callers saying how much they loved it.

I have a megawatt smile on my face. "Who do you think the seven negative people are?" I jokingly ask.

Jason lifts his shoulder. "What I really want to know is, out of almost three thousand members in this church, there were only one hundred and six positive calls? Me, Tabitha and the kids all called."

Bria laughs, "You had the young ones calling into the station too?"

"Sure did. They loved hearing daddy and uncle Gabriel on the radio."

"Well, I'm not ashamed to admit that me and Sabrina called in multiple times and had the girls call too."

Bria shakes her head and says mockingly, "Scandalous."

Sitting in one of the chairs in front of my desk, Jason addresses Bria sitting next to him. "It worked. The airwaves need positive faith-based topics. And if we keep getting great reviews, they will increase our days on-air."

"You're right. I'm proud of you guys."

"Thanks, Bria," I say to her then turn to Jason. "You want me to review your sermon notes now for the two upcoming Sundays?"

"Yeah. I emailed it to you before I came in here."

I hit the computer mouse to wake up my computer to retrieve his email.

"Right, your *trip* is coming up." Bria stands to leave.

Sabrina and I are leaving for our cruise in three days and I'm surprisingly excited. Especially since traveling, unless church related, was never a big deal for me.

"I'm happy you're finally taking your butt on a trip that's not church related. And I get to corrupt the congregation for two Sundays while you're gone." I chuckle along with Jason at his joke.

"Sabrina is excited and I'm looking forward to celebrating our anniversary on the sea." I log-in to my email.

"M'kay, I'm going back to my desk, I'll let you know when Ms. Urma is here." Bria leaves without waiting for a response from me.

I open Jason's email with his sermon notes he wants me to review.

Jason reclines back in the chair. "Who else is sitting in on this meeting with Ms. Urma?"

"Renee from the board and Kimberly."

"Bro, we need to pray things don't get ugly," he tells me with a straight face. And I must agree. You never know with Ms. Urma.

"For sure. But let's discuss your notes."

We spend the next hour going over his sermon notes and just bouncing biblical thoughts and ideas, in general, at each other. We also tossed ideas for radio show topics.

"Pastor Gabriel, Pastor Jason, Ms. Urma is here. I called Renee and Kimberly and they will be in your office shortly," Bria announces on speakerphone.

"Thanks, Bria."

Moments later, Jason and I are standing to greet Kimberly, Renee, and Ms. Urma.

"I got a bad feeling about this. Why am I meeting all four of you?" Ms. Urma nervously takes a seat next to Jason near my desk. Renee and Kimberly are sitting on the couch against the left wall. Because I conduct many meetings and counseling sessions in here, it's set up like a living room with my desk closer to vast window letting in natural light. Sabrina decorated it, choosing the pale blue paint for the walls, matching decorative pillows for the chairs and couch to go with the white coffee table and my white desk. I wasn't too fond of a white desk at first, I am now. The picturesque view of the pine trees outside is an added bonus.

After sitting, I address Ms. Urma. "I called you here today to follow up with our previous meeting a few months ago. We have received a lot more complaints about you Ms. Urma. And since our last meeting addressing said complaints things have not changed. Because of this, the board has agreed for you to go on a temporary break as a greeter –"

"What?! Absolutely not! I will not step down from the hospitality ministry." Ms. Urma shoots a vehement look my way.

I try to assure her. "We're not asking you to step down, we want you to take a temporary hiatus and pending satisfactory change in your behavior and comments to guests and members of the congregation you can resume your position."

Ms. Urma huffs, "Does senior pastor Dean and first lady Dean know about this?"

"Yes, Ms. Urma. Pastor Gabriel stated, the board, as a whole, decided that you should take a break." Renee lets her know.

"This is absolutely ridiculous! I have done nothing wrong but speak the truth to people. Now if they feel convicted of something that's on them." Her wrinkled face is red with anger.

Kimberly, in accounting, speaks up. "Ms. Urma, last Sunday I overheard you telling a male guest that he will rot in hell with ashy knees because he stepped foot in the house of the Lord in shorts." Ms. Urma pouts knowing that Kimberly is telling the truth. "And three weeks ago another greeter told me that you told a member that her low fade haircut was an abomination and ungodly."

"Women shouldn't shave their heads." Ms. Urma states without any remorse.

"Ms. Urma. Your comments and misconstrued religious beliefs are unacceptable. At Everlasting Love Ministry, we are to treat each other with the love of Christ. Jesus didn't shame, condemn or ridicule people, He loved them as they were. Your actions have not been displaying the love of Christ and unless you change you will not be allowed back in your position. Minister Jennifer, head of the hospitality ministry, will go over the ministry bylaws and expectations and the church membership guidelines with you again. We're hoping a two-month break will be sufficient enough."

Ms. Urma shoots up to her feet on her sturdy legs. She plasters on a smile that looks more like a sneer. "Fine. I understand where you're coming from. And I guess I can be a bit blunt at times, but it's not my intention to hurt anyone. I will graciously step aside for two months." She smooths down her red and green muumuu dress.

I fight to keep my face neutral because I was not expecting that response from her.

Jason speaks because I'm at a loss for words. "Ah… thank you Ms. Urma. We appreciate your cooperation and understanding on the matter. We look forward to you being reinstated to greeter in two months."

Ms. Urma nods lifting her purse on her shoulder, then turns and leaves the office without another word.

After a few seconds of silence Kimberly says, "Well, that went well."

***

Couple hours after the meeting with Ms. Urma, I'm alone in my office reviewing a stage play script that Judah, head of the performing arts ministry, wants my okay on for the church to produce this fall.

Bria bursts into my office letting the door hit hard against the wall. Alarmed by her entrance, I watch as she excitedly approaches my desk.

"Gabe…Pastor Gabriel, you won't believe who's on the phone to speak with you." I stare at her blankly and she quickly replies. "Pastor Jamal Bryant of New Birth church in Atlanta."

I sit up straighter. "What does he want?"

Bria reaches across my desk and picks up the phone. "Find out." She extends it to me, clicking a button to connect me to Pastor Bryant.

Bria stands in front of my desk for the fifteen minutes I am on the phone with Pastor Bryant. I hang up completely blown away. "One of the speakers for his Men's Empowerment conference had to cancel short notice and he wants me to take his place. It's a four-day event starting on Friday. I need to leave for Atlanta Thursday afternoon." This is huge! Not only will this be great exposure for the church, but it would be nice adding this speaking engagement to my resume. It will also be great networking with other church leaders. "How did he know to call me?" I ask out loud.

"I know you've been wanting to beef up your resume and it just so happens my cousin Trina in Atlanta is best friends with Pastor Bryant's secretary. Trina connected me with his secretary, and I asked her if there was a chance you could be considered for any upcoming events and it just so happen that this opportunity was open." Bria smiles proudly.

I lean forward resting my forearm on the desk. "Bria this is awesome. I can't thank you enough for reaching out and getting me this opportunity."

"You're welcome. I will go and book our plane tickets and rooms now." She goes to leave.

"Wait. *Our tickets* and *rooms*? Bria, I appreciate you getting me this speaking engagement but it will be highly inappropriate for us to travel together."

She seems a bit dumbfounded by the blank look on her face. "But I thought…I mean I am your secretary and it's church/business related."

"You've never traveled with me before and there's no need for you to do so now."

"Fine!" She replies a little too sharply. "Should I reserve tickets for you and Sabrina, seeing as you'll be *missing* your anniversary cruise?"

The cruise! My face falls. *How am I going to tell Sabrina we must cancel?* I'll also be busy most of the trip in Atlanta, I won't be much company if she tags along.

"Just book mine, for now, I will let you know if Sabrina decides to join me."

"Will do." I don't take much thought to the expression on Bria's face, she's leaving my office with a grin.

Sabrina's parents fly in tomorrow. Maybe with them being here, it will soften the blow when I tell Sabrina.

TWENTY-SIX – SABRINA

Gabriel's been acting weird since he got home last night. He called me yesterday afternoon at 4:30 telling me he was bringing dinner from my favorite Caribbean restaurant. I love me a good jerk chicken and peas n' rice with plantain. Living in Southern Florida it's hard not to fall in love with Caribbean cuisine. Just about any Caribbean island nation you can think of you can find a restaurant that sells their food.

Aside from the food he brought, which hasn't been unusual with him for the past three months with his kind gestures, he bought me a gift certificate for a luxury spa experience. I am so going to use that when we get back from our trip. I appreciate his sweet gestures and one may think it's because he's in early preparation mode for our 11th anniversary… but his vibe seems off. I can't quite put my finger on what it is though.

I can't dwell on it much now because I need to add some final touches to the debutante booklet before sending it over to the committee to proof. I need to do all that in the next twenty minutes before I need to leave my office to pick my parents up from Palm Beach Airport. They usually rent their own vehicle when they come to town and they own a rental property nearby where they usually stay during their visits. With Gabriel and I going on the cruise, my parents can drive my SUV and they are staying in our guest room.

"It feels really good to be here," my mom hugs me at the arrival terminal. Dad is hefting their luggage into the trunk of my SUV.

Both my parents look great for their ages, of 65 – my dad, and 60 – my mom. My mom is always dressed classy chic. Right now, she's wearing slim fitting dark jeans with a purple button-down shirt, tucked in, and designer black sandals. Her salt and pepper kinky hair is styled in a twist-out that reaches her shoulders. My dad has on khaki pants with a plain white polo shirt with grey Vans on his feet. Mommy keeps him on point. He's tall and since I was a kid, I have to lean my head back to look up at his 6' 7" height. He long ago lost the hair on his head which must have moved to his face because he has a long gray beard. It rivals Gabriel's.

"The weather in Maryland is frigid and it's the end of April," Mom continues while getting into the front seat.

My parents own a small general contractor business in Southern Maryland. It's not easy for them to *both* be away from the business, though they have a staff of seven. Running a small business the boss must be around often. Which is why I appreciate them coming to be with the girls for a week.

"Yeah, I'm going to enjoy these next few days. I want to get a tan from soaking up the sun on the beach," my dad joins in after getting in the back seat. I drive off before airport security shows up.

"Make sure you use the sunscreen I brought," mom advises him. "Black people get sunburn too."

"Yes sweetheart, I will use the sunscreen." From the rearview mirror, I see daddy shift his eyes to me. "How are you, baby girl?"

"I'm good daddy. I'm excited about our anniversary cruise." I focus on the road to make my exit for I-95.

"Good for you baby. I can't remember you and Gabriel traveling together before. This will be meaningful. You two will have fun," Mommy tells me.

***

"Mimi and Pop!" Genesis and Nehemiah both exclaim getting off the school bus greeted by their grandparents in front of the house. The girls knew they were coming just not when.

"Aren't you two the prettiest girls ever!" My dad says lifting them both in his arms at the same time. "I've missed you two." He places kisses on their foreheads. Genesis and Nehemiah are their oldest grandchildren. My older brother, Meko, waited longer to have his 6-year-old fraternal twins – a boy and girl.

"We missed you too Pop," Nehemiah says being brought back down to stand on her sneaker feet.

"We're going to have so much fun!" Genesis exclaims.

"Come give Mimi hugs." Mommy opens her arms wide to receive them. Afterward, we walk inside with the girls talking animatedly.

***

Gabriel and I decided to take my parents out to dinner as a thank you for them traveling here to take care of the girls when we leave for our cruise day after tomorrow.

We're at a local chained restaurant. We ordered our meals and our drinks and appetizers are on the table. The girls are trying to convince my parents to take them to a waterpark on Saturday.

I lean in closer to Gabriel sitting at my right at the rectangle table. "Are you okay? You've been noticeably quiet since you got home this evening." *And you've been giving me weird vibes since yesterday.*

He looks at me with something unreadable in his eyes, it has me on edge. "I ah…"

"Gabriel, how are things at the church?" Daddy asks sitting across from us. I see that Gabriel visibly relaxes because of the interruption.

What the heck is going on?

"The church is doing well, Henri." My parents insisted he calls them by their first names since way back then. "Membership has increased by twenty-three percent these past few months." My dad nods his head. "I was just about to tell Sabrina that I got a call from Pastor Jamal Bryant of New Birth Church in Atlanta." This captures mom's attention as well as mine. "He extended an invite for me to be one of the speakers at his Men's Empowerment Conference."

Mommy claps her hand. "That's wonderful, Gabriel. You must be excited."

Gabriel flashes his handsome smile. "Yes, ma'am I am."

Daddy adds, "That's great news, son. That's a big platform opportunity for a pastor."

"What does it mean daddy?" Genesis asks. Nehemiah pulled mom's attention back to playing tic-tac-toe on the back of the kid's menu.

Gabriel speaks to her. "It means I get to speak to a large group of men at a really big church in Atlanta."

"Okay," she nods and smiles.

I shift in my seat to look at him and ask, "When is it?"

Gabriel clears his throat reaching over for his glass of water, taking a sip. My eyes are like laser beams on the side of his head. I watch him painstakingly return the glass of water to the table. "I leave for Atlanta tomorrow."

It's my dad's turn to clear his throat.

I must have heard Gabriel incorrectly. Yeah, the chatter in the restaurant is a bit loud. "When do you leave?" I lean closer to him.

His eyes find mine. "I leave tomorrow which means we have to cancel our trip. But we can reschedule something a month or two from now to make it up."

I want to curse him out so bad it would shame the devil. Three things are stopping me; my children at the table, respect for my parents, and my faith.

My eyes turn cold. "Let me guess, you found all this out and *accepted* the invite, yesterday?"

"Yes. This is a big opportunity, Sabrina. I couldn't pass it up." He speaks where only I can hear him. My parents act like they're not trying to eavesdrop. "Opportunities like this for ministers don't come often. This can open doors for bigger and better things. The platform I will have to spread the love of Christ is phenomenal."

The waiter erupts by placing our food on the table. My parents both give me sympathetic looks from across the table. I ignore Gabriel as best I could for the rest of the night.

***

"Babe, I promise we can plan another cruise in a month or two." I walk past him as I exit our master bathroom. I just took a shower and changed into nothing but a sleeveless short pajama dress. I climb into bed. If my parents weren't here, I would take the guest room, it is what it is.

"Come on Sabrina, talk to me!" He has the nerve to raise his voice. But whatever. "It's killing me you're not saying anything. I know you wouldn't want me to turn down this opportunity. I've worked hard to even be acknowledged for something like this…Blah, blah, blah."

I turn on my side pulling the covers over my head. Like in the shower, the tears soon fall.

I feel his hand on my waist. "Babe, I'm sorry. I love you and I will make this up."

There he goes with that damn sorry, *again*.

TWENTY-SEVEN – SABRINA

11:08 a.m. Gabriel: Babe, I know you're upset. I will make this up to you though. I will search for cruise dates and get us the same itinerary for later. Why don't you use the spa certificate I got you? Take your mom or Tabitha with you for a spa day. I love you, see you in a few days.

After reading the text I place my phone down on the restaurant table. I purposely got up and left the house before Gabriel this morning. I parked near the beach and watched the waves. Thank goodness my parents are home to get the girls ready and on the bus for school. According to my dad, he dropped Gabriel off at the airport and he and mom are using his car. I'm now having an early lunch with Tabitha.

I feel hurt and embarrassed.

"We should go out on Saturday and have a ladies' night. We can invite Sunni and Aubree too." Tabitha picks up her soda and sips from the straw.

Saturday is my 11th wedding anniversary.

Tabitha is trying to cheer me up. She knew how excited I was about the cruise. How I wanted the opportunity for Gabriel and me to give each other undivided attention and reconnect. I'm the fool for letting my guard down.

"You know what? Let's do it. I need a night of letting loose and being irresponsible. I don't want to think about Gabriel, and my parents are here so I don't have to worry about the girls." I finally pick up my now cold fries and eat a few.

"How irresponsible are we talking?"

"Let's just say, I'm not going to be a church girl on Saturday." I dip my fries in ketchup.

She grins. "In that case, one of us still has to be. I'll make sure you don't get too drunk or end up in jail."

"You truly are a great friend."

***

1:44 p.m. Gabriel: I made it safe to Atlanta and I'm on my way to check-in the hotel. Later I'm meeting with some of the speakers and Pastor Bryant for dinner and to discuss the lineup for the event since I was added late.

5:03 p.m. Gabriel: I called your mom and she let me speak with the girls. I know you're upset but please don't ignore me. If you won't answer my calls at least reply to my texts.

5:03 p.m. Gabriel: I love you ❤️☐

I put my phone back in my jeans pocket after reading his last texts. He's been calling me all day and I have ignored all his calls.

"I brought in the mail. It's on the coffee table," mom says while walking into the kitchen. They just got back from taking the girls on a bike ride around the neighborhood.

"Thanks, I will look through it later." Mom had prepped dinner earlier – shrimp and fresh veggie stir-fry that I have cooking in the skillet. I can hear dad and the girls in the family room.

"How are you feeling?" She sits at the kitchen island.

I stir the shrimp and veggies watching them sizzle. "I'm okay. Sad, disappointed, but I will be okay." *Will I?*

"Ah, baby girl." I turn from the stove at the sound of daddy's voice. He's walking into the kitchen with a partially unwrapped small gift box. "Nehemiah thought this gift that was on the coffee table may have been for her from us and started to open it. I took it from her, letting her know it wasn't. She didn't see what's inside, but I did." He moves closer placing the gift box on the counter."

I place the wooden spoon down then reach for what looks like pictures. My hands shake viewing the four photos of a partially nude woman. Her face isn't shown in any. All I know is she's black and loves lacy underwear.

Mommy is cupping her mouth with her hand and her free arm is wrapped around her waist.

Daddy looks like his bald head is going to explode in anger.

We're all quiet as I pick up the handwritten note: Pastor Gabriel, hmmm that sounds soooo sexy. You know how I love calling you that. I thought you'll want something good to look at while you're on your trip with her. Hope you're miserable without me. Bon voyage.

I stuff the note and pictures back in the box along with the wrapping. Mom moves to turn off the stove because the food is starting to smoke up the kitchen.

I fight the tears because I'm sick of crying over him. "I'm getting a divorce." I quietly speak. "He canceled our cruise –"

"A divorce Sabrina, don't you think that's a bit much?" Mom asks.

I turn to face my mother. "This isn't just because he canceled our anniversary trip, this is for the years of my needs not being met. And then some woman has the audacity to send nudes to my husband –"

"The woman in the pictures wasn't completely naked."

I shoot daggers at my mother. "Really mom? Does that even matter?"

"No sweetheart it doesn't matter," my dad says from behind mommy. "Do what you feel you need to do, and your mom and I will support you."

"Henri, you're agreeing to her leaving her husband, who happens to be a pastor of a prominent church, and split up her family?"

"If she's unhappy she doesn't need to stay. There's evidence of why right in front of us." He gestures the gift box in my hand.

Mommy faces me, dismissing my dad. "How about you two going to see a marriage therapist?"

I shake my head, "Gabriel doesn't want to. I've suggested it before. He feels we don't need it, especially with his position. And honestly mom, I'm done. I don't want another year to go by with me being miserable."

"What about Genesis and Nehemiah? They need their father." Mommy pleads.

"They also need a mother that is happy and whole. I've been faking it for too long. This is my breaking point."

I pick up the gift and wrapping and head to my bedroom where I can lick my wounds in private.

Damn you, Gabriel! Damn you!

***

Three years ago I had my lawyer write up divorce papers but I didn't go through with it. My reason three years ago for divorce is still the same today, a day before our 11th anniversary – irreconcilable differences.

"Yes, I still have the papers on file, but are you sure Mrs. Dean?" My lawyer Lashan Dassie asks with concern. "Once I file and have Mr. Dean served it can be difficult to reverse."

"Yes, I'm sure." I uncross my legs and run my sweaty hand down my cream slacks. My heart is racing making me afraid of hyperventilating. "Please file."

You're doing the right thing. You have suffered too long in this marriage. You'll finally be free.

Lashan, a gorgeous BBW, settles her brown eyes on me. "Again, I have to ask as part of my duty, are you *absolutely* certain this is what you want to do?"

I briefly close my eyes and will myself to relax, breathe evenly. The nude pictures of the woman flash in my mind. I reopen my eyes, resolve back in place.

"Yes. I'm filing for divorce."

Back at home, Mommy is pissed with my decision but she's helping me pack me and the girls' things. I don't want to be here when Gabriel returns and since I'm filing for divorce it's only fair that I leave. I want to go about this as painless as possible.

"You're making a mistake, Sabrina," she says for what feels like the hundredth time. We're outside now in the blazing sun loading my SUV with suitcases. I'm only taking mostly our essentials for now. The girls are at school making this easier.

"Mom, please just know it's time I did this and it's not easy for me at all. But I just can't..." The floodgates break. My heart feels ripped to shreds.

Mommy pulls me into her arms right there in the driveway.

"Oh sweetheart, I'm sorry." I sob in her chest. "I didn't realize how broken up you are about this." She smooths her hand down my back.

I hear daddy's footsteps coming outside. He's probably carrying the last suitcase. Moments later I feel him hug me from behind. "You're gonna get through this baby girl."

We move me and the girls' things to my parent's rental property. We'll stay at our house until my parents leave early to return to Maryland on Monday. The day before Gabriel returns.

TWENTY-EIGHT – GABRIEL

It's 7:15 a.m. I have thirty minutes before I need to leave my hotel room to meet at New Birth Church for the breakfast session for the second day of the Men's Empowerment Conference. I'm dressed business casual in dark jeans, a blue button-down shirt with a tan sports coat over it.

Today is me and Sabrina's 11th wedding anniversary. I scroll way back through the pictures on my phone in search of the photo of us on our wedding day that I had saved for some time. We were so young. Sabrina looked beautiful in her floral off-white dress; she was so slim you couldn't tell she was pregnant. It was certainly a shotgun wedding. My dad married us in the empty church. My parents were our only witnesses. My mom took our picture afterward. Sabrina had a wide smile; I look like a deer caught in headlights. But this is some of my favorite pictures of us because it represents us boldly taking a leap of faith for each other.

I scroll through more photos on my phone. I honestly don't have much of us together. My fault because most of these are photos Sabrina sent me of her and the girls on vacation, school events, and social activities. Scrolling to more recent photos I have some I've taken with me and the girls and a few shots I took of Sabrina on dates these past three months. But no recent photos of us together. She declined whenever I asked for us to take an usie. She used to love us taking photos together.

It's now 7:30 a.m, I don't think it's too early for me to call Sabrina. I click to dial her number hearing it ring. It continues to ring unanswered. It's Saturday morning, she can very well be sleeping in– but she's also been avoiding my calls for the past couple days.

7:31 a.m. Gabriel: Good morning beautiful. Happy 11th Anniversary. I'm thankful to God for blessing me with you. You are an amazing wife. You personify the Proverbs 31 woman. I vow to fix my shortcomings in our marriage and do right by you and our daughters. I look forward to many more wonderfully blessed years ahead for us. I love you ❤️☐

She should have the flowers I ordered delivered today. I go back to looking at photos of my wife on my phone. I post a picture of her on social media announcing our anniversary.

7:38 a.m. Babe: Happy 11th!

I read her reply with mixed feelings. She finally responds to my texts, but her response is short and... dismissive.

I sigh loudly putting my phone in my jacket pocket. I know she's pissed we're not on our cruise but how long is she going to give me the silent treatment? I have a valid reason for canceling. I have to come up with a way to make this up to her a hundred-fold. I head for the hotel room door to take the elevator to the lobby to meet the driver.

I see a housekeeper walking towards me pushing a cart.

"Mmmm, yes, papi! You *are* a tall glass of hot chocolate." Her eyes balloon in size as I chuckle while walking past her. "Did I say that out loud?"

"Yes." I wink at her and keep it moving.

I needed that ego boost after the deflated text from Sabrina.

***

"Pastor Gabriel Dean," a gentleman that looks to be in his mid-twenties says shaking my hand. "That was a powerful message you taught today, Sir. I'm Wendell Brooks."

"Thank you. Nice to meet you, Mr. Brooks." I left the stage about forty minutes ago speaking on my topic, *Men Step up to Father and or Mentor-hood*. We're in the crowded lobby during a break in sessions.

"I was adopted when I was fourteen. And to this day I'm forever grateful to my adopted parents, especially my dad. At fourteen I was lost, man. I felt like the world was against me. I had no parents, no family, and at my age, I just knew I would never get a family because most people don't like to adopt teens. And when I finally did get adopted, I was a straight up knucklehead. I tried to buck the system in my new home and my dad put a stop to it real quick.

He put my wilding behind in a boy's detention center for one day – only eight hours. I was scared straight. Since then I'm always going to him for godly wisdom and advice. It's because of him I'm not in the grave or in prison– I was doing some messed up things to cope and adapt to my environment."

"Sounds like you should've been the one up there speaking. I spoke from a godly perspective and the influence my dad had on my life, but you're also living proof of what a great mentor/father can do." I tell him.

"Nah, man. I'm not comfortable with public speaking. I'll leave that to you. But I just wanted you to know that. And I live in Deerfield Beach, Florida. Not far from Everlasting Love Ministry. My wife and kids will visit one Sunday."

"Awesome man, that would be great. Please come and see me when you do."

I shake a few more hands and chat with some more people before going outside, finding a quiet spot off to the right side of the church entrance. It's past noon, I call Sabrina. I just want to hear her voice.

Babe, please just pick up my call. Her phone rings, going to voicemail, *again*.

I call Leah, my mother-in-law.

"Hello?"

"Hi Leah, I've been trying to reach Sabrina but she's not answering my calls. Is she with you?"

"No," I can hear she's a bit hesitant in her response. I also hear Nehemiah and Genesis in the background so that may be the reason why. "She and a girlfriend went to the spa."

Good, she's using my gift. "Okay, that's good to know. Please let her know I called. Can I speak to the girls quickly before I have to get back inside?"

"Of course, they're your babies." The phone moves away from her mouth. "Girls your dad wants to talk to you."

I smile hearing them exclaim my name.

TWENTY-NINE – SABRINA

The day at the spa has me feeling like a new woman. After being pampered Tabitha and I went shopping for an outfit for tonight and I bought the sexiest ratchet dress I could find. Tabitha tried to talk me out of it, but like I told her, tonight is my night to let loose and be irresponsible. I don't want to think about my problems.

"Sabrina, what the hell are you wearing?" I turn to find my mom holding the bedroom doorknob she just opened after I told her to come in.

I look myself in the mirror again admiring myself in the Sexy V-neck, backless halter black and gold mini dress. My B-Cups are sitting pretty in this dress without a bra. One of the many pluses of my weight gain is my breasts being fuller. After breastfeeding two babies they were sagging a little. I look good! I pick up my red lipstick. "You don't like it?

She closes the bedroom door then takes a seat on the edge of my made-up bed. From my view in the mirror I watch her scan me from my perfectly styled bob hairstyle to my four-inch strap heels. I'm opting not to wear my glasses tonight.

"Actually, you look, amazing." She shakes her head. "But a woman should wear a dress like *that* either for her man, with her man or trying to find a man. So what the hell? I know you're filing for divorce but you're still the pastor's wife."

I pop my lips after applying lipstick. I look at my mom through the mirror. "Mommy please, just let me be. For one night I don't want to be Gabriel's wife or Nehemiah and Genesis mother. I need to just be *Sabrina* right now. That's not saying I'm going to do anything as if I don't carry those titles."

She studies me for a moment. "I get it. And I understand. Have fun tonight, *Sabrina*." She smiles.

The doorbell sounds.

"Thanks, mom! That's probably Tabitha." I put the top on my lipstick and put it in my clutch that's on the dresser. I start for my bedroom door with mommy on my heels.

***

"Oh sh...damn! Boss lady got legs!" Aubree exclaims upon seeing me walk towards her and Sunni waiting at the Bar & Lounge entrance. There's a line to get in with impeccably dressed people ready to get their Saturday night started.

Tabitha is walking beside me dressed cute herself in a gold shimmer mini dress, but she's showing much less skin. Her dress is hubby approved.

Aubree looks flawless in a red halter jumpsuit. And Sunni has on a deep purple short pants suit with a black midriff halter top under the jacket - she cute.

"Watch out people, Sabrina Dean did not come to play." Sunni hugs me, then Tabitha. "You look smoking hot!"

"Girl you need to take a picture and send it to hubby to show him he's missing out in Atlanta." Aubree hugs me then Tabitha.

Maybe I should. Tonight is for me to get my mind off my troubles though. I haven't told my friends I'm filing for divorce and I have no intentions to do so tonight. I've been blocking thoughts of Gabriel as much as I could all day. He's called me five times without me answering. I read a text from him on the car ride here. I haven't replied to that either.

I look up at the clear night sky. The beats from the inside are making me hype. It's ladies' night!

"Thanks, ladies we all look great. Let's go have some fun!" I hook my arm with Tabitha right next to me and Sunni on my left. Aubree loops her arm with Sunni, and we strut into the lounge bypassing the line because Aubree has the hook-up.

"…Bang this in your whips, pack em call the roadie with the chips in the wrists, here's a French kiss…" I'm rapping Lil Kim's lines to her song *Ladies Night*. The two glasses of Hennessy I consumed has me doing things my sober mind wouldn't. Like grabbing the mic and doing karaoke in front of all these people. My girls have my back though singing and rapping the other artists' lines to the song.

I get real ratchet when Cardi B's song *Money* comes on. Karaoke is over, I'm on the dance floor allowing the now three glasses of Hennessy to take over. I don't know the words to the song but my drunk mind thinks I do. Sunni and Tabitha are on the sidelines shaking their heads gleefully being the mother hens making sure I don't fall flat on my face. Aubree is the real trooper at my side hyping my intoxicated mind up as if the Henny hasn't already done so.

I hope no one is recording this. Right now the Henny is making me feel like Cardi B. Tomorrow I will know better and I don't want physical evidence to prove it.

"Yasssss, get it, girl!" Aubree shouts while I gyrate my hips, popping my butt, moving to where I'm squatting, dropping it down low. Somehow I manage to make my way back up without falling on my butt. I do hear a crack in my knees though, oh well.

Tabitha shouts over the music, "Okay sis! I ain't mad at you." She looks impressed.

Sunni has her phone out recording giving me a thumbs up. So much for no evidence. She soon puts her phone away.

I feel a hand on my bareback. "Can I have this dance?"

I turn at the sound of Kian's voice. I throw my arms around his neck. "What are you doing here?"

He moves a little to the beat with me. "A little birdie told me you would be here tonight I came because I wanted to check on you. I thought you'll be cruising to the Bahamas."

He takes my hand leading me off the dance floor. We keep walking until we're outside on the back patio. The light breeze cools my heated skin from dancing and drinking. The lighting is poor out here but it's enough light to not be creeped out. We're two of a handful of people outside.

"Why aren't you on your cruise for your anniversary?" He looks me over. "You look gorgeous by the way."

I look up at him, watching his lips move. I step closer to him running my hands up his chest then looping my arms around his neck, cupping his neck. I inch up on my toes drawing his face closer to mine.

His minty breath washes over me. "I overstepped bounds with you twice and I don't ever want to do that again. *You* don't want me to do it again." He unhooks my arms from around his neck. Drunk and frustrated I push at his chest. "This isn't you Sabrina. You're the good girl. Don't let your relationship break you. Fix the problem or move on."

His words sober me a bit. Tears spring to my eyes. Why can't Gabriel love me the way I need to be loved? Why is my most important relationship after God tearing me apart?

Drunken cries are the worst. "I just wan... want himmm to loooove me.... how I need to be... loved.

Why did... didn't h...he choose me? I'm... always last." I slobber in Kian's arms.

"Is she okay?" I hear Tabitha's voice. I know she wasn't going to be far.

"I got her. We'll be back inside soon." He tells her.

"Okay. I got her a bottled water."

I still have my head buried in his chest, I feel one of his arms move, I guess to accept the bottle.

Kian hugs me with both arms again. "Everything will be okay," he assures me.

***

Why did I want to be reckless and irresponsible again? *Jesus, receive me home to glory.* Death would be better than this. My headache is on one hundred. My breath is kicking, and my throat is dry. My back and knees ache something fierce.

I moan trying to get comfortable in my bed. How did I even make it back here? Last night is fuzzy in my brain.

"Hmmmm," I groan. Moving my head makes my headache worse. *Damn you, Hennessy!*

Something smells good…like roses. I peak an eye open and slightly lift the covers. The roses Gabriel had delivered yesterday are on the nightstand on my side of the bed. Mom must have brought them up last night.

I close my eyes dropping the covers to take me back to darkness. I think I dozed off for a few minutes cause I'm startled awake by my cellphone ringing which sounds like a blaring siren.

"Make it stop!" I groan.

I blindly snake my hand out of the covers searching for my phone on the nightstand. I grab it answering the noisemaker without looking at the name of the caller.

"Hello?" I croak.

"Sabrina," Gabriel breathes with relief. "Thank you for answering. Are you okay, you don't sound well?"

I groan. I don't feel like talking to him. "I have a headache, but I'll be fine."

"You should probably stay home from church today," I mumble a response back to him. "Did you enjoy the spa yesterday?"

"I did. But my head really hurts I want to sleep it off some more before I take any meds for it."

"Okay, yeah." He sounds defeated, but my hungover mind doesn't care. "I know I keep saying it, but I'm really sorry we didn't get to celebrate our anniversary together."

Yeah, whatever! It's nothing new, we barely went to dinner last year since you had a crisis to handle at church that day.

"Okay, bye Gabriel."

"Bye."

THIRTY – GABRIEL

Sabrina continues to ignore my calls and texts. She must have really not been feeling well to have answered my call on Sunday. It's Tuesday. The conference ended late last night and this afternoon all of the guest speakers met up for lunch. This was definitely a great experience. I enjoyed the conference as if I was a regular attendee. I did a lot of networking and have some new awesome brothers in Christ that I will be keeping in contact with.

My flight back to Florida has me getting home late– close to midnight. Sabrina's parents left my car in the parking garage at the airport, so I can pick up my keys from an attendant when I arrive.

After checking in for my flight, sitting at the terminal, I try calling Sabrina again but she's not answering. My patience with her has expired. I get that she's upset with me but this is not the way to handle it.

I'm extremely tired when I turn on my street to get home. I look forward to sleeping in my own bed next to my wife. I pull-up in our driveway and hit the remote on my visor to open the garage. I notice instantly that

Sabrina's SUV is missing. *Where could she be at this hour on a Tuesday night?*

I park, closing the garage behind me. *Did she get the neighbor to babysit this late on a school night?* I shut off the car then pick up my cellphone from the cupholder. I grab my suitcase from the trunk then make my way inside. I dial Sabrina's number after disarming the alarm.

"Hello?"

I'm walking towards the family room expecting to find the neighbor's daughter sleeping. "Hey, babe. I just got home. Where are you?"

"The girls and I are sleeping out tonight."

I stop in my tracks releasing the handle to my rolling suitcase. "What do you mean you all are sleeping out tonight?" My tone is sharp. "I know you're upset but you ignoring my calls and text and now this is not the way to handle this, Sabrina." My jaw clenches. "And where the hell are you?"

"We are at my parent's condo. Please, just give me space right now. We can talk more tomorrow."

Knowing where they are releases some of my tension. "Fine. But this ends tomorrow, Sabrina. I'm serious."

"Ok, bye Gabriel."

She hangs up. I have the urge to show up at her parents' condo. But I'll give her one more night.

***

It feels good to be home and sleep in my own bed– though my wife's side of the bed is cold. I woke up after 9. Bria called letting me know she has me scheduled for a counseling session with a woman stating she urgently wants to meet with me and not any of the other pastors on staff. I agree to the meeting for 11:30, and afterward, Sabrina and I need to sit down and talk. The silent treatment ends today. When I checked my phone after the call with Bria, I noticed a text from Sabrina letting me know she's going to work and will be there until 2:30. We'll have to meet up on her break then.

Dressed casually for the day, since technically I was supposed to be on vacation, I make my way into the kitchen to start the machine for coffee. I'm looking in the fridge for the hazelnut cream when the doorbell rings. I check the security camera on the wall near the kitchen and see a middle-aged white man in a polo shirt and dark pants standing on my porch.

"Good morning, how can I help you?" I ask after opening the front door.

"Is Gabriel Dean available?"

"I'm Mr. Dean, what's this about?"

He hands me a large envelope. "You've been served." He states before walking away towards his late model pick-up truck.

I slam the front door shut and rip open the envelope. My world comes crashing down when I read the first few lines stating that Sabrina filed for divorce. I must be dreaming because this is not real, it can't be.

Dear God, please tell me this is not real!

I go to the kitchen to find my phone. I shut off the coffee machine, grab my keys and head for the garage.

I barge into Sabrina's office shutting the door behind me.

She looks up from her computer. "So you do remember where I work." Her sarcasm has me teetering on the edge to destruction.

"A divorce Sabrina? Really?" I hold up the papers. "Because I took the speaking engagement?"

"No, because you, as you've done for the majority of our marriage, put my feelings and desires on the back-burner. I've suffered through countless disappointments. As long as Gabriel's happy, as long as Gabriel's needs are met, as long as Gabriel's big man on the church campus, as long as I dutifully play my role, you couldn't care less about me. Well, I'm tired of showing up and showing face when I'm dying in this marriage. I want out!"

She might as well have put a gun to my forehead and blown my brains out. My heart and mind are racing. Hearing her words crushes me more than the divorce papers in my hand. Tears are burning the back of my eyes begging for release.

"That bitch you've been sleeping with can have you all to herself now."

"What?!"

"You heard me!" She snaps.

I near her desk. "You think I'm cheating on you?"

"It explains why just this year that I finally gained weight and have curves and fuller breasts you can't keep your hands off me. Was she making up for my lack? Was she coddling you, stroking your ego and telling you how great of a pastor you are?

I shake my head laughing humorlessly. "You know what. Yeah, I guess she can have me all to herself now."

I slam the divorce papers on her desk then stalk out of her office slamming the door behind me. Sunni and another woman named Aubree, from what I barely remember from the tail-end of Sabrina's business party, watch me cautiously. I move past them and out the building not uttering a single word.

Sitting behind the steering wheel of my SUV I freely let the tears fall, blurring my vision. It feels like I'm about to lose my mind.

How can she want to end our marriage so easily? I was making an effort to meet her needs.

And she's been waiting 11 years for you to do so. My conscious chastises me. *Your trip together to celebrate your anniversary was more important than you appeasing your ego by accepting the speaking invitation. Your first ministry is home.*

I shake my head trying to erase my thoughts. I angrily wipe the tears from my eyes. She doesn't love me anymore and she thinks I'm cheating on her. She's been waiting for whatever reason to end our marriage.

I start the engine then drive off.

***

I'm an emotional mess. I don't want to lose my wife and break up my family.

Jason walks back into my family room, that's void of my family's laughter, handing me a bottled beer. I should be in my office at church right now, the irony is not lost on me. The Holy Spirit made me aware. I accept the bottle taking a big gulp. I rest my head against the back of the couch closing my eyes with the bottle still in my hand.

"I take it she's not budging on the divorce?" Jason asks from the chair across from me. I called him on my way to and from Sabrina's office. I need my boy right now to talk me off the ledge.

I shake my head with my eyes still closed. I feel a headache coming on. *Jesus, please help me, Lord.* My eyes burn with tears. This hurts so bad. I have never felt heartbreak like this.

"I know you don't want to hear this, and I think it's a bit extreme for Sabrina wanting a divorce, but you shouldn't have canceled your anniversary trip for the speaking engagement. I've known you for years and I can only recall one trip you and Sabrina took alone together. Y'all didn't even take a honeymoon trip when you got married.

Tabitha said Sabrina was really looking forward to the cruise for you two to spend quality time together. You said it yourself three months ago that you wanted a better work/life balance. Taking the speaking engagement may have made her feel that you don't care about her and your marriage."

Opening my eyes, I lean forward and take another swig of beer. "I do care about my marriage. She's the one that doesn't love me anymore."

I watch his eyes grow in size. "She told you that?"

I nod. "Three months ago."

"I'm sorry, bro... I didn't know you two had issues like that. But regardless of what she said y'all can work things out. Eleven years of marriage isn't something you should give up easily."

My emotions keep fluctuating between heartbreak, bitterness, and anger. "It's easy for Sabrina especially since she thinks I'm cheating on her."

"What? You told her that's not true right?" He looks me dead in the eyes, "That's not true, *right*?"

"No it's not true but if that's what she wants to believe, it's on her." I gulp my beer.

"Don't let her think you're cheating, man. That will only make matters worse."

Frustrated, I push up from the couch. "She made matters worse by having me served with divorce papers and packing her and my children things out of our house." I kick the coffee table hard, knocking it against the chair opposite from where Jason is sitting. The remote and knickknacks on top crash to the tiled floor. After getting back home from her office I took a good look around our bedroom closet and the girls' rooms to find most of their clothes, shoes, and essentials gone. I also found an opened gift with semi-nude pictures of a woman and a handwritten note that Sabrina left on my home office desk. "If she wants a divorce, I'll give her a divorce." I angrily scrub my face with my free hand then tug on my beard. "I will see you later, man." I walk away not waiting for a response.

THIRTY-ONE – SABRINA

My parent's rental property in Delray Beach is a beautiful tropical oasis overlooking the beach. I'm fortunate that the place is vacant. The condo has two spacious master suites. However, after three days of being here, the girls aren't enjoying sharing a room anymore. Especially when they know the comfort of our home is only minutes away.

"Mommy, when are we going back home? I don't like sleeping with Nehemiah because she talks in her sleep." Genesis asks before popping a forkful of waffle into her mouth. We're sitting at the round breakfast table near the sliding door with views of the quiet shore from the second floor.

Miah protests, "Nuh-uh, I don't talk in my sleep. You snore!" She tells her sister.

"No, I don't! Mommy can we go home today. Isn't daddy back from his trip?"

Guilt has my mind racing for the right words to tell my daughters. This is precisely why I haven't left Gabriel before. I didn't want to uproot the girls and create chaos in their lives. But I couldn't stay any longer.

I place the coffee cup in my hand down on the wicker glass-top table. "We'll be staying here a little longer, but you'll get to go home soon." *God, please let that be enough to pacify them for now.* I need to have a civilized conversation with Gabriel and schedule mediation for us to come up with a plan. Yesterday when he confronted me at my office it didn't go so well.

"Are you and daddy breaking up?" Genesis asks shocking the heck out of me.

Miah's wide eyes turn to me for an answer as well.

Think fast, Sabrina! "Daddy and I have to discuss some things then we will talk to you both about it. Okay. We're still married we just had a disagreement."

"I don't want you to break up. And I don't want to live here forever. I like my room at home." Nehemiah's words rip my heart to shreds.

I push back from the table, move closer to Nehemiah and wrap my arms around her. "Baby, this is hard for mommy too. I just need you to trust me that no matter what I will always make sure you and your sister are well, happy and safe. I love you." I open my arms wider for Genesis to join us which she willingly does. "I love you too, Genesis." I kiss them on their braided heads.

After a few moments, "Come on, we have to get going so I can get you to school on time." Since we're not home for them to get on the school bus I have to drop them off and pick them up from school. "I will see if daddy can pick you girls up from school today, would you like that?"

"Yes!" They both cheer.

***

It's 10:30 a.m. and I haven't made it to the office yet. I just left my lawyer's office to discuss mediation. I don't know if Gabriel has a lawyer yet or not but my lawyer, Lashan Dassie, Esq. will contact Gabriel to find out and schedule our meeting.

I'm now sitting in front of my therapist, Dr. James Adderley. He's a black man in his mid-sixties, however, he looks a decade younger. He's always impeccably dressed in a suit, vest, and bowtie. His afro tapered salt and pepper fade is always on point. He's good to look at. But I haven't been seeing him for almost a year because of his looks. His wisdom, care and his way of forcing me to self-evaluate myself have me coming back. He keeps me levelheaded and I like having him as a soundboard.

"Do you think you were a bit hasty in filing for divorce and moving you and the girls' things out of the house?"

See, he makes me face the questions I want to avoid but shouldn't. *Darn him!*

I sigh with my hands resting in my lap. I look around his spacious, comfy, earth-tones decorated office. "Maybe I was?"

He lifts his brow.

I narrow my eyes at him. "Fine! Yes, I think I reacted too quickly. But I don't regret finally doing something to show Gabriel how fed up I am with his disregard for my feelings. And some woman sent him nude pictures and a note."

"And you think he's cheating on you?"

I push my glasses further up the bridge of my nose. "Isn't it obvious?"

"Is it?" He queries.

Grrr. I look down at my nails. I need to get a fill-in.

"Sabrina," Dr. Adderley prompts.

Okay, maybe I may have jumped the gun accusing Gabriel of cheating on me. As a pastor, people do send him gifts of support and appreciation. And that package could be from some desperate thirsty woman. *But Bria may be right, that something is going on with her and Gabriel. Maybe those photos are of her.*

"I don't know. But it doesn't matter. Whether he cheated or not our marriage hasn't been great for too long and I'm done. Loving him shouldn't be hard."

"You're in Love with him again?"

In the three months since I told Gabriel I wasn't in love with him anymore, his attentiveness, dates, gifts, and quality time allowed me to give my heart back to him. Which is why his canceling our trip hurt me twice as hard. He accomplished his goal of me falling back in love with him only to cut me deeper than before.

"I am. It doesn't mean we can resolve our issues though. My trust in him is nonexistent. And what is a marriage without trust?"

"No relationship can survive without trust, but trust can be rebuilt."

"There lies the problem, Dr. Adderley. I don't care to rebuild it." *Or do I?*

***

I've called Gabriel's cellphone five times since I left Dr. Adderley's office and he's not answering. Payback's a hurtful thing. I'm back in my place of business closed-off in my office. Because of Gabriel showing up yesterday my staff knows there's trouble in paradise and right now I don't want to talk about it, so they've been giving me space. Tabitha has also been blowing up my phone, I'm sure Jason filled her in on what's going on, he and Gabriel are best friends and are like brothers to each other. I'm not ready to talk to her about my marriage and divorce right now either.

"Good morning, you've reached Everlasting Love Ministry, this is Bria speaking, how may I assist you?"

Her perky voice grates on my nerves for many different reasons. One of which is my suspicion that she sent the photos to Gabriel. I'm not going to confront her without evidence, the last thing I need is for her to know Gabriel and I are on bad terms.

"Good morning Bria, this is Sabrina. I'll like to speak to pastor Gabriel, please."

"Oh, hi," she responds dryly. "How was the cruise?" I hear her finger snap. "That's right, you didn't get to go. Sorry about that. Hold, I'll see if Pastor *wants* to talk to you."

I bite down on my tongue to avoid going off on her, I have bigger issues to deal with right now. She'll be dealt with later.

"Yes, Sabrina," Gabriel sounds completely fed-up with me, which too starts to tick me off.

"I've been trying to call you –"

"Avoided phone calls doesn't feel nice, now does it?" He snaps at me.

I keep my mouth shut from voicing a response at his chastisement. It's well deserved on my part. "I deserve that. I shouldn't have ignored your calls and I won't moving forward. I don't want our divorce to be ugly." He makes a low growling sound when I say the "D" word. "I'm calling because the girls want to see you, I thought it would be nice if you can pick them up from school."

"And where shall I take them after, Sabrina. Home?"

I close my eyes, blocking the view of my office. Inhale, exhale. I reopen my eyes. "This isn't easy for me either Gabriel I–"

"It seems pretty damn easy when you have divorce papers written up, filed, moved you and my daughters' things out of the house and have me served with divorce papers in a matter of days, Sabrina!" He raises his voice and I can attest to the fact that in our eleven years of marriage he has never raised his voice at me like this before. And we've had our share of disagreements.

Tears pool in my eyes and my throat clogs. The pain in his voice and the memory of the defeated look on his face yesterday in my office guts me to the core. But dammit, I've been hurting for years. *Years!*

"I will pick them up from school and take them out and you can get them from school tomorrow because they're staying *home* with me tonight. I received the call from your lawyer, I will have my lawyer contact her so we can move forward with mediation and whatever it is you need to get rid of me." He hangs up without waiting for my response.

I pull my cellphone from my ear completely dumbfounded and hurt. I don't know how I'm going to handle him being dismissive to me. How dare he try to turn everything on me? He's acting as if he played no role in the demise of our marriage.

Another important question is if divorce is what I really want?

THIRTY-TWO – GABRIEL

"What do you think of this?" I ask Jason after he takes a seat in front of my desk. I'd gotten off the phone with Sabrina almost an hour ago and I'm still agitated. I didn't mean to go off on her the way I did but this whole situation is tearing me apart. I feel completely helpless. I know I need to get on my knees and pray, and I will, but I can't let go of the anger, hurt and betrayal I feel with her going about the divorce the way she did. I was completely blindsided. It was a proverbial sucker punch.

Help me dear, Lord.

Jason leans forward as I push the small box, torn wrapping and items towards him on the desk. "What is it?" He picks up the pictures.

"Someone mailed that to my house addressed to me. I think it's why Sabrina believes I've cheated on her."

I watch him look through the four pictures. Then he picks up and reads the note. "Does the handwriting look familiar to you?"

I shake my head. "I have no clue who could've sent this."

He puts the pictures and note back. "What about?" He motions with his thumb pointing behind him.

"Bria?" I stroke my full beard. "Nah man, I don't think she would do something like this."

"Look, I'm not trying to accuse her either. But this," he gestures to the incriminating items on my desk, "Probably pushed Sabrina over the edge. And Bria did come at you with that back in the day nonsense about you two getting married. You shot her down, maybe she's still salty about that. Why all of a sudden someone is sending you half naked pictures and a note?" He leans back in the seat as if he presented a powerful argument. And maybe he has.

I stare at the torn gift box, wrapping, note, and pictures. A lightbulb goes off in my head. I reach for the wrapping. "Does this look familiar to you?"

Jason looks at the ripped floral wrapping paper in my hand closely. Realization dawns on him. "Ms. Urma!"

"She used this same wrapping paper for the drawers she got us."

"Man," he shakes his head with a humorless chuckle. "You think she did this because we made her take a hiatus?"

"This wrapping paper has me convinced. I don't want to believe it, but it seems pretty obvious to me. This is Ms. Urma we're talking about. She doesn't like being knocked down a peg, what better way for her to get back at me?" My jaw clenches.

"That's messed up! That old woman would go to these lengths just because she was asked to check her behavior and she does this."

"I don't even know how to handle this. Can a church ban someone from attending? In some ways, she's costing me my marriage. Forget turning the other cheek!" I utter out of frustration. I take a calming breath. "I need to meet with Ms. Urma today to address this. Not only does she owe me an apology, but she owes Sabrina one too. The board would have to decide how to move forward with this."

"Do you want the board to know Sabrina filed for divorce? I heard what you said yesterday and I know you didn't mean it. Fight for her. Bro, that's probably all she wants. And we can address Ms. Urma with the board but I think you should hold off on the part about her sending these pictures. At least for now."

He's right. Why put a negative bug in the board's ear about my marriage? But would I just be putting off the evitable?

The Lord is my shepherd; I shall not want. He maketh me to lie down in green pastures: he leadeth me beside the still waters. He restoreth my soul: he leadeth me in the paths of righteousness for his name's sake... Psalm 23 runs through my mind.

I love my wife. I don't want a divorce. I don't want to be separated from my children.

"You and I can meet with Ms. Urma today and hopefully get it resolved without involving the board."

Jason nods. I pick up the phone on my desk calling Bria to set up a meeting with Ms. Urma as soon as possible.

***

A little over an hour later Ms. Urma walks into my office wearing a red design of one of her infamous dresses, she looks guilty as sin. She eyes her dirty work on my desk right away. I left it there for this very reason.

"The devil made me do it!" Ms. Urma exclaims.

I roll my eyes and stop myself from asking her if the devil can also make her stop wearing these hideous dresses.

I let Jason start the conversation because I need a few more moments to get right with the Lord or else I may say the wrong thing. I'm a man of the cloth but I'm still a *man*. What Ms. Urma did upset my home. Granted there was trouble in paradise before, this may have made it worse.

Jason addresses her after she takes a seat next to him in front of my desk. "Thanks for admitting to what you did, Ms. Urma. However, your actions were extremely wrong. Not only did you disrespect Pastor Gabriel, you disrespected his home, his wife and his children. The very reason we asked you to take a break from the hospitality ministry was because you were not exemplifying the love of Christ. And then you took things too far." He gestures to the pictures and note on my desk.

...forgive us our trespasses, as we forgive those who trespass against us, and lead us not into temptation, but deliver us from evil... I mentally recite the Lord's Prayer.

Ms. Urma surprisingly looks remorseful. She can't even look me in my eyes. This helps a bit with my anger.

Ms. Urma fiddles with her fingers in her lap. "I apologize pastor Gabriel for my actions. I was upset after the meeting last week and did what I did. Those photos are not of me," Jason and I look at each other, we're both fighting a smirk. I know he'll have something slick to say when we're alone. "Those are my granddaughter's photos that I found a while back that she was sending to some man in jail. I will also apologize to First Lady Sabrina when I see her." She lifts her head looking directly at me. "I'm truly sorry for my actions." She removes the pictures, note and wrapping from my desk, shoving them in her oversized purse.

I blow a breath. It's my turn to practice what I preach. "I accept your apology Ms. Urma. And I expect you to apologize to my *wife*." My heart skips a beat. "With that being said, your break from the hospitality ministry will be extended to six months."

"I understand pastor Gabriel. Again, I apologize for my actions. I thought you would still be on your cruise because I had planned to tell you the truth and apologize when you returned."

"I'm happy we were able to resolve this. I hope we won't have any other problems," I let her know.

"We won't. God has been dealing with me for my wrongs."

I stand and Jason follows. "Thanks for coming in Ms. Urma, see you on Sunday, he tells her while opening my office door since he's closer.

"See you both Sunday. I look forward to your message again this Sunday Pastor Jason. Will you still preach this Sunday?"

He nods. "Yes, I am. Pastor Gabriel is technically still on vacation."

"Good! I enjoy your preaching as much as I do his." Are her final words before she leaves.

Jason turns to face me. "Bruh, did she really think we thought those photos were of her?" We both laugh shaking our heads.

THIRTY-THREE – SABRINA

"Yeah, I'm here. I've had enough of you avoiding my calls. I got the address from Gabriel. We don't have to talk about it. I just want you to know I'm here whenever you do want to." Tabitha pushes past me into the condo. I lock the door behind her.

I'm here alone. Gabriel wanted the girls home with him another night, I didn't have it in me to refuse. It feels weird not having them around, though they drive me crazy sometimes. They've always been with me when I'm not at work and they're not at school.

Dressed in a onesie pajama I go back to my room with Tabitha following behind me. I climb back in bed getting comfortable. I un-pause the television to continue the movie.

"Aww man, this is really bad if you're watching Lifetime movies." Tabitha kicks off her flip-flops getting on the bed. She's wearing black yoga pants with a long yellow sleeveless tunic.

I crack a smile. She knows I find Lifetime movies super cheesy. This is better than wallowing in guilt, heartbreak, and confusion. I need a sappy love story to help uplift my depressing dilemma.

"Tuh! This chick is in love with her brother's best friend. The brother has no clue and the best friend is starting to notice her more in that way. But he's fighting his attraction. And we know how it's gonna play out but we're still going to watch."

"Oh yeah! That is super cheesy but should be good." Tabitha gets comfy against the pillows.

Three hours later her cellphone is blowing up with text messages. She and Jason are so darn cute. They've been married for seven years and still act like newlyweds. I could be bitter and jealous watching her caking on her phone, but I'm not.

She throws her leg off the bed. "Okay, girl I've got to go. Jason's complaining that he needs his pillow."

I frown. "His pillow?"

"Me, chica. I'm the pillow." She laughs and I do too. "I swear Jason acts like he can't sleep unless I'm right beside him."

See? They're so darn cute.

I want the cute and cheesy relationship. But then I feel maybe it's not God's plan for me. I did get a tiny taste of it the past three months and it was sweet. Maybe I was only allowed a taste. A taste I miss immensely. Maybe Gabriel just isn't suited to give me what I need. Maybe I'm not what he needs. Maybe he needs the wife that will work full time in the church while raising the kids. The wife that will freely give hugs and kiss the babies of the congregation. The wife that will give him pointers on his sermon notes. The wife that's content without quality time together and not traveling together and creating fun memories with each other and their children. The wife that's okay with him always choosing the church and work above her. Maybe she's who he needs.

"Tell Jason to take it easy on his *pillow* tonight, kay?" I wink at her.

She slips on her flip-flops giggling. "Will do. Love you girl. I will lock the door on my way out."

"Thanks. Love you too!"

Now I'm thinking about sex and my lack. Ugh! For a while, I had lost the desire to have sex with my husband, but he'd awaken the need something fierce the past few months. I really didn't think this divorce and separation through. Can women get blue clit? I'll have to survive sleeping through one tonight.

****

GABRIEL

"Wash your hands, Genesis, then you can add your pizza toppings." The girls and I are making homemade pizzas for dinner. This won over my choice of spaghetti. We're each adding our toppings to eight-inch pies.

Miah is overdoing it with the cheese, but I let her have at it. The cheesier the better, right?

"I wonder what mommy's eating for dinner," Genesis says absentmindedly.

Nehemiah replies, "Maybe she's going to order Bahamian food from The Caribbean restaurant. She said she wanted conch fritters then peas and rice with steamed crawfish." Miah adds cheese, pepperoni, and sausage to her pizza.

"Yeah, I think so too," the oldest replies.

"Daddy, are you and mommy broken up? I heard her crying one night. It wasn't the praying cry it was the sad cry."

My heart quickens at the thought of Sabrina in tears. Because of me?

"How can you tell the difference in cry?" I really want to know.

Nehemiah has a thoughtful look on her youthful face. "Well, usually when she pray cries she's speaking in tongues and she's either kneeling, sitting or standing. This sad cry she was lying in bed with her face in the pillow. It made me feel sad."

It makes me sad too.

"Okay, let's get the pizzas in the oven," I say as a distraction as I pick up the tray.

"And I will find a movie on Netflix." Genesis skips out of the kitchen. I chuckle. She's slick getting out of cleaning up the minimal mess. Nehemiah is more of a neat freak like her mama. She's already got most of the mess up.

I promised the 16-year-old babysitter extra pay for coming over on short notice. The girls and I ate our pizzas and watched two Disney movies. I couldn't get what Nehemiah said about Sabrina crying out of my head. When I noticed the girls dozing off, I called the neighbor.

I have a spare key to my in-law's condo, but I knock on the door instead. I don't want to invade Sabrina's privacy. Then the thought of her being in there entertaining another man... maybe Kian, causes my fist to clench.

After the second knock, I hear footsteps on the tile floor heading towards the door.

"That was quick, don't tell me–" Sabrina stops mid-sentence when she opens the door to find me. *Who did she think I was?* "Gabriel?"

I move to pass by her getting a good look around the living area. Empty. I look back at her still near the door. She has on a leopard print onesie. "I know you don't love me, and you filed for divorce, but I *need* you right now. Please." *If only for tonight I need to feel like you're still mine.*

Her back is facing the now closed door. "Okay." She replies softly but I hear it loud and clear. I pounce on her, zipping down the onesie and taking her right up against the door.

Later I carry her limp and fully satiated body to the bedroom, clean her up and tuck her in bed. She's out cold. I hate leaving but this was just sex, and I must accept it for what it is. She doesn't love me and no longer wants to be Mrs. Dean. I bend over, kissing her on the forehead whispering, "I love you."

THIRTY-FOUR – SABRINA

Today is character day in children's church. I barely get the car in park before the girls are sprinting for the church entrance. I smile while shaking my head. Genesis is dressed as some girl from a show on Nickelodeon and Miah is dressed as a character in her favorite book series.

It's weird not seeing Ms. Urma as a greeter at the door. I sure don't miss her unpleasant remarks. I smile politely at Lilly and a new male greeter whose name is AJ. I greet a few people as I'm walking through the church foyer.

"Wow, you do know when to arrive on time." Katherine, a Haitian lady on the church board boldly remarks as I'm walking past her.

I stop, turn, and face her. "I guess it's much easier for you to arrive on time since early Sunday mornings are the only time you can freely ride deacon Philips joystick without his wife finding out."

Her mouth drops open. *Checkmate!* She looks around to make sure no one heard what I said. I'm sick of people like her – judgmental sin police hypocrites. I turn and strut away.

Ms. Urma comes into my line of sight as I make my way towards the side doors that leads into the sanctuary. I prepare myself for her shenanigans.

She has a pleasant smile on her face. It matches the sunflower pattern on her dress. "Good morning First Lady Sabrina," *Harpo, who dis woman?* "I want to sincerely apologize for the pictures and note I mailed to pastor Gabriel." My mouth forms an O as she speaks. "I was upset with him and the board making me take a break as a greeter and I took things too far. I hope you can forgive me."

Whaaaattttt!!! She sent the pictures and note? Gabriel wasn't cheating on me? Who is the woman in the picture? Did Gabriel lie when he admitted to there being someone else? Did he say there was someone else?

"I understand if it will take some time for you to accept my apology. I also must apologize for the way I have treated you since you became First Lady. The good Lord has shown me the error of my ways. You were right about that scripture Acts ten verse fifteen, what God has called clean I and nobody else has a right to call unclean."

"I forgive you," I tell her truthfully. Because *this* truly is a miracle.

Ms. Urma pulls me into a hug, I cringe for a moment before relaxing into it. "Thank you!"

She releases me and walks away. I'm baffled standing here in the church foyer as people mingle by. *Did that really just happen?*

****

GABRIEL

I trip over my words talking to minister Tracey when I notice Sabrina walking into the sanctuary from the side doors to the left. She is a vision in her cream wide leg pants and pale pink blouse. We haven't seen each other since Friday night when I showed up late at the condo. When she picked the girls up on Saturday, she blew the horn and waited outside the house for them to get in the car.

I didn't expect her to show up at church. I figured with the divorce papers filed she wouldn't want to be here... around me. Seeing her awakens a hunger in me I thought I satisfied two days ago – who am I kidding? I'm always in need of her. She's my wife – soon to be ex. The thought sours my mood.

The choir gathers on stage for the start of service. I excuse myself from minister Tracey. Usually, I sit on the stage near the pulpit with the other pastors and church leaders, today I'm interested in sitting somewhere else. Next to Sabrina, especially since Jason is preaching today.

"Good morning," I greet Sabrina. She's standing at her usual spot in the front row, left section.

"Good morning, Gabriel."

I want to hug her, kiss her, but I refrain myself. Her hibiscus scented perfume enticing my nostrils makes the decision extremely difficult. I want to be buried deep inside her.

"I honestly didn't expect you to be here," I say for only her to hear.

She studies my face before replying. "I didn't think you would want the church to know anything," she whispers. "The girls are excited about character day today in children's church and despite everything, I love this church."

But you don't love me. She's also right, I'm not ready to let anyone know the status of our relationship. I'm barely coming to grips with it myself.

The choir starts the first song, "This is The Day the Lord Has Made", singing it upbeat.

Still standing, Sabrina turns to face the choir, clapping her hands to the beat. Most of the seats in the one thousand seat sanctuary are filled. This is the third and last service for the day. I notice her watch me from the corner of her eye as I move to stand by the seat next to her. She turns her head towards me lifting a brow in question, I smile as my reply.

Throughout the service, I am distracted by Sabrina. I've heard Jason's sermon twice already so I know he's doing a great job. I'm acutely aware of every move Sabrina makes. When she claps, when she picks up her bible and turn the pages. When she picks up her pen and write notes. I almost lost it when the praise and worship ended and Minister Tracey asked everyone to greet their neighbors, the few men who shook hands or church-hugged my wife had me seeing red.

I don't want to lose her.

Service ends. I watch Sabrina stand, placing the strap of her purse on her shoulder and bible in her hand. Again I want to reach out and touch her. I don't.

"Are you greeting guests or you're leaving that to Jason and Tabitha today?" Sabrina asks.

"I'm technically on vacation, remember?"

Her eyes dim, I realize I probably said the wrong thing. "Yeah, we would have been arriving back from our cruise."

There's an awkward silence.

She points with her thumb over her shoulder. "I'm going to get the girls..."

I interrupt her. "I want to take them out for lunch, would that be okay? I will bring them to you afterward."

"O... okay. They will like that." We stare at each other. "I'm going to head out then." She turns and leaves. I watch her until I can't anymore.

I feel a pat on my shoulder. "Fight for her!" Jason encourages before strolling away to meet Tabitha by the sanctuary main doors.

But how can I fight for someone who doesn't love me or wants me?

THIRTY-FIVE – SABRINA

My heart skips a beat when Gabriel walks into the conference room of my lawyer's office, followed by his lawyer. My heart has been doing that since I filed for divorce whenever I'm in Gabriel's presence. *What's up with that?*

Gabriel's dressed casually in relaxed dark jeans and a green plain t-shirt. So simple yet he makes it look so enticing. And I love it when he dresses down because it makes him look laidback as oppose to his serious pastor mode. He looks like he recently got a haircut and his beard is neatly groomed. I want to run my fingers through it.

"Sabrina?"

"Huh?" I blink out of my reverie looking up at Gabriel standing across from where I'm sitting at the oval mahogany conference table.

Gabriel has a smirk on his handsome face. "I was introducing you to my lawyer."

I push my chair back and stand to greet the black man in his early forties. "I'm Sabrina Dean." We shake hands across the table. "Nice to meet you."

"Same to you, I'm Lovell Jones."

Apparently, my lawyer, Lashan Dassie had already greeted Lovell while I was in la-la land.

Before I can take my seat again a Hispanic woman in her mid-forties walks into the conference room. "Good morning! Great, it looks like everyone is here right on time." She has a bubbly personality. "I'm Jhanielle Diaz, I'm the mediator." She walks over to me. "I am familiar with your lawyers. You must be Mrs. Sabrina Dean, it's a pleasure to meet you."

She offers her hand in greeting, I accept. "Yes, I'm Sabrina. Nice to meet you."

She walks over to Gabriel. "Mr. Gabriel Dean, nice to meet you."

Gabriel shakes her hand. "I don't like the circumstances, but it's nice to meet you."

"Yes, of course. And hopefully, with mediation, everything will work smoothly." She takes a seat at the head of the table resting her satchel on top pulling out a legal pad and pen. "Your lawyers Lashan and Lovell have briefed me on the divorce. As a mediator, I am a neutral third party to help resolve any issues during the divorce process. The first thing we should discuss is the welfare of your daughters and come up with a co-parenting plan."

My right leg is bouncing nervously under the table. *This is actually happening. I can't believe this is happening.* I look over at Gabriel. He has a solemn look on his face. *Dear God, am I doing the right thing?*

"Are you both okay with joint custody? You can do a week on and off schedule where you both alternate having the kids every other week. Or a bi-weekly schedule where you alternate every two weeks."

"I ahh," I look at Gabriel again. The sadness in his eyes is enough to bring me to my knees. He refuses to look at me. "I think bi-weekly would be less hectic."

"What do you think Mr. Dean," Jhanielle asks.

"Y-yeah. That would work." He clears his throat. "I would still like to see them when they're not with me, for dinner and helping with homework, things like that."

"Me too," I tell Jhanielle.

The mediator jots down notes. "Child support. Though you both agree to joint custody, one parent will still most likely spend more time with the children. Which one of you will that be?"

"In most cases, it will be my wi... Sabrina." Gabriel shifts his eyes to me, they no longer express hurt. He's angry.

"Okay, in that case, Mr. Dean you will pay some child support. I will have the calculations for you later."

The rest of the hour meeting we discuss exceptions that override the joint custody schedule, such as holidays and vacations. How we will communicate with each other about the children and rules and discipline in each home.

I feel sick to my stomach.

When the meeting ends, Gabriel gets up and abruptly leaves the conference room without saying goodbye to me. I mean, should I have expected him to?

***

Gabriel and I will start our bi-weekly custody schedule next week. It's not legally binding yet but during mediation today we agreed to start it. Tonight he has the girls, I will get them from school tomorrow. I'm thankful Tabitha invited me over for dinner because I don't want to be alone in the condo all night, especially after the first mediation session today.

I get to the condo after 5 p.m. from work. I shower then change into Bermuda shorts, a plain white t-shirt, and flip-flops. Tabitha said I didn't need to bring anything so I'm heading to her house early to help her cook. I need to keep my mind occupied anyway.

"Hey," Jason answers the door after my second ring on the doorbell. He's holding two-year-old Jason Jr. Five-year-old Taylor is clinging to her daddy's leg.

"I see you've got your hands full." I walk past him into the house.

"Hi, auntie Sabrina!" Taylor launches herself against me, I catch her in a hug.

"Hi, gorgeous girl."

"Hi, auntie Sabbie!" Jason Jr., exclaims. At two years old he has a hard time pronouncing my name. He has his arms outstretched.

I take him from Jason with Taylor still clinging to my waist. I kiss his chubby cheek. "Hey, auntie's baby boy." He giggles, melting my heart.

I look at Jason. "I came early to help Tabitha in the kitchen." I can smell the aroma of food cooking.

"She's throwing it down in there. I was keeping these two occupied in the playroom." He takes Jason Jr from me.

"Okay, I'm going to help her."

Tabitha sure is throwing down. She has 90s RnB music playing on Alexa while she stirs one pot while adjusting the temperature gauge on another.

I sing along to "I'm So into You" by SWV. She turns from the stove at the sound of my voice.

"What you cooking? It smells good. I smell the fried chicken, but what else?"

"Fried chicken, mac and cheese is almost done in the oven." She pulls a crispy chicken drumstick out of the fryer putting it on top of the other perfectly cooked chicken in a dish. "Green beans and I cheated and got a coconut cream cake from the bakery."

My stomach growls, the music prevents her from hearing it. "I came early to help."

"Thanks, but everything is pretty much done. Chicken is ready." She turns off the heat under the fryer then takes another piece of chicken out of it.

I sit at the kitchen island. "Thanks again for the invite. Not having the girls feels so surreal. And like I told you earlier, mediation was harder than I thought. Gabriel and I were sitting across from each other negotiating our children, it just didn't feel right."

"Of course it doesn't feel right, Sabrina. You didn't go into your marriage thinking one day you'll be getting a divorce. But I still think you and Gabriel can fix things in your marriage. He didn't cheat like you thought and he'd been making a better effort to meet your needs. Granted he messed things up big time by canceling the cruise." I finally told Tabitha why I filed for divorce a couple days ago. "Want something to drink?"

I shake my head. "I will wait until dinner... I hope Gabriel doesn't grow to hate or resent me in this whole process. I did what I felt I needed to do. I was tired of being disregarded."

She sits across from me at the kitchen island. "He loves you, Sabrina. He's hurt and in self-preservation mode. And despite everything in your marriage, you've got to admit the way you went about filing for divorce was a little underhanded."

The truth hurts.

"Maybe. But I have been suffering from neglect for years. I have had enough." I blow a breath. "But this divorce process hurts so much more." Tears sting my eyes.

Tabitha gets up from the stool and comes over and gives me a hug. "I understand. I'm so sorry."

"I didn't know this would hurt so badly."

She rubs my back. "You will survive this one way or another."

The doorbell rings.

I pull away from her embrace wiping tears from my eyes. "You're expecting more guests? I thought that was a lot of chicken."

She grins. "Jason invited Gabriel and the girls. I didn't know until before I started dinner. He didn't know you were coming either until then."

I hear Jason answer the door and the sound of Gabriel and my girls is music to my ears.

"I can't say I'm mad about it. I miss my family."

GABRIEL

I am shocked to see Sabrina's car in the driveway at Jason's house. He invited me and the girls over for dinner, but I didn't know Sabrina would be here too. The girls get excited in the backseat when they see their mom's SUV.

"Why didn't you tell me she would be here?" I ask Jason when the girls ran off to the playroom to play with Jason Jr. and Taylor.

"Tabitha told me a couple hours ago that she invited Sabrina too. What, you don't want to see your *wife*?"

I cut my eyes at him. "Soon to be ex."

"Not if you man up and keep your woman. Stop fronting, yes you're hurt but you love that woman. And you already know you were slipping in your responsibilities as her husband. Fix it. Point. Blank. Period."

"She doesn't love me anymore." It's always hard admitting that. We walk to the playroom to monitor the kids.

"Then make her fall in love with you again. Bet it's sweeter second time around."

He makes it seem so easy. But it's not.

"Mommy!" Genesis and Nehemiah shout at the presence of Sabrina. She and Tabitha join us in the playroom. It is organized chaos, toys are everywhere. The girls run and give their mother a hug.

"Dinner is ready," Tabitha announces. The kids line up at the hall bath to wash their hands.

My eyes stay on Sabrina. Despite my anger and frustration with her today because of mediation and the divorce nonsense. She's still the love of my life.

Jason and I wash our hands at the kitchen sink.

Dinner goes off without a hitch. Sabrina and I say no more than a few words to each other. But there's no tension just uncertainty and awkwardness.

It's almost eight, the girls have school tomorrow, so we say our goodbyes and leave. Sabrina stays to help Tabitha clean the kitchen while Jason gets their kids ready for bed.

The girls are asleep and I'm restless in bed trying to watch a movie. I'm still not used to not having Sabrina in bed next to me. The doorbell rings. I look at the clock on the nightstand – 9:16 p.m.

I climb out of bed and since I'm only wearing boxers, I put on my robe hanging on the back of the bathroom door.

Looking through the peephole I'm surprised to see Sabrina. I open the door. "Hey. Everything okay?"

"No. I need you to return a favor."

Confused, I ask, "what favor?"

"I need *you*." She nervously pushes her glasses up the bridge of her nose.

My heart skips a beat. I take her by her hand leading her inside then locking the door.

"Okay."

This time she's the one who pounces. I catch her in my arms carrying her to the couch. She unties my robe and has her way with me without any complaints on my behalf.

I wake up in bed after 2 in the morning to find she's gone. I reach for my phone on the nightstand to find she texted me to let me know she's safe at the condo. I lay my head back on my pillow not sure how to feel. I just know this is not the life I want.

THIRTY-SIX – GABRIEL

"What's up Pastor Gabriel?" Zaiden greets me after I step into DesignHer.

We dap. "I'm good. How about you?"

"All is well. The wife and kids are healthy and happy which makes everything good with me. Your wife pays me well too, so I can't complain."

"That's great to know, man." I look to the right where Sabrina's office is located. "Is she busy?"

"Not too busy to see her husband. I just left her office."

"Thanks." I walk to the right of the office suite. "Good morning, Sunni, is it?" I extend my freehand to her. She's sitting working on a design on her computer screen in her cubicle.

"Yes, and you're Pastor Dean, nice to meet you again." We shake hands.

"I want to apologize for my actions the last time I was here, I wasn't exactly friendly."

I hear a chair roll back from behind me. I turn to see Aubree.

"I want to apologize to you too, Aubree."

"No worries. We have our days." Aubree smiles.

"We forgive you...She's gonna love those," Sunni says pointing to the hibiscus floral arrangement in my hand.

"I hope so. Can you tell me what mood she's in?"

"She's been grinning like a fool all morning like she got some good d – good sleep last night." Aubree blurts.

I bite my lip to stop my laughter. "Okay, good to know. Thanks."

I walk away to knock on Sabrina's office door.

"Seriously Aubree, you can't be speaking vulgar in front of the pastor." Sunni tries to whisper.

"Girl, you know I've been saved for only a couple months. The Lord's work is not complete with me."

"Come in," Sabrina calls out after my knock.

I walk in and discreetly lock the door behind me. "Good morning."

"Gabriel, h-hi. Good morning."

I walk over to her desk placing the vase of flowers on top. "These are for you."

Her eyes light up. She picks up the vase to sniff the hibiscuses. "They're beautiful. Thank you."

"I wish you would've stayed last night."

She places the vase down on her desk. "I –"

"I don't want a divorce, Sabrina. I love you. I want you to remain my wife." I walk around her desk and turn the swivel desk chair for her to face me. She visibly swallows at my nearness. I like that I'm making her a little nervous, but not in a bad way.

I place my hand on each elbow rest on her chair, caging her in. "Please give me another chance. Give us another chance." I lean in close so our noses are touching. "I don't want to live without you. I don't want to separate my family." I run my nose across her face reaching under her ear. She smells like the flowers on her desk. Her body shivers at my touch. Her reaction to me is making me feel like a king. I kiss her neck. She moans awakening the beast inside me.

"Okay," she squeaks.

"Okay to what, Sabrina?" My mouth is still on her neck. I may not be playing fair right now, but I'll do almost anything to keep her as my wife.

"Le...let's try to work things out..."

My eyes close in relief at her words. *Thank you, Jesus!*

"...We have to go to counseling."

"Okay."

She nods her head.

"I'm going to kiss you now," I warn her.

"Please!" She tugs on my beard.

Our mouths clash, I devour her lips.

"I'm also going to need you to be quiet because you didn't allow me to get round three last night."

"Oh yes, please!"

I chuckle while lifting her to sit on her desk.

THIRTY-SEVEN – GABRIEL

"Pastor Gabriel, your nine-thirty appointment was waiting for an hour and left ten minutes ago." Bria chastises me the moment I step into the church office reception area.

After leaving Sabrina's office I ran home to get a quick shower and change into another suit. Sabrina had to leave too so she could freshen up and change after the mess we made. I have a stupid grin on my face that Bria notices.

"What's going on with you?" She's sitting behind her desk.

"I had a really good breakfast that I can't stop thinking about. What about you?"

"Oh, okay." She looks at me oddly. "I had oatmeal, but it wasn't memorable."

I walk closer to her desk. "About that appointment, did you reschedule?"

"Yes, I have them down for tomorrow same time."

"Okay, but I may need that rescheduled too, I will let you know. Also, find out if they would be okay meeting with another pastor."

"All right, I will and let you know."

I leave the reception area walking towards the office. I knock on a door before entering.

"You're slacking, I see." Jason greets me upon my entering his office. The space is white walls with leather and wood furnishings. "It's almost eleven and you are just strolling in." He's sitting behind his dark wood desk.

I sit in one of the guest chairs in front of his desk.

"Let me guess, you just left Sabrina?"

"How do you know?"

He chuckles. "Man, you look like King Kong ain't got nothing on you, that's how I *know*. Cause I know it can't be no one else but your wife."

"Yeah. And I want to talk to you before I bring it up at the board meeting this afternoon. I want to take a month's sabbatical. Sabrina agreed for us to work on our marriage and I want at least a month that I'm fully focused on us reconnecting and working through our problems."

Jason sits up straighter. "Bout time. I thought I would have to whoop your behind to knock some sense into you."

"Yeah right. You don't want these hands, bruh."

He waves me off. "Anyway. I think a month's sabbatical is good. It's not too long of a break where the congregation will have any issues with your absence. The board is a different story though. You know how your parents are."

"Exactly. And I don't want them to know what's going on with me and Sabrina. But I would just say that I need a personal break to focus on family without giving away anything specific. I'm not trying to hide anything I just don't want anyone's opinion. I want me and Sabrina to deal with us privately before letting others know."

"I agree. You know I've got your back."

"Good. Because that means you'll most likely be covering for me for the next month."

"Man, that ain't nothing. Don't feel bad when you get back and the congregation don't want you no more." He laughs.

"At this point, as long as I have my family, perfect health and strength, I'm straight."

"I hear ya."

***

I click on the television monitor on the wall in the conference room bringing my parents to life on screen. All thirteen of us board members are now present.

Mitch opens the meeting in prayer. Everyone says "Amen" when he finishes and take our seats around the conference table.

"How was the trip to Atlanta?" Dad asks me. I give him and everyone else a debrief. "...And because Sabrina and I had to cancel our anniversary cruise I want to take a month's sabbatical to spend time with my family. Since I've been on as senior pastor for two years, I haven't taken much of a break. I've also not taken a break prior to that as well. It will be beneficial for me and my family."

"I understand needing a break, but a whole month?" My mother asks from her living room in Barbados.

"Do you think the congregation will be okay with your absence for four Sundays? You know people have the tendency not to attend church when the Senior Pastor is away," Renee states from three seats to my left.

"Well, church attendance was great these past two Sundays with Pastor Jason preaching. The congregation loves his teaching too and our second weekly bible study on Thursday nights are high in attendance with his lessons." Colleen, a white woman in her mid-fifties mentions.

"I say take the month sabbatical. Family is important and the congregation should understand that. I know how hard it is being the leader of a church. It takes a toll." My dad shocks the heck out of me.

"Seriously Lucas? How is it going to look with the senior pastor taking a month break?" Mom huffs turning to show her face on the screen. "If that wife of yours would help with the load –"

"Mom." My voice is loud but controlled drawing everyone's attention to me. "Don't." She clams her mouth shut.

Eddie, a black man in his late thirties speaks up. "The congregation will be understanding. The fact that Pastor Gabriel wants to spend time with his family will further promote the importance of family."

"I agree," Katherine says in her Haitian accent. I side-eye her. I remember the comment she made about Sabrina always showing up late.

"Let's put it to a vote," Mitch says. "All in favor of Pastor Gabriel taking a one-month sabbatical say yah or nay. Yah!" He raises his hand.

I say yah, Jason says yah, Katherine says yah, my dad says yah, Colleen says yah.... only three nays including my mother.

"Thank you! I will preach this Sunday and next Sunday, the last two Sundays in May, then I will take the month of June off."

The rest of the meeting we discuss church business. But I'm sitting here daydreaming about being with my family tonight.

THIRTY-EIGHT – SABRINA

The evening after our rendezvous in my office, Gabriel and I have dinner as a family with the girls at the condo. After getting Genesis and Nehemiah to bed, Gabriel and I are sitting on the couch drinking a glass of wine. I have the sliding door open to enhance the view and sounds of the ocean at night. The cool ocean breeze feels amazing. I'm wearing black yoga pants and a t-shirt. Gabriel's wearing basketball shorts with a white t-shirt.

"I want you and the girls back home?"

"And I don't want to confuse them anymore than they are." I shift on the couch folding my legs under me.

"What do you mean? We agreed to work things out."

"Yes, but I don't think we should move back permanently, yet."

"How is us living in two homes going to help?" He is getting frustrated.

"Gabriel, I don't like this situation any more than you do, but we're in this place because my needs weren't being met as your wife. I have us scheduled for a marriage therapy session with my therapist–"

"You've been seeing a therapist?"

I nod. "For almost a year."

He shakes his head. "Why didn't I know that?" He asks almost to himself.

I lift my hand to touch his face drawing his attention to me. "I have been going to help me deal with the neglect I've felt from you. I'm happy you have agreed to go to therapy. We have a tentative appointment for tomorrow at twelve-thirty. Will you be able to make it?"

"Yeah, babe. I will be there. Text me the address."

I blush. I really do like him calling me babe. I sip from the wine glass in my hand.

He chuckles. "You're blushing?" Gabriel brushes my cheek with his fingers. "You are so beautiful." He kisses my cheek. I blush again. "I love how responsive you are to me again. I knew something was wrong in our marriage when that stopped, but I have selfishly been too focused on one day becoming senior pastor, then getting the position and further pushing you away with my need to be successful at church. Please forgive me."

I see the sincerity in his eyes. "I want to."

"That's good enough for now." He leans forward, gently pressing his lips against mine. "So, a sleepover is out of the question?"

"Yes. But we can have a playdate." I gently tug on his beard keeping his lips against mine.

"I love playdates." He removes the wine glass from my hand, and we proceed to *play*.

***

I leave the office at 11:10 a.m. to make therapy on time. After starting my SUV I click a button on the dash to call my lawyer through Bluetooth. The number connects me straight to her office bypassing her secretary.

"Lashan Dassie, how can I assist you?"

"Good morning Ms. Dassie, this is Sabrina Dean."

"Good morning Mrs. Dean how are you today?"

I merge onto the highway.

"I know you cautioned me about being completely certain about filing for divorce, and I'm calling to ask if you can withdraw the filing with the courts." I anxiously chew on my bottom lip.

"That won't be a problem. In our practice, we typically wait two weeks after meeting with a client before filing the divorce papers. From experience, clients withdraw often for one reason or another and having a waiting period helps avoid unnecessary paperwork."

I blow a sigh of relief. "Wow. I guess I'm a couple days shy before the waiting period ends."

"Yes. I hope the reason you're putting a hold on the divorce is positive and, on a personal note, I hope you and Mr. Dean are able to work things out."

"Thank you. I hope we're able to as well. We have a counseling session in a few minutes."

"I'm happy to hear it. All the best."

"Same to you, thanks."

As soon as I hang up with Lashan a call comes through the Bluetooth. I click the button on the screen in my dashboard to accept. "Hi, Mommy."

"Hey, Sabrina. Your dad and I would like the girls to spend a month with us."

"Wow, a whole month?" Typically they only did two weeks in the summer.

I turn on James Hastings Ave which will take me to Everlasting Love Ministry.

"We'll do two weeks here and they can go to camp while we're at work. Then another week we're going to rent a camper and drive to Niagara Falls, Canada and stay overnight a couple stops along the way. Then we'll fly down to Florida to bring them home. Would that be okay with you and Gabriel?"

I pull up to the church, parking alongside the church office entrance.

"The girls will love spending a month with you and dad."

"Thanks for picking me up, babe." Gabriel gets in the passenger seat then leans over to kiss me on the cheek.

"Sabrina Olivia Dean, I know good and damn well you are not entertaining another man while you're still married to my son-in-law." Mommy snaps on me. Dang, she switches up quickly.

Gabriel chuckles while buckling his seatbelt. "Momma Leah, I'm happy to know you're rooting for me. How are you?"

The line is dead for a moment before she speaks. "Gabriel?"

"Yes, ma'am."

I shift the car in drive moving away from the church.

"So, are y'all not getting a divorce?"

Gabriel looks at me. "That's the plan."

"Oh, thank God! Don't get me wrong, I wanted to whoop your behind when I saw those pictures, but I knew in my heart that you wouldn't cheat on my daughter. And whatever issues y'all have I am confident you can work it out."

"Thank you for the confidence. You're right, I would never cheat on Sabrina." I feel his eyes on me.

"Keep it that way... I called to ask about Henri and I getting the girls for a month this summer. Henri can fly out to get them."

"Let us know the dates and itinerary but it shouldn't be a problem. They're out of school in two weeks."

"Good! Thank you. We'll be sure to send them back spoiled rotten."

I chime in. "Absolutely not, mom."

"Oh, hush. Those my babies."

I roll my eyes with a smile on my face.

THIRTY-NINE – GABRIEL

The call with Sabrina's mom ends right before she turns into the parking lot of the therapist's office. It's a pink two-level building that houses several professional suites. I notice signs for a dentist's office, law office, a private investigator, among several other businesses.

Sabrina finds a spot in the almost full lot, reversing into the space. Even though she drove I hop out first and open her door for her, taking her hand in mine as we walk to the therapist's office.

The therapist, Dr. James Adderley, puts my suits to shame. I'm going to have to ask him where he gets his suits from. This gray with yellow pinstripes suit he has on is on point.

"Sabrina, welcome," Dr. Adderley shakes her hand. "And it's nice to meet you, Mr. Dean." He and I shake hands.

"Nice to meet you. You can call me Gabriel."

"Certainly. Please, have a seat."

Sabrina and I sit on the couch and Dr. Adderley sits in one of the three armchairs in front of and adjacent to the couch. "I've been meeting with

Sabrina for a while and I'm happy that I finally get a chance to meet with you together, Gabriel. Tell me how I can help?"

"I don't want a divorce. I want you to help my wife and I have an open dialogue about issues in our marriage and give us help on ways to work through them." I pick up Sabrina's perfectly manicured hand, threading my fingers through hers and placing it on my lap.

Dr. Adderley notices the action with a neutral look on his face. "What do you want Sabrina?"

"I...want the same thing."

"One of the first things I would like to address is Sabrina and the girls moving back home. She doesn't think they should now, but I feel if we're taking steps to work things out, moving home will be best."

"Typically, most couples in a similar situation aren't able to live separately while pending a divorce or working on reconciliation. However, I recommend you continue living apart while you learn to reconnect. In your case, absence can make the heart grow fonder. Sabrina has given me the liberty to bring up some of the things she and I have discussed during her sessions. With you living apart you can learn or relearn to date your wife."

I thought he would've jumped on my bandwagon with my family moving back home. But he... has a point. I do want to relearn to date, Sabrina. I can admit I'm not good at it.

I nod my head. "You've got a point. I do want to date my wife."

Sabrina looks at me with a smile.

"I'm taking a month sabbatical from church. I want to relearn everything about you." I tell her.

"Really? A whole month off?" She leans back a little giving me a doubtful look.

"Yes. The board voted yesterday. I understand if you can't take time off from work because of any projects you're working on and I'm not expecting you to. I just don't want the distraction of church business to interfere with my desire to earn your love again. I also want to use the time to come up with a strategy to better manage work and family."

"I want to believe you so badly. I'm honestly scared, Gabriel. I want you to strive for and accomplish all of your goals as a minister for Christ, at the same time I want to not feel taken for granted. I've given my all to you only to be given scraps and pieces of you in return. I'm afraid of trusting you because you've let me down too many times."

"That's what I want, babe, to earn your love and trust. Dr. Adderley has a point, being away from you, not having you and the girls at home, made me realize nothing I accomplish is worth it if I don't have my family with me. I'm also sorry for sometimes making you feel like I don't support your business as a graphic designer. You are talented and gifted in what you do. I want you to pursue that to the fullest. You don't have to work at the church if you don't want to. And you don't have to be a part of most ministries. Continue to do what you're already doing at and for the church. All I want is your love and support."

She squeezes my hand that I'm still holding in my lap. We stare at each other.

Dr. Adderley draws our attention. "Sabrina, is this the first time you've expressed to Gabriel your fear of trusting him?"

She nods. "Yes."

"Good. You both should be completely open and honest with each other. It's neither of your responsibility to guess how your partner feels. In time you won't even have to ask because you will *know* in most cases. But never stop verbalizing how you feel, even if you think it may hurt the other's feelings. Holding on to that emotion won't help matters at all."

"You are right, Dr. Adderley. I think I've built up some resentment towards Gabriel because I wasn't always fully expressing how I felt or just pushing it aside."

"Gabriel, what do you think about what she just expressed?"

I look at Sabrina, then Dr. Adderley. "It hurts, but it makes sense because of the way she withdrew from me over the years. And recently when I started to make a better effort in changing my actions, she still had and *still has* a wall up."

"Sabrina, for you to fully give Gabriel a fair chance in you two reconciling, you will have to take those walls down. Yes, you are afraid and rightfully so, however forgiveness plays a pivotal role in you two having the marriage you desire. One of love, trust, intimacy inside and out of the bedroom and unity."

Sabrina shifts uncomfortably next to me. I hold her hand in place on my lap not wanting her to pull away. "I want to let my walls down, and I will. Gabriel agreeing to therapy has pushed the walls down some."

I smile. Participating in marriage counseling for my marriage is starting better than I thought.

Dr. Adderley smiles. "Good. Gabriel, you will have to be patient with her as she relearns to trust you again."

I nod in agreement.

"There's something I need you to do while we're working on our marriage," Sabrina says to me. "I don't like Bria being your secretary. She's made comments to me hinting at something going on between you two and her attitude towards me is just nasty in general. Can you find her another position?"

That may be easier said than done. My eyes move from Sabrina to Dr. Adderley. I know I'm taking far too long to respond.

"Okay. I will find her another position." I say looking at Sabrina again. Her shoulders relax at my response.

She smiles. "Thank you."

"If possible, I want you two to take a trip together without the kids."

"I was going to mention that." I shift on the couch to speak directly to Sabrina. "While I was in Atlanta, I was looking up an alternative trip for canceling our cruise. How about we just fly to the Bahamas and stay at the Atlantis Resort?"

"Yes! I would love that! We can leave when my dad takes the girls to Maryland."

The bright smile on her face makes my day. *God, please let her always smile for me.*

FORTY – GABRIEL

"It feels good to be back." I'm standing at the podium addressing the congregation.

The church shouts their responses:

"We missed you, Pastor."

"Welcome back!"

"It's good to have you back!"

I chuckle, I'm happy I was missed. "Pastor Jason did an amazing job so y'all got to give him some love." I turn around motioning for Jason to stand, he does. The congregation erupts in applause. "Awesome. I know I'm the Senior Pastor, but we have many other amazing, Holy Ghost filled pastors and ministers in the church. This church would not be the blessing it is without *you* and *them*."

There's more applause.

"With that being said, I want you all to know that I will be taking the month of June off to spend quality time with my family. We teach the importance of family often here. I would be remiss if I don't practice what I preach. Pastor Jason and the other Pastors will fill in during my absence. It's only a month, I won't be gone long."

"We understand, Pastor."

"Be with your family."

"We will be right here when you get back."

I lift my hand to settle the congregation. "Thank you. I appreciate your support and understanding. It's now time for us to get in the Word." I open my bible.

***

It's Monday morning, three days since Sabrina asked me to find another position for Bria, and I haven't figured it out yet. I want to avoid unnecessary drama but the possibility of having to go to the board regarding this may create that. Plus, I'm uncertain of how Bria will take the news. Pastoring isn't easy sometimes.

I stare out the window in my office while sitting in my desk chair.

Maybe I can convince her to take on another position in the accounting department. Though there isn't a position to be filled.

Or I can convince her to find a job elsewhere.

I will also need to get another secretary.

A tap on the door jolts me from my thoughts. "What's got you looking forlorn?" I turn in my chair to see Jason strolling into my office. He sits in one of the chairs in front of my desk.

"Sabrina doesn't like Bria as my secretary and wants me to find her another position. But there isn't anything available that fills her experience."

Jason whistles. "How you think Bria is going to take the news?"

I massage my jaw. "I honestly don't know. And I want to get the ball rolling before I go on my break."

"Man, I don't even know what to tell you. This could get a bit tricky."

"Exactly. Maybe I can look at some job sites for open positions and put in a good word for her."

Jason lifts his hand in surrender. "Like I said, I don't know what to tell ya. You should've done this when she came at you sideways. Doing so now, I don't know." He shrugs his shoulders. "Pray for guidance before you move forward."

"Of course."

"We need to go to the music room to meet Drake to start recording our radio segments." Jason stands.

I push back from my chair doing the same. I pick up the manila folder, with our notes for the show, off my desk heading for the door.

I pray in the spirit the entire walk to the music room. *Dear Father, help me resolve this dilemma with Bria without any issues…*

"Welcome to 15 minutes with Senior pastor Gabriel Dean and Associate pastor Jason Forbes of Everlasting Love Ministry in Boca Raton, Florida." Drake plays the radio DJ's announcement which will be played at the beginning of each segment.

"I'm Pastor Gabriel."

"And I'm Pastor Jason."

"There are a few misconceptions about Christians. One of which is that because we may disagree about a person's lifestyle, beliefs or practices, because of our faith, it means we don't like said person. This is false! For instance, because Christians believe in traditional marriages doesn't mean or shouldn't mean that we don't value couples in same-sex relationships.

There is so much more to a person than their beliefs. We need to separate *who* a person is from what they do. Jesus loves all people regardless of their sexual orientation, beliefs, economic status, race, etcetera. Which means as Christians we are to love everyone the way Jesus loves."

"Pastor Gabriel is correct. Just because a Christian may not agree with certain things doesn't mean we hate and or not respect other's opinions or persons. As Christians, our job is to display and spread the love of Christ. Not to be judge and jury to people's lives. Like Romans three verse twenty-three states, *'all have sinned and fall short of the glory of God'.*"

I interject. "In turn, Christians shouldn't be ridiculed for their beliefs the same as those that are against said beliefs don't want to be ridiculed either. We can agree to disagree and still keep the love and respect. This is precisely why God gave us free will. Our Heavenly Father wants us to have a *personal* relationship with Him. That's what He truly wants. He doesn't care *who* or *what* we are. Jehovah couldn't care less about our lifestyle, beliefs or practices – He just wants us to *know* Him."

Jason chuckles. "See folks, as followers of Christ, we're lovers, not haters." I laugh along with him. "I'm going to quote another Scripture for you, first John four verse sixteen. 'We know how much God loves us, and we have put our trust in his love. God is love, and all who live in love live in God, and God lives in them.' So stop hating on us Christians!" Jason states the last part jokingly. "But for real, we know there are some said *Christians* out there that truly aren't living the love of Christ. They abuse the Word of God for their selfish and evil agenda. Please know that *true* Christians, *true* followers of Christ are not like that. We love!"

"That's it for us for now. Join us again next week same time, same place. And you can also join us every Sunday or during one of our weekly services or groups, at Everlasting Love Ministry, seventy-seven James Hastings Ave, Boca Raton, Florida. Check us out on the web – www.everlastingloveministry.nas. I'm Pastor Gabriel."

"And I'm Pastor Jason."

Simultaneously we end with, "Good night!"

Drake claps from his spot in front of the soundboard. "That was great, guys!"

***

After recording four 15-minute radio segments I'm ready for lunch.

"What are you doing for lunch today?" Jason asks as we walk down the hallway heading towards the office reception area.

"I was just thinking about lunch, I'll probably Uber Eats a sub. I've got lots to do before my month break."

"Speaking of..." We see Bria walking out of an office heading towards the reception area too. "You need to handle that."

"I will. Today."

"Okay. Order me my usual sub. Lunch is on you today." He pats me on the shoulder before walking off.

Sitting at my desk, I use my cellphone to order subs for me and Jason.

"Jason said you wanted to see me?" Bria stands in the doorway of my office.

This dude! I'm going to choke him out when I see him.

"Yeah, have a seat." I place my cellphone on the desk.

Give me your wisdom Father, and the right words to handle this. "Bria, since you revealed to me that you have feelings for me, I feel it would be best that you no longer be my secretary. I know I said that I wouldn't dismiss you from your position, but you remaining makes things uncomfortable for me and my wife."

Bria sits up straighter folding her arms across her chest. "Are you uncomfortable or is it your wife?"

"Both! I would move you to another position on staff but there are no openings that meet your qualifications. Which means you will have to look for a job elsewhere. Of course, I will give you an outstanding reference to aide in your finding another administrative position. I will be taking a one-month break, so from today to the end of June I hope will be enough time for you to secure another position."

She unfolds her arms resting her hands in her lap. "You're serious? You're firing me?"

"What you revealed placed me in an awkward position and moving forward it's best you're not working under me…for me as my secretary."

"You're going to miss me working under you, won't you?" She moves to the edge of the seat leaning forward seductively.

"Bria, this is precisely why I'm letting you go." I shift my eyes to the door, glad that it's open. "This is inappropriate."

"It wasn't inappropriate when –"

"Oh, hey Bria, Pastor Gabriel," Katherine says in her Haitian accent sticking her head in my office. "Sorry to interrupt. I'm waiting outside for us to go to lunch, Bria."

"Okay. Just a second. Pastor Gabriel is firing me."

I cock my head to the side. Bria's showing out right now. Katherine's eyes balloon in size, but she moves away from the door leaving us alone.

Bria abruptly stands. "I will find another position by the time you get back from your break. If not, unemployment compensation will have to do." She sashays out of my office without a second look.

I blow out a sigh of relief.

FORTY-ONE – SABRINA

"You can talk yourself into greatness the same way you can talk yourself out of greatness. What is it that God wants you to do that you are talking yourself out of...?"

"Yasss! Talk that shh... stuff Pastor." Aubree shouts. I'm shaking my head laughing. *Lord, continue to work on my girl. And me.*

Aubree, Sunni, Tabitha and I are sitting together at a round table. We're at the Women's Ministry monthly brunch. Gabriel is preaching a message about *allowing God to use us as the women of God we're created to be*. Usually, Tabitha or a female pastor on staff teaches a message, this month we wanted a message for the women from a male perspective.

"That man can preach!" Sunni applauds Gabriel as he exits the room leaving us ladies to continue our event.

I'm clapping too along with everyone else. Gabriel did a fantastic job. Preaching is his calling.

Tabitha takes the podium. "Alright ladies, after that powerful message by our Senior Pastor, it's time to eat! Today's meal is catered by Laverne Nelson owner of Ma's House Foods." We rotate using regular catering vendors every month to give support to our local businesses.

The food is smelling good, it has my stomach growling. "Okay ladies, I can't front. I'm hungry!" I push my chair away from the table.

"Ha, me too." Aubree stands with me followed by Sunni. We head toward the long forming line for the buffet tables.

"You know that fake looking *you* over there?" Aubree nudges me on the shoulder.

I turn to look where she's looking across the room, by the side doors of the church event hall. Bria is still sporting a similar bob hairstyle as me. She's dressed in a cute yellow jumpsuit looking right at us and starts to walk our way.

"That's Bria. Gabriel's soon to be ex-secretary."

"Why is she walking over here like something about to pop off?" Sunni talks slang and with her being white it doesn't sound weird coming from her. Aubree has rubbed off on her some.

"Man, since joining the church this is the second brunch I've been to where someone keeps trying to test my newfound faith. Boss lady, if she says the wrong thing I'm going to need you to turn a blind eye and ear to what I will say and do."

I grab Aubree's hand pulling her to stand closer to me at Bria's approach. "Good morning, Lady of the Church." Bria sneers but keeps her voice low enough where only the four of us can hear in the crowded room. "Guess you're happy you convinced *our* man to fire me."

"Bitch! You–" Sunni covers Aubree's mouth with her hand, reminding her in her ear that we're at church.

Jesusssssss

I lean in close to her ear. "Bria, I suggest you find yourself a psychiatrist and get on some meds because I promise you the next time you come at me sideways I *will* beat some sense into you. *My man* doesn't want or need you. Be a good mommy to your son and get your own life."

"And I will be in line to pass out the beatdown!" Aubree snaps on Bria.

Bria huffs and trots her yellow jumpsuit behind away.

Being the bigger person when it comes to Bria will cause me to snap one day.

"Dear Lord, forgive me for almost choking Big Bird out..." Aubree starts to pray cracking me and Sunni up.

We continue toward the buffet line. My stomach is still growling.

"Why do I keep getting tested?" Aubree outburst throwing her hands up.

Ms. Urma stops in front of us with her plate filled with fruit, Danish, bacon, shrimp and grits and something that looks like quiche. She must be hungry too.

"Good morning Sabrina. I like your dress," I'm wearing a sleeveless plum colored maxi dress. My forearm hibiscus tattoo is on display. "It looks nice on you. And the color compliments your brown skin complexion." My mouth hangs open. She addresses Sunni and Aubree. "Good morning Ladies. Don't you look cute with your little diamond nose ring," she tells Sunni. "And you, that color lipstick is a perfect shade for you." Ms. Urma compliments Aubree.

"Thank you," the three of us say in unison. Shocked. Completely shocked.

"Y'all better go get your food. It smells divine. I'm going to dive in face first." Ms. Urma walks away.

Not going to lie, Ms. Urma being nice gives me the heebie-jeebies. I shudder as we continue to move towards the buffet line.

Sunni picks up a plate. "Uh, is it just me, or was that weird. I've only encountered that woman once before. But if God can change her from what I experienced last month, to what we just witnessed, I'm putting a bit more in offering on Sunday."

Aubree nods. "I second that."

***

My dad flew in this morning, he, Genesis and Nehemiah will be flying back to Maryland tomorrow afternoon. The girls and I had their bags packed for days. They are beyond excited to spend a month with their grandparents for the summer. I'm going to miss them.

"You and Gabriel are back together working things out but you're still living here?" Daddy's holding a mug filled with steaming black coffee.

We're sitting in the living room of the condo. I'm on the couch with my legs stretched out sipping on a glass of red wine. Daddy's stretched out in the recliner. He's the only person I know who drinks coffee at night. We recently finished eating baked chicken with garlic red potatoes and a salad that I made. The girls are with Gabriel for the night.

The television has The Jeffersons playing, one of daddy's favorite throwback sitcoms.

I take a sip of wine. "Our marriage therapist suggested we live apart for a while. I think it's a good idea for letting us rediscover each other."

Daddy shakes his head. "I say a man and a woman should work out their problems together at home." He sips his coffee. "And are you sure Gabriel didn't cheat?"

Now that I think about it, I never directly asked Gabriel if he cheated. I trust that he didn't. "I'm sure. We're moving in the right direction."

"I'm happy as long as you're happy. I never did like the way y'all had a shotgun wedding without me and your mama present. But Gabriel seems to have been a good husband and father these past eleven years. I hope it stays that way."

I simply nod sipping my wine.

FORTY-TWO – GABRIEL

"That was a quick flight. I'm kicking myself we haven't visited the Bahamas sooner." I get our carryon luggage down from the overhead compartment. To sweeten the experience, I booked us first class tickets. We don't have long to wait to deplane. Sabrina is standing in the airplane aisle in front of me wearing a short floral sundress with sandals. She got her hair braided in those poetic justice style box braids. I'm loving the look. I have plans with those braids wrapped around my arm later. I'm dressed for vacation too in golf shorts, a Nike plain t-shirt and Nike slides on my feet.

Sabrina bites down on her bottom lip while accepting the handle to her carryon from me.

I lean close to her ear. "Thanks for not making a smart comment." I nip her ear which makes her giggle. I know she wanted to make a comment about me never being interested in travel unless it was for church.

Brotha man is learning the error of his ways.

The airplane door opens and seconds later we're walking off. I reach for Sabrina's free hand, intertwining it with mine as we walk towards immigration, luggage and customs checkpoints.

"We just got here but thank you so much for this." Sabrina graces me with her beautiful smile.

I lift the back of her hand to my lips, kissing it. "I want this to be our normal. From this moment forward it will be."

We're now driving in the taxi from Lynden Pindling International Airport to the Atlantis Resort on Paradise Island which is over the bridge from the main New Providence Island. Calypso music is playing on the radio. Driving on the left side feels weird, but I have experienced it before on past church related international trips. It's been a few years though.

There are some similarities here to Florida yet so much isn't the same. I felt the laidback Island vibe the moment we exited the airport. Then there's the unique Bahamian dialect that isn't hard to understand. The weather is warm, but the ocean breeze makes it bearable. And from flying over and now driving by the beach, the water is way better than our beaches in Boca Raton. It's clear! Tranquil. I'm looking forward to swimming in it. I make a personal vow to get in the water every day of our seven-day vacation.

"Dat's Fish Fry, y'all want to go visit there to experience some Bahamian food. Especially conch salad if ya not allergic to shellfish." Ethhean Cox, our taxi driver, points out. Fish Fry has multiple colorful booths and restaurants. There are also a couple straw market vendors and people selling fresh coconuts and tropical fruits.

"I have heard about conch salad, we definitely have to try that, Gabriel." Sabrina is sitting beside me in the passenger van looking out the window as we drive by. Her excitement is almost childlike and infectious.

Lord, please forgive me for neglecting my wife and myself of moments like these.

***

After checking into our room, we took pictures in the infamous Atlantis Chair. We had to do it for the gram. And we wanted the memories of it.

"Mmmm, this is so good!" Sabrina exclaims after a spoonful of tropical conch salad.

It is good. It has the right amount of spice, lime, and sweetness from the added chopped mango. "The vendor said conch's an aphrodisiac. I hope to test that theory soon." I wiggle my eyebrows at Sabrina. We're on day three of our Bahamas vacation. We finally made it to Fish Fry to try conch salad. It's chopped raw conch with herbs, lime and orange juice with options for fruits added like pineapple and mango.

Sabrina stares at me seductively. She lifts her hand to run her fingers through my beard. "I don't need an aphrodisiac to want to have sex on the beach with you." She bites down on her bottom lip knowing what that does to me.

There's a rumble in my throat at her response. I'm ready to go! Or these other tourists and locals gone see something. My wife has been so relaxed and responsive this entire trip. I'm feeding her main love language of quality time and in return, I'm receiving my main love language of physical touch. I want to touch all over her with my tongue.

"Babe, don't make us get arrested in a foreign country for indecent exposure," I warn her. She's already looking edible in her yellow bikini under her white shorts romper.

Sabrina giggles before eating another spoonful of conch salad. She thinks I'm joking.

***

God, you are magnificent. This view you created with Your hands is breathtaking. Sabrina and I are sitting on the balcony of our hotel room overlooking the Atlantic Ocean and this beautiful sunset.

Sabrina is sitting between my legs in the lounger with her head against my chest. Old school group Jagged Edge is playing on my cellphone setting a romantic mood. It's our last night in paradise. I didn't realize how much I needed this…we needed this until we got here. We disconnected from our world only accepting or replying to calls or texts about our daughters. Aside from that our phones are set to "do not disturb". This trip can be considered the honeymoon we never had. I hate that it's coming to an end.

I run my fingers along Sabrina's tank top covered belly. "Thank you for being my wife and mother of my children." I kiss the side of her face.

Sabrina shifts in my arms turning her head to face me. "Thank you for being my husband and father of our children. I love you." The truth in her eyes has me wanting to shout her love from a mountain top. I didn't know if I would hear her say those words to me again.

It almost killed me when she confessed she no longer loved me. *Thank you, Father! I pray she never falls out of love with me again.*

I position Sabrina where she's straddling my lap. "Thank you! I will love you forever, babe. You're it for me, Sabrina. My helpmate, my rib." I kiss my wife with every ounce of passion I possess, making love to her lips… then her body with her moans as my praises.

FORTY-THREE – SABRINA

"I know Dr. Adderley said we should live apart for a while, but I think I should move back home."

Gabriel has a Cheshire smile on his face. "Can you do it tonight?"

I giggle like a schoolgirl. We just flew back from the Bahamas. We're in his SUV heading home from the airport. It's close to ten at night.

"Tomorrow after I leave work. But I will stay with you tonight."

"There was no doubt you're staying with me tonight." He looks over at me briefly before refocusing on the road. "I've had you in bed with me for seven nights straight, no need to switch up now."

"Of course not."

Our trip was amazing. I've craved this attention and quality time from my husband for so long I feel like I'm on a high of happiness. My love tank is overflowing. I hope I'm riding this high for a long time.

"You can't play hooky from work tomorrow?"

I shake my head. "As much as I would love to, I have projects that have deadlines that I need to finish working on. And you have things to do around the house like cut the grass."

"Okay. But 6 p.m. tomorrow you're packing you and the girls' clothes to move back home."

"Done."

***

With my Wawa coffee in hand, I make my way inside DesignHer. When you enjoy what you do for a living, showing up to work isn't a burden. I walk in the office a little after nine on a Tuesday morning. I find all five of my employees and friends huddle around Zaiden's computer.

"Y'all watching porn on company time?"

I startle them with my presence. I bit down on my lip to stifle a laugh at the deer in the headlight looks on their faces.

"Oh hey, boss lady," Tyreke says. "We didn't know you were coming back today." He moves to block Zaiden. But I see Zaiden quickly close out of a screen on his computer. I still can't tell what they were looking at.

"How was the trip?" Josh asks.

Zaiden stands from his desk chair. "You look refreshed and a shade darker from lounging on the beach I bet."

Sunni and Aubree are both pretending to be enthralled with studying their nails. *What is going on?*

Tyreke takes me by the arm trying to guide me away. "Tell me all about the Bahamas…"

Shaking my head, I pull away from Tyreke's grasp. "Nuh-uh. What are y'all trying to hide from me?"

Aubree looks at me. "Girl, we were watching this couple do some freaking stuff on –"

"Aubree spare me. I know you all weren't watching porn. Now please as your boss and your friend, tell me what's going on."

Aubree looks over at Sunni, they both share a look before Sunni speaks. "An email from an erroneous email address was sent to everyone on the church's email list…there's an ultrasound picture and a note stating that Pastor Gabriel fired Bria because she's three months pregnant with his baby and he took a month sabbatical to get you to forgive him."

And just like that my world crashes into a brick wall – obliterating me. The hot coffee slips from my fingers crashing to the hardwood floor. The burning from the liquid on my wedged sandal feet doesn't register.

"Get a mop Josh," Zaiden calls out.

Tyreke directs me to sit in Zaiden's vacant desk chair. Sunni and Aubree grabbed paper towels to wipe the hot liquid from my exposed feet.

"We didn't want to tell you because we thought you and Gabriel were dealing with it." Zaiden reasons standing in front of me. "The email went out six this morning."

It can't be true. It can't be true!

I stand. "I have work to do. I'll be in my office if you need me." I walk away not caring what else they have to say.

I make it to my office and lock myself in. At my desk, I rest my head on the wooden furniture willing my emotions not to lead me astray. After the time we had in the Bahamas I want to give Gabriel the benefit of a doubt, but a niggling feeling has me wanting to believe the email is true.

Bria's slick remarks rush like a tsunami to the forefront of my mind. Then when I asked Gabriel to fire her, he hesitated. Why did he hesitate? Was it because he'd been cheating on me with her and didn't want to get rid of his side chick? Is she why he always put church business before me?

Was the Bahamas trip just to help soften the blow of this discovery?

I lift my head from my desk and wipe the tears from my eyes. If I call or see Gabriel right now I may say or do things I may regret. I boot up my computer in hopes doing some design work will be a good distraction.

Satan, I rebuke this attack in the name of Jesus!

FORTY-FOUR – GABRIEL

I probably should've waited until the sun went down a bit before tackling the yard. But no matter when it did, it would still be hot. I have a quarter acre of grass to cut. With my baseball cap on and earbuds in my ear listening to a gospel mix, I push the lawnmower to make the perfect diamond pattern.

It's after eleven in the morning by the time I'm done. In the garage, I look for the weed eater. I vaguely hear a car pull up in the driveway with my earbuds still in my ear. I turn around to see Jason getting out of his car.

"Bruh, I've been calling you all morning. You're out here cutting the grass, which means you are taking the news better than I thought."

I pull one of the earbuds from my ear. "What news?" I pull my cellphone from my cargo shorts pocket. "I forgot to take off the do-not-disturb on my phone." I go to settings to take the notification off. Followed by continuous binging of text messages flooding through my phone. "What's going on?"

"Bria."

"What about Bria?"

"Bruh!" Jason leans against the rear of my SUV in the garage. "An email was sent out to everyone on the church's email list. It says Bria is three months pregnant by you which is why you fired her and took a one-month break so you can try to patch things up with Sabrina. There was also a legit looking ultrasound included in the email."

Son of a b – This can't be happening.

"The board is going nuts. I'm surprised you haven't heard from your parents yet. Tina in marketing has been trying to do damage control by drafting up a statement about the church emails being hacked and that the allegations are false. She sent it out because we hadn't heard anything from you. The church office phone has been ringing nonstop."

I hope Sabrina hasn't found out about this yet. I want to tell her in person. Right now I need to clear things up with the church. Find Bria, because it's obvious she's behind this or knows who is. I groan at the thought of having to deal with my parents.

"Has anyone reached out to Bria?"

Jason nods. "She showed up for work like normal since she hasn't found a new job yet. She denies having anything to do with it. She said maybe someone at her gynecologist office leaked the ultrasound photo..."

"Man, she's got to be lying. It's not by coincidence that this is happening after I fired her."

My cellphone rings, looking at the screen I see it's my father calling.

"Yes, dad. I'm about to handle the situation," I tell him knowing exactly why he's calling.

"Son, your mother and I have been calling all morning. Please tell me allegations are false."

"Yes dad, they are false."

"Good. But this looks bad. Why would someone do this to your reputation? Bria said she has nothing to do with it."

"You spoke to Bria?" I try to tap down on my anger towards her. Give her the benefit of the doubt. My spirit is telling me she has a lot to do with this mess though.

"Yes. This affects her too. Everlasting Love Ministry does not need a scandal, especially one regarding the senior pastor. And right now, that's what we have, a scandal. There are many truths in the matter: you are on a one-month break, you fired Bria, she is, in fact, pregnant, it's not going to be hard for people to assume you got her pregnant. Major damage control needs to be done, now. Your mom booked us a flight we'll be in Florida tonight. Hopefully, by then your mother has cooled down enough to have a conversation with you."

"What did they say?" Jason asks after I ended the call.

"They're flying in tonight. And they believe Bria has nothing to do with this. I know better. Bria is messing with my reputation and my family."

"I think she's guilty too. She's been cool as a cucumber all morning."

I turn and walk towards the door to the house from the garage. "I'll meet you at church."

"All right, see you in a few."

***

The sight of Bria behind her desk boils my blood. I walk right past her and ignore her afternoon greeting. There's no way I can be her brother in Christ right now. *Why is she even still here?*

I head to Tina's office. She's head of marketing and public relations. She's a 37-year-old biracial woman, half black, half Japanese.

Tina puts up her finger when I step into the open door to her office. She's on the phone.

"No, Pastor Gabriel isn't having an affair with his secretary and he's not the father of her child...no you're not attending and giving tithes to a heathen church...he took a month break to spend time with his family..." I tune out the rest of the conversation while sitting in the chair in front of her desk.

I had to silence my phone because it's been going off nonstop with calls and texts regarding the allegation.

Tina hangs up the phone. "I have been taking calls like that since I got in this morning."

"Thanks for handling it. And thanks for trusting my innocence in this. You haven't asked me and you're letting people know I didn't do what I am accused of."

"I will trust you until I have a reason not to. Plus, it's my job to protect the church's image."

"Thanks! What can we do to fix this?"

"I sent out a statement and received replies back from people supporting you and believing the allegations to be false. But it's not enough. We need something bigger. I think you should do a live broadcast on social media."

I shake my head at Tina. "No. I want this contained within the church."

"It's too late for that. Copies of the email allegations and ultrasound pictures are floating on Instagram, Facebook and Twitter with hashtags *#everlastingloveministryFL #cheatingpastorGabriel* it's only a handful of posts. I haven't seen anything on Snapchat yet or any gossip blogs. But people love scandals, especially scandals in the church. Everlasting Love Ministry is a big church with three thousand members it won't be long before a gossip blog posts something. We need to get ahead of it before it goes viral."

I massage my temples. "Okay, let's do a live broadcast about me denouncing the allegations."

"Yes. It would be good if Sabrina is with you while..."

I shake my head. "No. I don't want to drag her in this any more than she already is. This situation is embarrassing enough." The look on Tina's face lets me know she doesn't like that answer but I'm not budging.

"Okay fine. We can get Bria to also deny the allegations and stick with the email hacking as a reason for mass email."

"Fine." I bite out. The thought of being near Bria tap dances on my nerves. But I'm willing to do so to put this drama to rest.

Moments later Bria and I are sitting aside each other with a chair at the conference table between us. Tina's cellphone is propped in front of us along with a laptop to start a live video on the church's Instagram and Facebook accounts. Jason, Tina, and Kimberly from accounting are with us.

I adjust my necktie while silently praying in the spirit for this to go well.

"We'll go live in five minutes. It will be brief. Pastor Gabriel, you speak first denying allegations and informing everyone that someone hacked into our email account and sent out a bogus email." Tina says to me then looks at the Snake next to me. "Bria, you will confirm that you and Pastor Gabriel are not having an affair and he's not the father of your unborn child."

"Got it," Bria says.

Tina starts typing on the laptop and Kimberly gets the cellphone ready for the live video.

Tina breaks the silence. "Okay, we'll be live in a sec."

Jason gives me an encouraging head nod.

"And we're live on both accounts," Tina whispers.

"Good afternoon Everlasting Love Ministry members and friends, I'm Pastor Gabriel," already 30 people are watching on Facebook and 40 on Instagram and more viewers are coming on. "Some of you may be aware of the bogus email that was sent out earlier this morning. I'm here to let you know that the allegations against me in that email are false. I'm happily married and faithful to my wife. I'm not having an affair with my secretary. Bria Smith who is sitting beside me is my secretary *only*. We have a professional relationship that she can confirm herself." Now we have 180 viewers on Facebook and 1006 on Instagram. That's a lot of views for 1:50 p.m. on a Tuesday. I turn to Bria.

"Hi everyone," Bria waves. "Like Pastor Gabriel said there was an email sent out this morning that's one hundred percent true. We're having an affair and he's my unborn baby's father." She smiles.

What in the hell?

A thousand angels must be holding me down from reaching over and choking the life out of Bria. "What are you doing?! I'm not having an affair with you or anyone else!" I snarl at her. Kimberly, Tina, and Jason are standing before us in complete disbelief. "Why would you make up a false allegation like that?"

Bria pushes her chair away from the conference table. "Bye baby daddy." She winks at me while standing then walking out of the conference room.

I will myself to calm down. I can't afford to have these people see me lose my cool while streaming live. "I must be getting punked. This can't be happening." I shake my head closing my eyes briefly then reopening them. "Viewers I assure you that I am not an unfaithful man. I love my wife and family and wouldn't do something like this to destroy it. It seems, unbeknownst to me, that Ms. Smith has a vendetta against me for her to lie like this. Because I am not having an affair with her and I am not the father of her unborn child. I hope you trust my innocence in this. Thank you for your time." I single for Tina and Kimberly to end the live video.

"What in the world?!" Kimberly's mouth hangs open. "Why did Bria do that?"

"She's behind the email that's for sure. We need to get the police involved for what she's doing. Not only did she send out an email to the church email list without permission, but it was slanderous. She's trying to ruin Pastor Gabriel's reputation which also greatly affects the image of the church," Jason states with his nostrils flaring.

"I would have to agree," Kimberly says. "Bria and I are friends but this is a low blow."

Tina nods her head. "Getting the police involved would further show your innocence Pastor Gabriel and that we're taking the matter seriously." She blows a breath. "I was not expecting things to go left like that. All of this because you fired her?"

I massage my temples. "Apparently. She was inappropriate towards me and I felt it best she finds another job."

The phones start ringing, my cellphone in my suit jacket pocket. Jason's cellphone. Tina's cellphone and the office phone.

"Okay guys, we need to put out some fires and assure the congregation that all is well. Because things will be." Tina gives me a pointed look. "Stick to the script I gave y'all. Deny allegations and assure all is well with the church." Tina picks up the laptop and her ringing cellphone. She answers the call on her way out of the conference room.

Jason answers his call stepping out of the conference room. Kimberly walks out. I answer my cellphone from an unfamiliar number praying this whole thing will blow over soon.

***

I think I have a migraine from today's drama. I'd been at church for hours trying to deal with the circus Bria created. Looking at my wristwatch it is a little after six in the evening. I needed to get ahead of the scandal first before talking to Sabrina. And before my parents arrive later tonight. They built Everlasting Love Ministry from the ground up, starting with only twenty members in 1980. I don't want to be the cause of shame to the church. To their legacy. Though it seems I already have.

Standing in front of the condo front door I can hear music playing on the inside. I use my key and let myself in. Sabrina has music by Mary J Blige playing.

I'm a thousand percent in the doghouse. The aroma of food cooking pleasantly greets me. I turn the corner of the short hallway.

Sabrina is at the kitchen counter cutting vegetables. Something is cooking in a pot on the stove. She glares at me not saying a word then looks away to continue chopping. I walk closer to her keeping a few feet distance.

There's an intense silence between us. Mary J Blige croons through a speaker I don't see.

"Sabrina –"

"Bria's having your baby?" She picks up a banana from the fruit basket on the counter, pointedly looking at me, and starts chopping it with the knife.

"I did not have sexual relations with her."

"You sound like Bill Clinton and we both know he was lying. So let me ask it this way. Has there ever been any kissing, rubbing, touching, going on between you and Bria?"

I look away from Sabrina while tugging on my beard.

"Answer the question, Gabriel. Or God forgive me I will use this knife on you instead of this banana." Sabrina's voice thunders in the kitchen putting the fear of God in me. And I'm not considered as being a punk but losing my wife frightens me.

"We... Bria and I sort of dated in high school. We kissed and did other things back then except full on intercourse." The truth tastes bitter on my tongue.

Sabrina's face is a mirage of emotions as she processes what I said. I take a step back fearful the knife in her hand will fly in my direction.

"Let me get this straight. You and Bria dated as teenagers. Y'all kissed, dry humped each other and gave each other oral?"

I nod my head taking another step back.

"You did all that with her yet I'm just finding this out and you hired that bitch to be your secretary. Is that what you're saying, Gabriel?"

"There's no need for you to cuss –"

"Nah, my potty mouth right now is the least of your worries. You don't need to be Pastor Gabriel right now because you're the trifling husband. You hired your mentally unstable ex-girlfriend as your secretary who may or may not be pregnant with your third child –"

"I never had sex with Bria! I didn't cheat on you. I love you too much to do that."

"Save it! Get out! I don't want to deal with you right now."

"We need to talk about this Sabrina."

"I said to go! Now!"

"Okay I will leave, but when you cool off we have to talk. I'm sorry for not telling you about my relationship with Bria before. But it was nothing but a childhood fling and it's so far in the past."

"So far in the past, it's biting me on the ass. Leave!"

FORTY-FIVE – SABRINA

"Good morning, Sabrina. Kian's in the shop with your order," The clerk, Nikki, says when I walk in the door of Best Prints.

"Thanks, Nikki." I head towards the shop doors. Inside, several printing machines are running with a person managing them. "Good morning everyone!" I greet loudly over the noise of the printers. The two that hear me wave back. The others don't.

Kian is standing by a long stainless-steel table filled with color sorted and compiled stock cards. "Good morning."

"Hey. You got something for me?" I'm anxious to see the printout of the debutante booklet. I love seeing the final product of my designs. It's a much-needed distraction from the drama in my personal life.

I was completely blindsided by Gabriel's confession of his and Bria's prior relationship. It makes him even more guilty about their alleged affair and baby. Because why wouldn't he tell me, his wife, that his secretary was once his high school girlfriend? There's no way I would have been okay with him hiring his ex to be so accessible to him. And why did he think hiring her was a good idea? *Maybe because she really is his side chick?*

I push the thought aside. I'm here because I don't want to deal with my personal problems right now.

"Yeah, I got the printout. Come to my office."

I follow him out of the noisy printing shop. He opens the door for me to enter first into his quiet office. I immediately spot a copy of the debutante booklet on his desk. I go right over to it picking it up.

"This looks better than I thought it would."

Kian chuckles taking his seat behind his desk. "You always say that."

"Well, it's true. Especially with this." I take a seat in front of his desk flipping through the pages of the booklet. "They're gonna love this!"

"Of course. It was designed by DesignHer herself."

"Thanks. I will look through thoroughly then give you the okay to start printing all one hundred copies."

I study the booklet some more before getting up to leave.

"How are you handling the drama at church?" Kian breaks the brief silence. Of course, he knows about the scandal. Everyone knows. I'm out here looking stupid.

I sigh deeply. I lift my head to look at him. "I was trying to give my mind a few minutes of not thinking about it." I shake my head. "Kian, I don't know what to believe. Bria has had a personal vendetta against me since I met her and I finally know why. Yesterday was beyond embarrassing. And the live video on Instagram and Facebook only made it worse."

"Gabriel isn't cheating on you with that woman."

"Really, Kian? Is this a *protect the bro code* moment?"

"No, it's not. But as a man, I can tell you from watching the live video that Gabriel was telling the truth. And he would be a fool to cheat on you with her or anyone else."

"I guess he's a fool then. And your attitude about Gabriel has certainly changed."

"Your husband loves you, Sabrina. Hell, he came in my office ready to kill my black behind over you." Kian chuckles but I find nothing funny. He sobers when he sees I'm not participating in his humor. "Look, I don't know the insides of your marriage and it's not my business even though we're friends. But as your friend, I say don't count Gabriel out just yet."

I stand. "I can keep no promises." I wave the booklet in my hand. "I will let you know about this by the end of today."

"Cool."

In the parking lot halfway to my SUV, my cellphone rings in my crossbody purse. "Hey, Tabitha."

"Hey, so are we having our Waiting to Exhale moment tonight or sometime this weekend? I can swing by the store to get some kerosene."

I can't help the bubble of laughter that floats from my mouth. I'm picturing the movie scene in Waiting to Exhale when Angela Basset blew up her cheating husband's car. *Classic.*

"For a preacher's wife, you are a bad influence." I laugh and Tabitha joins me. I unlock my car and get in. "As tempting as blowing up Gabriel's car may be, I love my freedom."

"Yeah. I'm not sure we would be blessed with a biblical Paul and Silas experience where there's an earthquake and all the prison doors are opened for us to be set free."

I start the engine. "Yeah, I'm pretty sure God doesn't want us to take that route. But thanks for the laugh. I needed it." The call connects to the car's Bluetooth. I set my cellphone down in the cupholder, then reverse out of the parking space to head to work.

"Anytime. I'm here for you girl. Let me know if you need anything."

"Will do. Let's do dinner on Friday."

"Okay."

FORTY-SIX – GABRIEL

God knows I love my mother, but she can be too much to handle at times. Case in point, we're in the conference room in the church office having a board meeting, she's red in the face hollering.

"Pressing charges against Bria will only make matters worse! And her parents are good friends of mine personally and they are great supporters of the church." Evelyn Dean bangs her manicured hand on the conference table.

Dramatic much?

Thank goodness my parents own a one-bedroom condo in Delray Beach and aren't staying at my house. It seems since my mom retired as the first lady, I can only take her in small doses. I'm 34, almost 35, and she still tries to micromanage my life. I also love the fact that they're not staying with me because they would find out Sabrina's no longer living there. Who knows how long my wife will be gone with this drama unfolding. After Sabrina snapped on me last night and asked me to leave the condo, I haven't seen or spoken to her and it's almost noon. I'm going to give her a few more hours of space, then this evening we have to discuss things. I'm not losing my family over this. I just got my wife's love back.

"With all due respect, Mrs. Dean, it would further prove Pastor Gabriel's innocence with pressing charges. What Bria did was malicious. She not only defamed Pastor but also the church. And she illegally sent out that email to everyone on the church's email list." Tina states from her seat next to mine to my left. She's typically not in on the board meetings but considering the reason for the meeting and her position in the church as a marketing and public relations officer, she's present.

"Not everyone believes he's innocent," Katherine says under her breath in her thick Haitian accent. She's two seats from me to my left and I hear her loud and clear.

I turn my head in her direction. "What was that Katherine?"

She clears her throat sitting up straighter. "How do we know you're innocent in all this? Why must we automatically assume Bria is lying?"

"Yes," Mitch chimes in. "Of course I do have trust in you as Pastor. But Katherine brings up a valid point. How do we know you're not having an affair with Bria?"

The fact that they are questioning my integrity upsets me, but I push my fleshly pride aside. "All I have is my word. Which is why I agree with Tina on getting the authorities involved. Bria took things too far yesterday with the email then her stunt during the live video. I'm even willing to take a DNA test to prove I am not the father of her unborn child. I did some research yesterday and there's a safe way to do so."

"Hmph!" My mother pouts loudly. "Fine! Go ahead with pressing charges. Despite my reservations, we need to clear this situation up quickly."

"Now we need to discuss your position as Senior Pastor," Renee says.

"What about my position as Senior Pastor?"

"Should you step down or not?" Renee replies.

I look at her like she has two heads.

Jason interjects from my right. "Whoa! Pastor Gabriel's position shouldn't be on the table. He's done nothing wrong and is willing to prove it."

My father speaks, "The perception of his involvement in this scandal is a problem."

"Perception is different from reality and the reality is Pastor Gabriel did no wrong," Colleen defends me. I smile at her.

"Because I'm perceived to have done something wrong I should be punished as such?" I can't believe I'm having this conversation.

"Image is important. And right now you look like a cheating baby daddy pastor," Katherine mocks, she at least has the decency not to look my way, or maybe it's cowardness.

Lord, you must be refining me for some great things to come in my life really soon. My faith and patience have been getting tested too much in these past two days.

"Now that's uncalled for Katherine!" My mother chastises. "Gabriel is still Senior Pastor and he's my son and I'm not having any of the negativity."

Kathrine speaks to my mother, "I apologize. However, I only said what some members of the congregation may be thinking."

Eddie draws attention to himself by rapping his knuckles on the conference table. "We need to vote. Should Pastor Gabriel step down for now or not?"

I don't miss the smirk on Katherine's face.

"You're seriously doing this?" I have a desperate urge to walk out of here.

Tina interjects, "You will only make matters worse by having Pastor Gabriel step down from his position, temporary or not. It would make him look guilty and the whole point is to prove his innocence. He's already on a month's leave and has three weeks left before he returns. That's hopefully enough time for us to get this matter resolved and for the hype to die down."

"Vote!" I'm done with this meeting. If they want me out, I'm out.

"All in favor of Pastor Gabriel taking a longer hiatus say Yay," Eddie gets the voting started. "Yay."

Out of all thirteen of us, eight votes keep me as senior pastor. I know my parents are on my side, Jason of course, Renee, Colleen, and others…

***

There's a light tap on my closed office door. My head is against the headrest of my desk chair and my eyes are closed. I needed a moment to meditate after the board meeting.

Opening my eyes, I sit up straighter. "Come in."

Tina steps into my office. "Hey, I have something I need to show you."

Just by the tune of her voice, I know it's something I am not going to like.

"Okay."

Tina takes a seat in front of my desk then taps on her cellphone before holding it out across my desk for me to take. "There are some pictures and a video you need to see."

Taking the phone from her, I see the first photo of Sabrina scantily dressed in a deep V-neck short dress. She's in some night club of sorts on stage with a mic in her hand. I've never seen her dressed that sexy before outside the bedroom. There's a caption: **Looks like First Lady Dean is finding ways to cope with her husband's infidelity. #everlastingloveministryFL #cheatingpastorGabriel**

Despite the dress I don't see anything that's concerning. Though the caption suggests this was recent it is not. Sabrina still has braids in her hair since our trip. In this picture her hair is styled in her signature sleek bob. I swipe to the next picture. Sabrina is on the dance floor in a provocative squat position like someone off a rap music video. Aubree is next to her and Tabitha and Sunni are on the sideline.

Okay, she was out with the girls having fun. No harm, no foul.

The third slide is a video. Sabrina is dancing seductively to a Cardi B song. I would be impressed by her moves but not in public, in that dress. The dress leaves almost nothing to the imagination and the provocative dance moves don't help. *What was she thinking? Is she drunk? Why would she embarrass herself...and me, like this?* I'm about to lose my cool with Tina silently watching me.

I swipe to the fourth picture. The phone violently shakes in my hand. Sabrina has her arms around Kian's neck, looking up at him with a radiant smile on her face. I'm ready to launch the phone across the room. I look up realizing Tina is still in my office and this is her phone.

"There's ah... one more," Tina nervously lets me know.

I look back down at the phone swiping once more, the last photo is with Kian holding Sabrina's hand leading her towards a door. A low growl makes its way up my throat. I slam the phone down on the desk.

"Do what's necessary to fix this." I push away from my desk to stand. "I need to handle something."

I leave my office not waiting for Tina's response. I storm towards the reception area blind to whomever else are around. I head out of the church office building.

"Hey, Gabe! Wait up!" I vaguely hear Jason calling after me. "I've got to show you something."

In the parking lot, I jog to my SUV, unlock the doors and hop in. I touch the push start then pull out of my parking space like a madman. I see Jason running towards his car from my rearview mirror.

While speeding away, Ephesians 4:31 comes to the forefront of my mind. *"Get rid of all bitterness, rage, and anger, brawling and slander, along with every form of malice."* Not now Holy Spirit. I need to be pissed. I warned Kian about my wife. *"People with understanding control their anger; a hot temper shows great foolishness."* Proverbs 14:29 chastises me but I'm too stubborn to take heed.

Twenty minutes later I pull up to the parking lot of Best Prints. There are about ten other cars in the lot. I step out of my SUV when a car screeches to a halt behind my vehicle.

Jason hops out of his car. "Nah, bruh. I'm not letting you go down like this." He steps in front of me blocking my path.

"I've warned that fool about messing around with my wife. Move!" I step aside Jason nudging him hard with my shoulder.

"Bro, nothing happened with Sabrina and Kian."

I stop in my pursuit of the building, turning to face Jason. "How do you know?"

"That's what I was coming to tell you before you drove out of the church parking lot like a scene in The Fast and Furious. When I saw the pictures and videos on Instagram, I called Tabitha to ask her what happened. I remember Tabitha, Sabrina and two of Sabrina's friends went out the night of your anniversary when you were in Atlanta. Tabitha said the picture is nothing like it seems. There's nothing going on with Sabrina and Kian."

"And I'm supposed to believe that?"

"Same way you want Sabrina to believe nothing is going on with you and Bria. Perception is different from reality, remember?"

And just like that, I get a reality check. I'm still pissed, but maybe my beatdown for Kian isn't necessary.

My shoulders relax a bit. I look up at the clear blue Florida sky. *Help me Lord.*

FORTY-SEVEN – SABRINA

"I just knew that thot dress was going to come back to bite you in the butt."

"Really mom? Gabriel is the one who cheated, not me. Someone only posted those pictures and videos from the club because of his mess."

"He didn't cheat on you. He told you so himself and in the video, he looks sincere and blindsided by that woman accusing him."

"Hmm." I'm sitting on the balcony of the condo overlooking the beach. It's a little after four in the afternoon. I just finished catching up with Genesis and Nehemiah, they're enjoying their time in Maryland with their grandparents and making friends at summer camp. Now I'm chatting with my mom. The scene out here is beautiful and soothing: the ripple of the waves, the seagulls flying high and the sailboats floating by. I take a bite of one of the tacos I purchased on my way home from work.

Sunni came to my office this afternoon and showed me the pictures and video of the night of my anniversary that was posted on Instagram. I know none of my friends had anything to do with the footage of that night being exposed because we were all captured. I also trust them.

"Hmm, nothing. You don't look so innocent in those pictures hugged up on another man. If anything, you look more guilty than Gabriel."

"Which one of us is your child, *mom*?"

"He is my son-in-law and I want the best for you both and despite all this mess you both are dealing with I feel all is not lost in your marriage."

I take another bite of the crunchy taco.

"Stop all that smacking in my ear."

I giggle after swallowing a mouthful of taco. "Sorry."

"Sabrina, have a conversation with your husband. You filed for divorce weeks ago under false pretenses, granted you both had issues that led up to that. Anyway, what I am trying to say is, get all the facts. And after you get that, if you can't or don't want to handle it; you feel your love for each other isn't enough for you both to work things out, then this time follow through with the divorce.

A thriving relationship needs love, respect, trust, commitment and loyalty from *both* partners to stand the trials of life. If you don't have anything in you to give, walk away. And I don't say that lightly. But if any reason you decide to stay doesn't make you happy it's not worth the heartache of being in a relationship that doesn't fufill you."

Tears sting my eyes. Her words resonate deeply. I'm back in love with Gabriel, but do I have anything left in me to work through our problems and save our marriage?

I sniffle. "Thanks, mommy. I needed to hear that."

"I love you, Sabrina. I want the best for you. I love Gabriel too. And you both have some things you need to discuss and figure out. Stop overthinking like you usually do. And talk through things with your husband because whatever decision you make affects him too."

I pick up a napkin off the outdoor small table, where my tacos and drinks sit and wipe my nose. "I will…soon. I'm still dealing with my anger. It's best I get that in check before I attempt to have a civilized conversation with him."

Mom laughs. "Ha! That I can understand. Ain't nothing good will come from having a conversation you need to have while angry. But don't wait too long."

I hear the front door of the condo opening. "Speak of the devil, Gabriel's here."

"Now you know better," Mommy laughs. "That man ain't no devil."

"You know what I meant."

"I did. Go have a civilized conversation with my son-in-law. Love you."

"Love you too, bye mom."

Placing my cellphone down on the table. I pick up my taco to take another bite while looking out at the sea.

"I made us an appointment with Dr. Adderley for tomorrow morning at ten," Gabriel announces from behind me. I roll my eyes. He steps onto the balcony and takes the seat in the wicker chair next to mine.

He snatches the second taco off the table. "You got this for me?" I look over at him watching him take a bite of my taco, looking so darn sexy. My fingers itch to run through his thick beard. I take in the navy suit he's wearing with a white dress shirt and dark tie. I hate myself for finding him so attractive at this moment. I'm angry with him and this whole Bria situation. But this is the same man less than a week ago I was on a romantic vacation with in the Bahamas.

"I was going to eat that."

"You want it back? I'll rather eat something else anyway." Gabriel smirks at me and my parts down south thump with excitement. I tap down the excitement though.

"You can eat it… I mean have it." I bite my tongue to stop my laughter. Gabriel doesn't and chuckles before taking another bite of taco.

We both silently eat our tacos and enjoy the quiet out on the balcony.

"I have never cheated on you, Sabrina. And I trust you have not cheated on me."

"I haven't… though I was tempted to."

"With Kian?" Gabriel tries to hide his anger, but I hear it in his voice.

"Yes. He stopped it from happening though. The night of our anniversary."

"I would've killed him today for nothing?"

I look over at Gabriel, his eyes were already on me. He has a serious look in his eyes. "What do you mean?"

"When I saw those pictures, I lost it. I drove over to the print shop out for blood. Jason talked me out of it."

I look away from him, back to the ocean. "Why is this happening to us? Why is our marriage getting tested?"

Gabriel sighs. "I don't know why. But I do know if we vow to make it through this, we will see our reward." I feel him pick up my hand from my lap. I look over at him. He intertwines our fingers together. "I love you, Sabrina. I don't want this stuff that's going on to end our marriage."

Tears freely flow from my eyes. "I don't want it to either. I love you."

Gabriel motions for me to stand then he positions me across his lap, then wastes no time kissing my lips, which I eagerly reciprocate. "We're going to make it through this, babe."

FORTY-EIGHT – SABRINA

Bria has been MIA. There's been radio silence from Bria since Gabriel pressed charges against her and sent out a public request to have a DNA test done to further prove he isn't the father of her unborn child.

Whew child! I know I agreed to work things out in my marriage but having to publicly deal with our issues is tough. I don't like having people in my business. And although I now trust that Gabriel is telling the truth about not having an affair, this situation is still hard to deal with. Therapy with Dr. Adderley on Thursday was beneficial because it's Sunday and I am standing next to Gabriel at the podium in church and all I want to do is run. Run out of this church, away from him, away from the public scrutiny and drama.

"...Thou preparest a table before me in the presence of mine enemies: thou anoints my head with oil; my cup runneth over. Surely goodness and mercy shall follow me all the days of my life..." I mentally recite my favorite scripture the 23 Psalm to calm my nerves.

I squeeze Gabriel's hand for comfort for both myself and him. He addresses the congregation.

"Most of you are aware of the email that Bria Smith sent out with false accusations against me. And you may have seen the stunt she pulled on live video on Instagram or Facebook. I promise you I am not guilty of the accusations..."

"We believe you, Pastor!" A woman shouts from the filled congregation. It seems more people than usual showed up to all three services today to get the scoop on the scandal. The sanctuary seats one thousand and today more than ever, the overflow room is filled with all three hundred seats taken.

I try not to look in the sea of curious faces looking back at me and Gabriel. I don't know how he does this every Sunday. It's draining. I have been here for all three services today in support of him addressing the church about the drama. I want people to know I'm standing with my man and Bria is a liar. If it makes me look stupid, I will get over it. Dr. Adderley made a strong point on Thursday that if I am going to work on my marriage I can't keep retreating every time some type of diversion comes up. Until proven otherwise, I am to trust Gabriel, and he and I are to be a team and fight our battles together.

"...Because of the route, Ms. Smith is going with these false allegations I had no choice but to press charges against her. I have also made a public request to Ms. Smith to have a safe DNA test done to further prove I have not had an affair with her, and I am not the father of her unborn child. Ms. Smith has yet to respond." Gabriel pauses and looks at me by his side. "I love my gorgeous, amazingly talented wife. She's blessed me with eleven years of holy matrimony, and I want so much more." He gently squeezes my hand. I give him a genuine smile. Gabriel winks at me causing me to blush. He looks back at the congregation.

"I'm not a perfect man, every day I have to die to self and ask God's forgiveness and guidance. But I am not unfaithful. It would go against my character. I love my wife and two daughters too much to destroy my family. I had fired Ms. Smith because of her inappropriate behavior and I believe this attack is her way of getting back at me. I ask that you please pray for my family as we deal with this matter and also pray for Ms. Smith. Thank you!"

There's loud applause as the congregation stands. Gabriel and I leave the podium to take our seats in the front row. Jason takes our place at the podium to begin his sermon. Gabriel is continuing his June leave which I am thankful for because we're going to need it.

My mother-in-law gives me what looks like a genuine smile. She and her husband are sitting in the front row with us and have attended all three services as well. Since my in-laws came to town, I only meet up with them today. Lucas Dean always received me well, Evelyn Dean on the other hand, not so much. Today I feel for once I have gained her devotion.

"Thank you for supporting Gabriel in all this. I imagine it can't be easy, but your support makes a big difference in how you both will get through this," Evelyn says after giving me a hug after service.

"I love him and I believe him." I smile at my mother-in-law.

"And he loves you," Lucas Dean interjects. "How are our granddaughters?"

We're standing near our seats in the front row of the emptying sanctuary. "They are thoroughly enjoying their vacation in Maryland. My parents have them signed up for camp and in a few days they will be taking a road trip to Canada."

"I'm jealous." Evelyn fake pouts. "Lucas, we're going to have to get the girls during one of their breaks from school. I want to create grandchildren memories too."

Lucas chuckles. "Yes, we should. Sabrina, let us know which school break will work for you and Gabriel."

"I will. Genesis and Nehemiah will love going to Barbados for a visit."

"Excuse me, Pastor Lucas and First Lady Evelyn, it's so good to see you since you retired." Ms. Urma makes her presence known.

"Ms. Urma! So good to see you." Evelyn hugs her. Followed by Lucas.

Ms. Urma moves over to me. "First Lady Sabrina," she then hugs me. "That Bria woman is lying. I saw her out and about with some man, months back being a thot," Ms. Urma whispers in my ear.

My eyes widen in surprise as she releases me from the hug. She turns and loops her arm through Evelyn's guiding her and Lucas away as they all catch up on each other's lives.

FORTY-NINE – SABRINA

"I love waking up to you in our bed where you belong." Gabriel snuggles his face in the crook of my neck, under the covers. He wraps his arms around my waist pulling me closer for me to feel his morning surprise.

I wiggle. He groans then snatches the covers off me…

Now it's the afternoon and we're just getting out of the house to go on a lunch date. I took the day off from work for us to spend the day together. The easygoing romantic vibe we've had on vacation in the Bahamas is back. Every day since I told Gabriel I want to fight for our marriage, I have to mentally push aside the drama surrounding Bria. It's been ten days since that email was sent out and there's still been no word from Bria. It is a blessing and a curse.

As Gabriel is driving, he reaches over for my hand, clasping our fingers together and resting our joined hands on the middle console. "We didn't do our prayer yet for the day."

"Yeah, because someone was too busy being fresh this morning," I tease. Since our therapy session with Dr. Adderley, Gabriel and I both agreed to pray together every day. And when the girls return home we will do so as a family. Some may think he being a pastor of a church that doing this before now would have been a no brainer– apparently not.

We're growing and learning though. Our prayers together these past few days has helped in my growing admiration and affection for Gabriel. It's also strengthening my faith in God. Gabriel and I are doing the very thing I've prayed for many years ago. To be living it, without the hurt, is amazing.

Gabriel begins to pray with his eyes on the road. I close my eyes. "Dear Heavenly Father, thank You for blessing us with another day of life. Another day of marriage and love. Help us to always be aware of Your presence in our lives and to not take it for granted. Continue to help us grow in love, affection, respect, and trust for one another. Help us to communicate better with each other and for us not to take each other for granted. We want our marriage to be what you created it to be, dear Lord. We rebuke the attacks against our union. Strengthen us so we can always stand strong against the trials of life. Thank You, Father, for your grace and mercy which are new for us each and every day. We pray Your will be done in our lives, amen."

"Amen!"

"Have you decided what you want for lunch yet?"

"I don't really have a taste for anything. You pick."

"Cool. Let's try that new restaurant on Pineapple Ave."

"The seafood place?"

"Yeah. Jason and Tabitha tried it. Jason said the seafood boil is really good."

"I suddenly have a taste for something. Seafood sounds like a winner."

A little over an hour later I'm stuffed from eating delicious seafood and ready to take an afternoon nap.

"I can't take you no where. The itis kicked in already." Gabriel laughs at me yawning as we're walking back to his SUV.

"The food was so good. Plus, I did get a workout this morning." I wiggle my eyebrows. "So yeah, I'm ready for a nap."

"Thirty-five is also less than a month away for you, maybe that's the real reason."

I playfully slap him on the arm. "You trying to say I'm getting old?"

Gabriel tries to act nonchalant while hiding his grin. "What? If you're getting old, I am too. We're the same age."

"Hmmmhmmm, guess who's going to be sleep right next to me soon as we get home? Trying to act like the itis hasn't kicked in for him too."

My cellphone rings in my purse soon as I climb into the front passenger seat after Gabriel opened the car door for me.

"Hey, Tabitha."

"Girl, Bria just uploaded a video to her social media pages. You and Gabriel need to watch it. I sent you a message on IG."

"Okay, thanks." I quickly hang up with her and anxiously go to my Instagram account. "Tabitha said Bria just uploaded a video on social media."

"Yeah. Jason just sent me a text too. You pull up the video?"

"Yes. Here it is." I click on the link Tabitha messaged me on IG for the video.

Bria looks a hot mess with a bedhead and red eyes. She's wearing a pink bathrobe and from the background, she looks like she's in a bedroom. She made the post less than an hour ago and already it has 800 plus views.

Bria wipes tears from her eyes. "Since it was revealed over a week ago that I have been having an affair with Pastor Gabriel. I have gotten verbal attacks and harassing calls and emails calling me a liar and homewrecker. As a result of the stress, I suffered a miscarriage. I tried to call Pastor Gabriel to inform him his third child had died but he has my number blocked…"

"This woman has got to be mentally insane!" Gabriel says next to me and I can't agree with him more. Then there's that nagging feeling that wants me to believe Bria, I push it aside.

"…For the past few days, I have been dealing with the loss all on my own. But you people don't care about that. You want to believe he's innocent because he's a pastor. But whatever! Go tell him his son died. And maybe now y'all can leave me alone!" The video ends.

I'm left feeling confused. The part of me that wants to protect my heart wants to lash out at Gabriel for bringing this drama in my life. Then I remember his prayer from earlier and my vow to work through our problems without retreating.

"God, when is this nightmare going to end?" Gabriel questions. "I wasn't having an affair with that woman, and she wasn't carrying my baby."

I close out of my Instagram account and reach over for Gabriel's hand. "God is our vindicator. When we are distressed, He will set us free." I vaguely recall Psalms 4:2.

"Thanks babe. I hate that we have to be dealing with this. I know this is hard for you and I appreciate your trust in me."

"It's not easy. But I love you and I trust that you haven't cheated on me."

"I haven't." Gabriel leans over and gives me a quick kiss on the lips.

"Keep it that way and we won't have any problems."

"Absolutely."

FIFTY – SABRINA

I nervously take my spot at the podium to address the women for this month's Women's Ministry Brunch. I push my glasses further up the bridge of my nose. My mother-in-law is sitting at the table directly in front of me which heightens my anxiety. My girls: Tabitha, Sunni, and Aubree are at the table to my left giving me thumbs up.

I have never done the keynote speech... teaching before. Never had a desire to. Quite frankly I don't feel I have enough biblical knowledge to do so. But I felt led to do so today.

Help me Lord

"I gave my life to Christ many years ago. For those of you that don't know how to surrender to God, it's pretty simple. Romans ten, verses nine through ten states *"If you declare with your mouth, "Jesus is Lord," and believe in your heart that God raised him from the dead, you will be saved. For it is with your heart that you believe and are justified, and it is with your mouth that you profess your faith and are saved."* Being a child of God isn't easy sometimes. Some people have the misconception that being a

Christian makes your life easier. That's a lie. Trouble and heartbreak don't end. If anything, it may seem like life has gotten harder. For instance, in the past, if someone cussed me out, I'm going to cuss them back and not feel one ounce of guilt about it..."

The ladies laugh. Helping me relax some. It's good to know they're laughing with me and not at me.

"...Now though, I'm consciously aware of how I respond in times of trial to honor God with my response. But how many of you know that we may be saved but God still has a lot of work left to do in us?" I raise my hand followed by many of the women. "We cannot live a Christian life or a successful life in general, in our own strength. Cause I'm saved and still feel the desire to curse some people out."

"Girl, you ain't never lied!" Someone hollers which creates a chorus of "Hmm…hmm" from the attendees.

"We need our Heavenly Father, Jehovah, to help us each and every day, every second. I have come to the realization that God uses the trials in our lives as a way of teaching and refining us. He uses our brokenness to piece us together into the people He has created us to be. Honey, I think I am in AP classes for Refining 101." The women laugh heartedly. I do too. "These past few weeks must have been coursework for me." I subtly mention the drama with Bria which all these women pretty much know about.

"You passed the test!" A woman near the back shouts.

I nod with a smile. "Thank you. Let me clarify though, God does not tempt us, ever! He doesn't. Life just naturally comes with its troubles – some we create on our own and others are by happenstance. Life isn't fair. Which is why the term "we live in a fallen world" makes sense. But our complete reliance on God will help ease the burden…"

One of the side doors to the church hall loudly opens. I can't help looking to my right to see Katherine and Bria walk in. My words stutter a bit watching them strut to the front of the room. *She can't be serious.* Both are dressed nicely in dresses and their faces are beat to perfection. They grab chairs from a vacant table and bring them to the table my mother-in-law is sitting at.

Evelyn's face is tight as Bria and Katherine make room for themselves at the full table set for six. I hear some of the women close by murmur in shock of Bria's presence.

My eyes shift to the table where my girls are sitting. They are staring holes on the side of Bria's face. Aubree is taking off her large hoop earrings and putting them in her purse.

"...*Thou preparest a table before me in the presence of mine enemies: thou anoint my head with oil; my cup runneth over...*" I continue trying hard to not let the uninvited guests steer me off course. "...Having that godly peace that surpasses all understanding helps a great deal. It doesn't mean we bury our heads in the sand during adversity, it means we don't allow what we are facing to overcome us. We rely on God's guidance, protection, peace, and joy to see us through..."

Minutes later all the women stand, except two, giving me applause. I humbly take my seat at the table with Tabitha, Sunni, and Aubree. Evelyn takes my place at the podium to address the women briefly, followed by her praying for the food for us to start brunch.

"I thought she was banned from entering the church?" Sunni whispers across from me.

I reply in a whisper. "She is. But it's not like we have security at every door. Katherine also brought her as a guest."

"I always got a bad vibe from Katherine, especially how she thinks people aren't suspicious of her and deacon Philips. And she's sitting at the table with the deacon's wife. Katherine is messy for bringing Bria here today," Tabitha mentions.

"Real messy but from what you just said she and Bria are two peas in a pod. Wanting other people's husbands. After unknowingly being a side chick to a married man, I don't get how women willingly go after a man that has a wife at home," Aubree says with a scowl on her face. "All I know is they better not try to dump any dirt here today because it will be on and popping. Father God, forgive me in advance."

"You know faith doesn't work like that, right?" I ask Aubree. "You shouldn't ask God to forgive you in advance for doing something that you consciously know you shouldn't do…" I think it over some. "Well I guess maybe you can, but there's going to be consequences because there's a reason God wants you to avoid doing something."

"I'll take em. Messy women irritate my soul. And those two need to be taught a lesson." Aubree looks over to the table where Bria and Katherine are sitting. "Bria is over there acting like she didn't almost destroy your marriage and possibly Gabriel's career. Not to mention the doubt she placed in people's hearts about Christians and the church."

"I agree with Aubree," Sunni says. And I do too.

Tabitha says with a straight face, "Just make sure they swing first so you're not held liable."

I laugh. "Tabitha, I swear sometimes I don't know how we're married to pastors."

She smiles. "Like you said today, God is still working on us."

We turn our attention back to my mother-in-law at the podium. She begins to pray for the food.

The prayer ends and I open my eyes.

"Now you know you ought to be ashamed of yourself showing up here like you didn't create all kinds of drama with your whorish lies." Ms. Urma is loud and clear all up in Bria's face standing over her.

"Get out of my face old woman!" Bria shouts.

"Jezebel, watch your tone with me," Ms. Urma snaps on Bria. "I'm not too old to knock some sense into you." Ms. Urma gets in a fighting stance and I almost fall out my seat in shock.

"Oh snap! Ms. Urma a G!" Aubree starts laughing beside me. "If Bria buck I'ma knuck with Ms. Urma."

"I'm here to participate in the brunch like I've been doing for years," Bria tells Ms. Urma.

"No. You're being messy. You were banned from being on church grounds," Evelyn tells Bria walking over to the table.

Bria laughs. "Seriously? The church is public property. I can be here if I want to."

"No, you can't. As an organization, we can refuse people that means no good. And that my dear is you. You need to leave." Evelyn flicks her wrist towards the same doors Bria entered.

"First Lady Evelyn, Bria's my guest –" Katherine is cut off.

Evelyn looks over at Katherine in her seat next to Bria. "Oh, I'm aware. So, let me be clear, you are no longer part of the church board. As a founding member, I have every right to terminate your involvement. You can find yourself another church too, Ms. Messy."

Katherine hops up from her seat. "Excuse me? I'm not –" She doesn't finish because deacon Philip's wife, Patrice, snatches her by her long weave ponytail and starts dragging her towards the exit. Katherine beings hollering in Creole.

"I've been wanting to do this for a long time. You think I didn't know you've been sleeping with my husband?" Patrice asks. She's a tall solid built black woman in her mid-forties, Katherine is no match to her. "I finally have the video evidence I need to divorce him, so don't worry he'll be broke and available real soon."

"Girl, where the popcorn at?" Sunni asks in amusement.

"Yes! And I need some Raisinets too," Aubree loudly replies.

Tabitha and I look at each other trying to hide our laughs. She and I at least should set a better example – right?

The other women at their tables are amused too. Some have even gotten up and returned to their table with their plates filled with food as they watch the show.

"Wow! Y'all acting real Christian up in here," Bria sarcastically replies while standing and picking up her and Katherine's purses from the table. "I just lost your grandchild and this how you treat me?"

Evelyn bitterly laughs. "Somewhere in that delusional mind of yours you know that's not true. My son never slept with you and he definitely wasn't the father of your child, if you were in fact pregnant."

"Tuh! That's the question of the day," Ms. Urma remarks while mean mugging Bria.

A woman in the middle of the room speaks up. "She right about that. What woman tries to knock another woman down like you tried to do to First Lady Sabrina? Lying about having an affair with the pastor and pregnant with his child. Now you show up here today, for what? Being dirty and further incriminating yourself."

The ladies start clapping after the statement.

I stand up feeling like I'm able to speak my peace without launching on the tables to dropkick Bria in the throat. *God is good.* "Bria, you came here today thinking you can hurt me. As if the stunt you pulled wasn't enough. You tried to break me, but it didn't work. You tried to ruin my marriage, when in fact I have to thank you for making it stronger. I'm falling more and more in love with my husband, and he with me. Your tricks and schemes did not work. With any dignity, you may have left I suggest you leave to allow us to enjoy the rest of the brunch."

Bria turns up her nose. "Whatever! When Pastor Gabriel's with you I know he's thinking about me." She turns to leave and stumbles on Ms. Urma's purposely positioned foot. Everyone starts laughing as Bria catches herself holding on to the back of a chair. She hightails out of the hall with a chorus of laughter.

"And people think church folks are boring," Sunni says thoughtfully.

I shake my head with a smile. Sunni, Aubree, Tabitha and I make our way to the buffet line.

FIFTY-ONE – GABRIEL

Yesterday was my first Sunday back preaching at the pulpit and I couldn't help noticing that all three-service attendance was significantly less than weeks before. Transparency is one of the difficulties of being a pastor of a church. Ideally, people know that the pastor isn't a perfect Christian yet expects them and their families to behave so. The moment a "situation" arises pastors are viewed through harsher lenses. It's unfair but it's something I've come to accept.

Am I now trying to win the approval of human beings, or of God? Or am I trying to please people? If I were still trying to please people, I would not be a servant of Christ. Galatians 1:10 describe my feelings to the T.

"What do you think about the initiatives the board suggested for helping to stop the decline in church attendance?" Jason is sitting behind his desk and I'm lounging on the futon against the left wall in his office. Church attendance is down twenty percent.

I run my hand along my jaw and beard. "It's what the church has always been doing. They only suggested increasing social media presence in a much more positive light to help drown out the negative. I'm all for it. But my thing is, people are going to form their opinion and do as they please – which they have every right to. I'm not interested in creating any gimmicks to draw people in.

The Word of God is enough. I like the idea of short sermon videos with a positive message attached to a post. The stage play Judah is producing is great. I think if we hype that up enough it will draw a lot of positive attention. People love to be entertained and a free five-star worthy stage play should do the deed."

"Yeah, I'm with you on that. As long as we're fulfilling God's purpose everything will line up."

"Exactly."

"You and Sabrina have any plans for both of your upcoming birthdays?"

I shake my head. "Nah, after dealing with this Bria drama, we want to keep things simple." Sabrina and my birthday are this month. Her birthday is July 10th and mine is July 20th. "There's a Beres Hammond concert in Miami on the fifteenth that I know Sabrina will love. She loves reggae music and love songs and Beres sings both."

Jason nods his head. "Sounds good."

Jason and I both turn to look at who is at the open door after a knock. "Sorry to interrupt, Pastor Gabriel there's a Mr. Sommers here to see you." Emmanuel, my new secretary... assistant says he prefers the title of assistant. He's twenty-five attending bible college with the right experience to fill the position. After the debacle with Bria, I'm playing it safe with a male assistant this time.

I stand. "Did he say what it's about?"

"No, just that it was important."

"Okay. I'm heading to my office, send him in."

"Okay." Emmanuel leaves.

I turn to Jason. "I'll catch up with you later."

"Aight."

I make my way to my office right before Emmanuel shows a man dressed in army fatigue inside. He's a black man around my age and it looks like we stand at the same height of 6ft even.

"Thanks, Emmanuel."

"You're welcome." Emmanuel leaves.

"Mr. Sommers," I extend my hand in greeting, he accepts. "Thank you for your service."

He humbly nods. "Pleasure. Call me Jay. Thanks for meeting me on short notice."

"Not a problem, Jay. Have a seat." I gesture with my hand, then make my way around my desk to sit. "How can I assist you?"

"I'm here about Bria Smith."

I can't help the immediate scowl I'm sure that's showcased on my face at the mention of that woman's name. "What about Ms. Smith?"

"Last I knew before I went on assignment two months ago, she was pregnant with my child. I doubted it because she was messing around with another dude I found out about. I told her I needed proof with a paternity test before I gave her any money for doctor's appointments and vitamins or whatever else she would need during the pregnancy. The results came back that I was the father.

Then a few weeks ago she called and told me she had a miscarriage. I got back in town not long ago and I got caught up on what's been happening. That's when I saw the videos. I don't know why she lied about our baby being yours. I can only imagine the drama it may have caused you and your family. And the church. So I wanted to come and let you know that the baby she lost was mine."

It's like a thousand angels are singing "hallelujah". *Thank you, Jesus!* "Drama is an understatement. I'm thankful my wife believed my innocence. I did not have an affair with Bria. I fired her for inappropriate behavior, and she decided to lie on my name in retaliation. Thank you for clearing things up. Is there any way you can make some type of statement to help me clear my name?"

"I don't want to do any videos. But I do have a copy of the paternity test. Text messages and voicemail from her telling me about the baby and her miscarriage. You can use those but cross out my last name. What she did was foul. As a man, I just can't let another man go down like this."

"I appreciate it. You have truly blessed me with this today."

FIFTY-TWO – SABRINA

Aubree shakes her head. "I feel bad for her son. Bria so busy running around from man to man, lying about having an affair with a married pastor and pregnant with his baby, she should be home making sure her child is taken care of. Can you imagine how embarrassing this may be for him?" She picks up her soda and takes a sip.

We're having lunch in the breakroom. It was revealed yesterday that Bria was pregnant by a man named Jay. Gabriel had called and told me right after he met with Jay in his office, Bria was being dragged on social media and I kind of feel bad for her.

Apparently, she has a habit of sleeping with or lying about sleeping with other people's men. Yeah, she did me and Gabriel dirty, but the Christian side of me has sympathy for her. I'm not saying I'm ever going to break bread with her, because that's not going to happen, but people on social media are going in on her, hard. I pray she stops her destructive behavior, repent, and get her life right with the Lord.

"I bet she didn't see this coming. You can't go around messing with people's lives like's it's nothing."

Sunni pops a French fry dipped with ketchup into her mouth.

"She is the reason some men don't trust women," Tyreke says sitting beside me to my left. "She was with dude A, then got with dude B, then met up with dude C, got pregnant, told dude A he's the father but after the paternity test, it was actually dude B's baby, who we now know is Jay. Then she lies and says it's Pastor Gabriel's baby." Tyreke shakes his head. "Dating is so messed up nowadays. My fiancée was cheating on me with her baby's father, makes me nervous about dating women with kids. I think my parents had it better back in the eighties."

"I'm happy I'm married and faithful to my wife and I know she's faithful to me. I can't deal with the drama in the streets." Zaiden takes a bite of his hamburger.

Tyreke replies to Zaiden. "Believe me bro, I'm trying to get tied down too to the right one. But I don't know who to trust out there."

"That's why I'm going to wife my girl. I bought a ring last week." Josh's admission gets us all quiet.

"What? When? That's great, man!" Zaiden pats Josh on the back.

I smile brightly. "Way to go Josh!"

Tyreke fist pumps Josh. "That's what's up!"

"Awwww, I'm jelly. But I'm so happy for you Josh," Aubree congratulates him.

"Good for you!" Sunni claps cheerfully.

Josh chuckles. "Thanks, but I haven't asked Trina yet. She could say no."

I shake my head. "Na, I think she's going to say yes. You two make a lovely couple and you will have a wonderful marriage in Jesus' name!"

"I receive that one thousand percent. Amen," Josh smiles.

"You've got to show us a picture of the ring…" Aubree says, and we spend the rest of lunch talking about weddings.

***

"I'm not feeling this," Gabriel grumbles from the driver's seat.

"It's a couple's date night."

"With homeboy that was trying to get at you."

"Kian and I have a platonic relationship. No lines were crossed. He and I have a business partnership and will be around each other and I need you to be cool with it."

"Nothing happened but it could have."

"It didn't though. I was in a bad place in our marriage. Things are much better now."

"And what happens when things aren't good? I'm not saying I want our relationship not to be. But life happens."

"We will work at it every day for that not to be the case, especially not for things to get as bad as they were. And we have to trust each other."

"I do trust you. Him? Not so much."

"That is why we're meeting him and his girlfriend for dinner. Jason and Tabitha will be there to make things less weird which honestly having them there isn't necessary, but it will be nice."

"Only because I love you babe, and this is about your business. But the second I get a vibe I don't like I'm going to need you to find another printer."

"Deal!"

We get out of the car and make our way into the upscale restaurant.

Seeing Gabriel shake hands with Kian causes butterflies to go wild in my belly. For my husband to do this for me has my love tank filling up.

"I'm only doing this for my wife," Gabriel tells Kian under his breath. Kian's girlfriend Cici isn't paying attention because she is greeting Tabitha and Jason. "Keep things kosher and we cool."

"There's nothing but respect," Kian lets him know.

Gabriel gives him a head nod. We greet everyone else before Gabriel pulls my seat out for me at the table.

I can see why Kian is in love with Cici, his ex-fiancée. She's beautiful. Her dark skin is glowing from happiness. She looks to be around the same age as Kian in her early forties. And I've picked up on a positive vibe from her. I can see her and I being friends if things ever lead that way.

"And just like that, the men folks huddle together to talk about what men talk about," Cici laughs.

Tabitha and I smile nodding our heads in agreement. Soon after the table was cleared from dinner, Kian, Gabriel and Jason exchange seats with us to further their conversation about sports, politics or whatever it is they're heavily debating.

"Can't take them no where," Tabitha teases.

"Hmmmhmm. So Cici, where you got those shoes from, they're cute!" I look down to check out the red open toe booties she's wearing.

"Yasss! I've been admiring them since I saw you," Tabitha says.

"I snagged these beauties online on sale for thirty dollars. I'll give you the website, I'm not sure they're still having a sale, but the regular price is sixty-nine dollars." Cici reaches for her phone in her purse.

Tabitha pulls out her cellphone from her clutch. "Cool. They have any other colors?"

"Yes. Black, white, blue and there was a leopard print one too."

"I'm getting leopard print!" I singsong pulling out my cellphone.

FIFTY-THREE – SABRINA

"Does this look first date appropriate?" Sunni walks out of the dressing room in Macy's for us to inspect her outfit. She has on a zebra print, spaghetti strap, wide-leg jumpsuit.

"It's cute!" Tabitha exclaims.

"This one is a keeper," I tell her.

Aubree steps out of the other dressing room door dressed in a flowy white maxi dress. The frown on her face says it all.

I shake my head. "It's a no for me."

"Yeah, I don't like it. The first outfit you tried on is my favorite," Tabitha tells Aubree.

"I agree. The first outfit you tried on was perfect," Sunni says.

Aubree smiles. "That's my favorite one too." She checks Sunni out in her outfit. "Yup, that's the one. I love it."

Sunni excitedly claps then starts playfully doing the booty dance. "I'm getting this outfit."

"Yeah, but you better not be twerking on anythang tonight," Tabitha tells her.

Aubree and I laugh. "You neither Aubree," I point at her.

Aubree and Sunni are going on a double date tonight with men they met at the church's singles ministry.

"Which is why we're doing a double date to keep me from doing something I will regret. Brother is fine, saved, actually single, and he's an accountant. He funny and makes me laugh. That's the first thing that attracted me to him. The old me would have thrown him the cookie jar by now. We have been getting to know each other for a month, talking on the phone almost every day. Tonight's our first official date."

"Tonight's my first official date with Steven too and I'm nervous. Like Aubree, Steven and I have been getting to know each other by talking on the phone and when we have a single's ministry get-togethers. But tonight's different. It's us saying– *I want to date you*. And it's different dating now because sex is officially off the table. Steven may be saved too but I don't know if he'll be okay with celibacy until marriage if we do decide to exclusively date each other one day."

"Just know if either of them isn't okay with your stance on dating and sex then maybe they're not the ones for you. Stay true to yourself. Stay true to your beliefs. Ask God to help you through any moments of doubt, guilt, and weakness you may have. God doesn't want perfection He wants your heart that truly loves Him."

"Exactly. Tonight will be fun. Don't stress it," Tabitha says.

"You're right." Aubree swirls around in the flowy white dress. "And we will be looking cute too." She returns to the changing room to change out of the dress. Sunni goes to change too.

After Sunni and Aubree pay for their outfits, we leave Macy's to enter the mall to stroll to another store to look for shoes for their outfits.

"Oh look, Sabrina and her minions." Bria stops five feet in front of us with her hands filled with shopping bags.

"Oh look, it's the Bria Train. All aboard men!" I call out getting curious looks from people walking by. *Why Lord. Why won't this woman just leave me be? I'm not going to stoop to her level again. I won't stoop to her level again. I'm a grown 35-year-old woman.*

Aubree, Tabitha, and Sunni laugh at my remark.

"Ha, ha. Funny." Bria scowls. "The attention I got on social media has been very profitable." She lifts up the bags in her hands.

This is so sad.

"Maybe you should use some of the money to buy you some dignity," Tabitha tells her.

"Y'all, please let's go." I start to walk away.

"Glady." Aubree walks forward and slaps the taste right out of Bria's mouth causing her to stumble. Aubree gracefully slips to the floor. "Oh my, I slipped and fell."

The slap was so loud I can still hear the echo.

Bria drops the bags out of her hands to hold her face. "Security! Security!" She hollers backing away from us like we're about to attack her. She points at Aubree. "You did that on purpose."

Sunni and Tabitha are trying to stifle their laughs.

I'm shaking my head biting on my bottom lip.

"Ow, ow. I think I may have sprained my ankle," Aubree fakes when two security officers show up. Somehow, she convinces them that she fell and accidentally hit Bria then they escort Bria away because she said she is afraid to be near us.

"Aubree, you tripped and fell?" I ask her as we continue to the next store.

She gives me an innocent face. "What? You saw it happen."

Tabitha gives Aubree an amused look. "Your hand just happened to land against Bria's face as you fell?"

Aubree hunches her shoulders. "How am I supposed to know how I'm going to fall?"

"No, what happened was you molly whopped the taste right out of Bria's mouth." Sunni cracks up laughing. We all do too.

FIFTY-FOUR – SABRINA

"It's a horse!" Nehemiah calls out.

Gabriel playfully groans. "Really Miah? A horse. Baby, look at it."

Nehemiah scratches her chin as she studies the large dry erase board trying to make out what it is that Gabriel drew. I know what it is but I'm not on their team. "Is it a zebra?"

"Time!" Genesis excitedly calls.

After praying as a family before dinner, we're now playing Pictionary. Genesis and I are in the lead by eleven points. The girls got back from their visit with my parents a few days ago.

"Can we guess what it is now?" I bite down on my lip to help stop my grin. Gabriel's being a sore loser with a pout on his handsome face.

"Yes Sabrina, you can guess." He falls onto the couch next to me.

"It's a donkey."

He looks over at me with a baffled look on his face. "Man, you be cheating!"

I laugh. "Nope. I just have a good memory. The girls and I have played this game a million times."

"Yeah, so you say. But I still think you're cheating."

"Don't be a sore loser daddy. We can play Heads Up now if you want," Genesis offers.

"Okay. Me and Nehemiah are going to beat you two in that one for sure."

"Hmm-hmm, we'll see," I reply.

Gabriel pulls me closer to him and starts tickling me. "Oh, you talking smack," he tickles my sides and I start laughing uncontrollably. The girls join in.

"This is so much fun, can we do this every weekend?" Nehemiah asks.

I somber up after they finish tickling me.

"Yes, we can do this every weekend," Gabriel tells her.

"I'm so happy we're all living together again," Genesis adds.

"Me too." It's almost hard to think just a few weeks ago I had filed for divorce. Now look at us.

"For I know the plans I have for you," declares the Lord, "plans to prosper you and not to harm you, plans to give you hope and a future." Jeremiah 29:11 pops into the forefront of my mind. *Thank you for not*

giving up on me God. Thank you for not allowing me to give up on my marriage and my family.

We play Heads Up then Monopoly before the girls get too sleepy to continue.

"They are out for the count," Gabriel says walking into our bedroom.

I press play on the song on my cellphone for the Bluetooth diffuser/speaker in our bedroom to start playing *Cater 2 U* by Destiny's Child. I step out of the bathroom wearing the infamous, thot dress, dubbed by my mom. Gabriel strokes his beard as he watches me strut seductively towards him near the bedroom door. I guide him to sit in the armchair I pulled from the corner and positioned in the middle of the room, between the California king-sized bed and wall for the flat screen TV.

While he got the girls in bed, I freshened up quickly before slipping into the dress and heels and applying red lipsticks to my lips. I had gotten my hair re-braided last week for my birthday, they are long and hanging down to my hips. Gabriel loves the braids and since tomorrow is his 35th birthday I wanted to get them for him too. And it's also the reason I'm lip-syncing the song and doing the dance moves Beyoncé, Kelly, and Michelle did during their live BET performance that I watched on YouTube for days just to get it right.

Gabriel says no words, but his body is telling me he's enjoying the show. I playfully slap his hands away when he tries to touch.

"You're killing me, babe," he finally says. I signal with my finger to my lips for him to keep quiet as I continue to perform.

I lift my leg over the back of the chair onto his shoulder, just like the ladies did on stage to the men they performed for.

Months ago, I couldn't stand the thought of my husband touching me because my love for him was gone. Today I am in love with Gabriel more than I ever have before. Thoughts of him make me smile. I look forward to being near him. We are both taking the initiative in making our marriage work. No more taking the other for granted. No more ignoring problems. We're going to win in this marriage game.

"Babe, if you don't want me to die of a hard-on, please put me out of my misery," Gabriel moans near my ear while I lean over him lip-syncing and dancing.

"Okay," I purr.

A message from the author:

Thank you for reading and making it to the end! That means you liked it, right? I ask one favor of you if you connected in any way with the characters– if you laughed, cried, if they broke your heart, or you cheered them on– **please leave a review**. I would appreciate it, greatly. Reviews are beneficial for authors to not only improve our craft and learn your likes and dislikes as a reader, it helps us connect with you. Take a few short minutes and leave a constructive review for me. Thanks!

Read you later! (Corny, I know. I couldn't help myself □)

Let's connect on Instagram: @introvertedkhara

Check out other titles by me if you haven't already…

Printed in Great Britain
by Amazon